HOLDING on to HOPE

A MILITARY ROMANCE

CLAIRE CAIN

HOLDING ON TO HOPE

A MILITARY ROMANCE

CLAIRE CAIN

Copyright © 2021 by Claire Cain

All rights reserved. No part of this book may be reproduced or transmitted in any form, including electronic or mechanical, without written permission from the publisher, except in the case of brief quotations embodied in critical articles or reviews.

In accordance with the U.S. Copyright Act of 1976, the scanning, uploading, and electronic sharing of any part of this book without the permission of the author is unlawful piracy and theft of the author's intellectual property. Thank you for your support of the author's rights.

This book is a work of fiction. While reference might be made to actual historical events or existing locations, the names, characters, places, and incidents are either the product of the author's imagination or are used fictitiously, and any resemblance to actual persons, living or dead, business establishments, events, or locales is entirely coincidental.

Cover design by Jess Mastorakos - Jess@jessmastorakos.com

E-Book ISBN: 978-1-954005-15-0

Print book ISBN: 978-1-954005-22-8

To Italia and the magic therein. (Thanks for pasta. And gelato. And Chianti. And Parmigiano. You know what? Let's blanket statement "Thanks for the food and drink" there to cover all the bases.)

CONTENT WARNING

Dear reader,

Holding On to Hope is a military romance about two adult long-time friends falling in love while living in Germany. While it's generally lighthearted, it may contain content not suitable for some readers.

The heroine's background includes an abusive relationship. This book takes place several years after that relationship has come to an end, but she does work through some of her feelings. There is also mention of death of a parent.

I hope readers who find this content to be particularly sensitive can make the best decision for their health and happiness. I want you to walk away with only happy, lovely feelings, and I hope you'll feel safe proceeding with this information in mind. If you have questions or need more information, contact me at claire@clairecainwriter.com.

My very best to you,
Claire

A NOTE FROM THE AUTHOR

This series focuses on soldiers stationed overseas. OCONUS is the military acronym that stands for Outside the Continental United States. So really, it's what military personnel say when they're stationed somewhere other than the 48 continental states.

Any posting in Germany is an OCONUS duty station.

This series was formerly titled the OCONUS Bonus Series, but since that's not very clear for civilian readership, we've got a fresh series title. I couldn't skip this little intro, though, because the OCONUS setting is such a big part of the series. Being a service member outside the US is unique!

I hope you'll enjoy a peek at my fictionalized version of being stationed in Germany, which is based on my time living in Bavaria as a military spouse—truly some of my favorite years so far.

PROLOGUE

Last Summer

Ariel

Nate's brown eyes glittered back at me. The bubbles from that last glass of champagne seemed to slip through my veins and create a floaty, light feeling in my belly.

"They're so happy," I said, a little sigh in my voice at the sight of Livie and Eric dancing a few feet away.

"He's been ridiculous since the day they met. I'm glad they got here as soon as they did." He glanced at the couple whose eyes hadn't left each other for a second during the song.

By *here*, he meant on the island of Malta, less than a

year after they'd first met last August, newly married and crazy in love.

"Me too. From the outside, it might seem fast, but knowing them, it fits."

Eric didn't do things impulsively, nor did he make a decision like this lightly. His past with his ex-wife and kids meant he weighed things with Livie carefully at every turn. Nate and I had borne witness to their love story. I was honored to have seen almost all of it happen.

"It does. It's been just about perfect this weekend." He smiled broadly over at Eric, who'd come down from cloud nine long enough to realize there were other people in the room.

I chuckled low. "It has. I'm glad so many people made it."

Livie's parents were here, of course. My mom, too, because she wouldn't miss it. And then a crowd of about ten other people aside from me and Nate, mostly comprised of Livie's friends, but one or two couples who'd come from Eric's friend group too. It was small, intimate, and lovely.

Nate pressed gently on my shoulder blade and raised his opposite arm. After a handful of dances already, I knew what to do. I hadn't known this about my friend before tonight, though I could've guessed: Nate had moves. Like, the man could dance.

His eyes skated over my shoulder. "You should've worn the suit, though. As best woman, it seems only fair you'd match the best man and groom."

The wedding party had been small—me and Nate on Eric's side, and Jen and Nina on Livie's. Delia made an adorable flower girl, and Robby was the happiest little ring bearer I'd ever seen. He'd talked to every person in attendance on his way down the aisle.

I brushed a hand over the linen of Nate's shirt. He and Eric had both ditched the suit jackets immediately after the photographer had finished the formal photos. Their khaki suits and white linen shirts had been surprisingly appealing. I liked a more traditional tux, but for the beachy locale and the midafternoon ceremony of this little destination wedding, they made sense.

And no surprise, Nate wore it well. He looked good in his uniform, too. He looked like a model with a sense of humor at almost all times thanks to the quirk of his lips that never seemed to leave his face outside of work. Most of the women at the wedding and resort the last few days had noticed the same.

"No? No suit for you?" he prodded.

I must've taken too long to respond. After the champagne and the long day, tiredness had started to tug. "You don't like my dress?"

His eyes flicked down over me, then met my gaze. "I wouldn't go that far."

"So, you do like it?"

Something in his eyes shifted, and his tone dropped. "Very much."

Heat snaked through my belly at the unmissable appreciation in his voice. I matched the bridesmaids—all of us in cheery coordinating tropical colors. Jen wore coral, Nina yellow, and I had a darker shade of bright pink I'd never wear in any other circumstance but that somehow fit here. Each dress was a cut that flattered the woman wearing it— mine a halter style with an open back, fitted around the waist and ending right at the knee.

Before I could respond, the DJ announced that Livie and Eric were leaving. I hadn't noticed them slip over and give the kids hugs. Nate and I hurried to distribute the small bottles of soap bubbles to everyone. Robby cackled with glee as he blew furiously, mostly breaking the soapy solution and failing to make any bubbles. Livie and Eric hustled down the walkway toward their honeymoon suite, and we all cheered and waved and sent iridescent little orbs floating after them.

My heart felt too full. I could hardly breathe when I looked at Eric and Livie together. It made joy leap in me to see him so utterly in love and centered. Not that he'd become complete with Livie, but that they'd found each other, and they already clicked as a family so beautifully.

Had I ever been that happy? If I had, it'd been so long ago, I could only grasp at a vague feeling of it.

"Come on, Wolfe. Let's get in another dance or two before we call it."

Nate grabbed my hand and led me back to the small dance floor, effectively breaking through my thoughts.

And I followed. He pulled me close—closer than we'd been while dancing, anyway. I let him. Of course I did. Nate was a great dancer and one of my best friends. Maybe *the* best. The small group celebrating my brother and sister-in-law had stuck close, but everyone danced with their own date. And tonight, Nate served as mine. He'd danced with Nina and Jen too because he was sweet like that, but mostly, he stuck with me.

My mom signaled to the exit, then shuttled Robby and Delia along to their room. They'd made it until after ten, and they would crash within seconds of getting into bed.

"Off they go. They did great today," I said, watching my niece and nephew leave.

"They did. I'm going to remember Robby's walk down the aisle for the rest of my life."

His lips formed a soft smile that spoke of his fondness

for the kids. I loved that he cared for them so much. It made my insides turn gooey and warm whenever he said stuff like that.

We danced through one song, then another. Nate's ease on the dance floor, and with me in his arms, made it feel natural to stay there and enjoy the night. I wasn't a terrible dancer, but I felt downright skilled when paired with him. He could actually lead a woman. The little flutters of excitement I'd felt on and off all night when he'd nudge a shoulder blade or tug on my hand proved it—I loved to dance with Nate.

It made sense. I felt safe with him. He'd been such a haven for me since I'd arrived full-time in Germany ten months ago. I'd missed our friendship while with Jim—missed it so much it hurt. But so many things hurt then. I'd almost forgotten Nate counted among the top.

Couples had drifted off over the last half hour, so only Nate and I and two other pairs remained. At the end of the current song, we mutually broke apart, sensing the time had come.

"Thanks for dancing with me all night," I said, suddenly feeling oddly embarrassed I'd monopolized him.

"Wouldn't have it any other way."

He grabbed his suit jacket from the back of his chair while I gathered the little wrap I hadn't needed and the small purse that held lip gloss and a room key.

We wandered along the same path everyone else had, back toward the hotel's main building. My feet ached, and exhaustion settled over me as we walked. He held the door for me, and the blast of cool air made me shudder when we entered the lobby. Our rooms were two floors apart, and he usually took the stairs since his was only one floor up. At the elevator bank, he pushed the call button.

"Great night."

"It was," I agreed.

He held out his arms, and I stepped into them. We hugged all the time—this was nothing new. Our bodies pressed together, close, and his chest expanded against me. He smelled like his crisp cologne and warm skin. And we stayed there for a moment.

And another.

The hug kind of... lingered.

You know that kind of hug; the one you'd share with someone who was *more*. Not a *friend* hug. And it sent a spike of awareness through me, sharpening the delicious feel of his warm body against mine. Alarm chased in its wake, a siren obliterating any sensation. I jerked with that feeling, my back going ramrod straight.

He bent his head, pressed a kiss to my cheek, then released me and took a huge step back with both hands up. "Night, Wolfe."

"Night."

And that was it. All my crazy weird feelings faded off, slinking away into the warm Mediterranean night outside.

The elevator came and got me, after which I dragged myself through a quiet nighttime routine and slipped into bed next to the one my mom slept in. In an adjoining room, Delia and Robby were quiet.

And thank goodness I'd been so tired, because otherwise, I suspected my mind would've been hung up on that hug. On the strange anticlimax it left in its wake that tingled and jostled me in equal parts. I woke feeling like maybe... maybe we should talk about that. Or maybe I just needed to see him and make sure everything was normal and that it had all just been in my head. Lord knew I couldn't trust that one where feelings and men were concerned.

So, when he didn't show at the brunch in the morning, an itch settled deep against my bones to set eyes on him and assure myself we were fine. This wasn't helped by the absolute bliss that surrounded me. Livie and Eric practically glowed with happiness and peace. Robby and Delia seemed grounded in getting to see them first thing this morning—Eric had been right about waiting a bit to take a honeymoon. Everyone who'd attended the wedding came to the brunch... except Nate.

He might've gone to the resort bar last night and gotten picked up by someone—he'd looked amazing in the linen shirt and khaki suit pants. Plus, he always had dates lined up—ever since I'd known him, he'd been out with someone every weekend. Not necessarily girlfriends, but "friends" he went out with. He never stuck with one woman for very long, but I could hardly recall a time when he didn't have someone he was dating. Never one for commitment, either, based on historical evidence, which always struck me as strange since he was such a faithful brother and friend.

If that sent my stomach through the floor now, and every time I'd thought of it over the years, it was only because I felt so far removed from something like that myself. I couldn't dwell on what he might or might not be doing. I'd had to put those kinds of thoughts far from my mind for years. And the farther into the day after the wedding we got, the harder it was to ignore that Nate had been a no-show.

At a little after noon, I knocked on his hotel room door. It took a minute, but when he swung the panel open, he leaned against it like he required assistance to stay upright. His eyes were bloodshot and dark—no trademark Nate glimmer of mischief or fun to be seen. Even his hair, mostly gray at the sides and close-cropped, had dulled somehow.

His skin looked sallow, and when he said, "Looks like I had one too many, huh?" no humor rang in it.

Unease flooded my belly. "Are you okay?"

He nodded in a way that made me think it hurt him—slight movement, tight expression.

"Do you need a hug?" I asked, like we often asked each other these days.

He watched me with those darkened eyes, so serious and unfamiliar. A beat passed.

My heart twisted. Tendrils of last night's alarm slowly snaked a path from my legs to my chest.

He swallowed, though it seemed like it took effort. When his gaze flickered over my face, then met my eyes, my stomach bottomed out and my throat closed up. That off feeling, that newness, returned ten-fold this time.

He gave me this *look*. It felt like something had slipped and shattered on the hallway floor where I stood. All the sparkling shards glinted back at me, shouting the warning.

"No, I'm good," he scratched out.

My breath became shallow and a whooshing sounded in my ears.

"Okay. Well. Feel better," I said before nearly running to the elevator to get to my room. The doors clanged closed, and I shut my eyes against the thundering in my chest. No need to acknowledge the shrieking distress hounding me as the lift rumbled to my floor.

No. No. No.

He'd said too much with that look. He'd let me see a raw, agonized piece of him I wanted to banish from my mind, but there it had been. Whether it'd just come up—maybe even this weekend—or it'd been there a while, everything between us had shifted in the last thirty seconds.

Now I knew.

Now I recognized it, even if I was oceans away from even attempting to acknowledge it.

The elevator yawned open, and I stumbled down the hall to my room. When the door closed behind me, I slid to the floor and hunched down on my heels. My head floated, almost like I might be graying out with little salt-and-pepper speckles behind my eyes.

I shouldn't be shaken like this over a look. Logically, some distant part of my mind shouted at me to get a grip and woman up, to block it out. If I pretended it wasn't there, I wouldn't have to see it. I'd done that so many times in my life already. So many times with Jim.

But the core of me, that part that had always needed Nate, had wanted him despite logic and what felt like a life-time of his disinterest... she was the one here on the floor.

This changed everything. We couldn't touch like we had before. I couldn't hug him and feel that calming of my battered heart. We couldn't sit close on the couch and relax for an evening of watching movies.

That safe, precious space he'd made for me was gone. Because when I looked now, I could see the possibility of something else, the silhouette of a future I had never dared to dream of.

Those hazel eyes looking back at me moments ago told me that somewhere along the line, Nate must've started feeling something for me. Something new and different and unplanned. That miserable expression spoke to how much he regretted it, and yet he hadn't been able to hide it. He'd shown me the truth, and it'd gutted us both.

And now that he'd gone and done that, he'd ruined everything.

CHAPTER ONE

This Winter
Nate

The moonlight glittered off slick pavement mottled with little dots of melting salt I'd just sprinkled. My breath came out in white puffs. I shouldn't have been breathing like this, like I'd sprinted a half mile under Masters' watchful eye. Yet here I stood, haunting Eric's front step like a huffing ghost after slipping out the front door from the New Year's party, wishing she didn't do this to me.

Not that I could blame *her*. No, Ariel Wolfe had no part in my idiocy. Somehow, for the last fifteen years, I'd managed to keep my shit together. Relatively. With the exception of Eric and Livie's wedding, and most of that lapse happening in the privacy of my hotel room thanks to one too many Bajtra cocktails in the wake of holding Ariel close for the first time and straight up not handling it. It was amateur hour at its finest, getting broke-ass drunk off the local liquor because I was in love with my best friend's completely unavailable sister and couldn't hide it anymore.

That, and the idiot move of opening the door to her knock the next day and getting weird. Not even just *weird*, but I let all the desperate longing for the woman show on my face, and then I saw her literally run away from me. *That*.

But now, I had to be done. She'd had chance after chance to express interest. She hadn't seen me that way when we met years ago, and there was just no chance of that changing. If divorcing her absolute jackhole of a husband and recovering from that hadn't opened her eyes, then nothing would. This was officially me putting a stake in the ground and saying I would move on. I'd waited this long, but when things changed between us the morning after the wedding, I'd lost hope. Because she'd never attempted to patch things up, or talk about it, or do anything. And this needed to be her call. After all she'd been through, I would not jump in and assume anything. It had to come from her.

And it hadn't. Instead, a line had been drawn, one neither of us would step over.

Time to accept reality and give myself a chance for happiness somewhere else.

If only my stupid, slayed heart could get that message. I shook my head at myself and gazed up at the moon, huge and bright in the wintry Bavarian sky. At least it was cold enough out here to cool me down.

How pathetic that, as a thirty-seven-year-old man, I could look at Ariel and be lit on fire. *Still*.

"You okay out here? Eric sent me to check."

Livie's voice interrupted my self-flagellation.

"Yep. Just taking a breather." If my voice came out a little too cheery for the occasion, well, *oh well.*

She folded her arms and shivered. The dress she wore did little to keep her warm. "You coming back in?"

"In a minute. You go ahead."

She squinted at me, her eyes inspecting. Over the last year or so, Livie and I had become friends. I was grateful for that, especially since she'd married my best friend. But she was building up to something, and I knew where she'd take it. She hadn't outright asked me about Ariel yet, but I'd noticed her watching us—Ariel and me—more and more.

"Really, I'm good. I overheated, and now I'm just taking a breath." *Making sure I don't do anything stupid.*

"Okay. See you in a minute."

She raised her brows as though to warn me she'd be keeping tabs, and I nodded, unable to keep from smiling at her as she slipped back inside.

I exhaled another breath just to watch it billow out in front of me. The door opened and a family tumbled out, all bundled to warm against the chill of the night.

"See you after leave, Reynolds!"

A fellow major, his wife, and their two little girls scuttled up the walkway toward their car. Each adult held tight to a child's jacketed arm as they slid around on shoes that looked like they might belong to dolls. Eric insisted on making the New Year's party a formal occasion. His oldest child, Delia, had suggested it one year, and they'd kept the tradition. This meant all of us wore our best dress, just shy of black tie.

One of the girls squealed as the woman tossed her in the air before settling her into the car seat.

Something rattled in my chest—one more thing to ignore tonight. I pushed away that echoing *want, want, want* dripping into me at the little family scene—the squeal and giggle of the kids, the look exchanged between husband and wife as they slipped into the front seats.

"Hey. You've got to be freezing out here."

Damn. I didn't have to turn to know Ariel had come out to find me. And because I had only so much self-control, I did turn to see her.

I'd never actually been sucker punched, but looking at her tonight was exactly like what I imagined it'd feel like. The air left my lungs; pain sliced through my gut. The only difference? The glowing senses of pleasure, aching need, and longing that rushed in immediately after. I doubted that had much to do with a sucker punch.

She wore a fitted black dress. Really simple, and yet it hugged her glorious curves like the person who'd made it had lovingly wrapped her in it and then sewn it on. Not too tight, not showy, but just... *killer.* Her hair had grown a bit since she'd moved here a little over fourteen months ago—it fell past her shoulders and looked shiny and soft. It was. I'd touched it. Not in a weird way, I swear.

We'd hugged plenty of times. Less so now, though. Not as often since Eric's wedding, and I had only myself to blame for that. But this physical distance proved to be for the best. She looked especially beautiful tonight—like she had a little more confidence. I loved to see that. God, how I loved that the shadows under her eyes had lightened over the last year. Maybe it was that, or the dress—whatever it was, I ached when looking at her. She was stunning.

Of course I thought that. I found Ariel attractive in all possible circumstances. But she was an objectively beautiful woman, as evidenced by every available man's eyes on her tonight, and some of the taken ones too. Livie drew eyes as well; she was also an objectively beautiful woman. Good for her. Good for Ariel. The problem was, looking at Livie didn't make me feel like my heart might explode all over the wall and create a gruesome rendition of a Jackson Pollock painting.

Actually, no, that wasn't a problem. It'd be super weird if I felt that way about my best friend's wife. But that I did feel that way for my best friend's sister... *not ideal*.

"Yep. Wanted to salt the walk once more before folks started heading out." Partly true. I did do that as an excuse to get some air.

"That was thoughtful," she said, her voice so melodic it hurt.

Maybe something was wrong with me. I shouldn't have been in physical pain just by talking to a woman—especially not one I'd known coming up on fifteen years. I was a bit young for a heart attack, and I was probably fitter now than I'd ever been in my life thanks to Masters' PT program, but still. Had to be something.

"You know me. Mr. Nice Guy." I flashed her a cheesy grin and gestured to the door. "Let's get back inside, though. It's too cold for you out here in that dress."

That mind-melting dress I needed to stop mentally slobbering over like a creep.

"Can we stay out for a minute? It did get stuffy in there. A lot more people showed up this year than last." She glanced over her shoulder like she could see inside, then back at me.

"Of course. Yeah. I'm good as long as you want." *Sucker.*

"Thanks." She smiled a sweet closed-lip smile, then let out a sigh.

"What's that for?"

She glanced at me, and her brow furrowed. "I don't know what to do about my mom coming."

"How so?"

Eric and Ariel's mom would be arriving in a month or so, last I heard. She'd lived with them most of the first year until Ariel took her turn. Though Mama Wolfe had always planned to come back, she hadn't made a visit in a while. Last time I'd seen her had been at the wedding, in fact. But now, from what I'd heard, she was coming back to stay until Eric, Livie, and the kids—and I guessed that also meant Ariel—moved back stateside.

She looked up at the moon and tucked her arms close. "I feel like I should move out. Honestly, I've felt that way for a while. I'm the third—or fifth—wheel. But I don't want to leave Germany until I have to, and I love taking care of the kids. With my mom coming back, I don't *have* to do that. And you know her—she's fine if I want to keep doing it, but she suggested I find another job I think I'd like."

"Your mom's the best."

She nodded. "She is. But I don't think I can stand to live with her for four months. I already feel like I've..." She trailed off, and her breath froze in front of her.

"Like you've..."

She didn't fill in the gap immediately. This was a more detailed discussion than we'd had in ages. I held my breath, hoping she'd continue—willing her not to clam up and leave. Not yet.

"Like I'm stuck. And crawling into bed next to my mother is not going to work against that feeling." She chuckled and shifted her blue-eyed gaze to me.

I should've laughed at the comment. I should've agreed, all good-natured and understanding. But instead, before I could stop them, the words shot out of me. "Move in with me."

She blinked. Then again. "What?"

I swallowed down the panic clutching at me and cleared my throat. "I—"

"What did you say?"

I shoved my hands into my pockets for fear they'd continue the stupid streak and reach out to grab her, keep her from running. Bolts of anxiety shot through my chest, but I repeated those words, completely barreling past that stake I'd supposedly set up as my plan to move on. "Move in with me."

Her lips parted, but this time, nothing came out.

And that did it for me. I had approximately ten seconds to make myself clear before she disappeared. "It makes sense. You need a room. I have a spare one. Two, actually. And in the next few months, I've got so many rotations and TDYs, I'm barely going to be home. You'd practically have the place to yourself."

Her expression didn't change. She just blinked back at me. I might've broken her with my stupid suggestion. Or maybe she froze out here in the cold. With that thought, I stepped closer to her and nearly set a hand on her arm before I remembered our unspoken agreement *not* to touch each other. There's that line in the sand.

But now that the words had come out, I couldn't erase them. I wouldn't.

"Just think about it. No pressure, and you won't hurt my pretty princess feelings if you decide you don't want to. But don't feel stuck. You have at least one good option, and I want you to really think about it before you say no."

Her shoulders rose as she took a breath.

"Will you think about it at least?"

She nodded, then said, "Yes."

And though it wasn't the yes I ultimately wanted, it would work for now.

The door swung open and out came another family, bidding us goodnight. I followed Ariel back inside, wondering how long she'd keep me waiting before she told me no.

CHAPTER TWO

Ariel

The last hour of the party dragged. Maybe because when Nate suggested I move in with him, the words shoved my brain into a jar of mud and closed the lid.

He'd seemed serious. He would've broken by now and said *just kidding* like he had a million times before if it had been a joke. And this wouldn't have been funny. It would've been cruel. That wasn't Nate.

He hadn't so much as looked at me since we came inside. Finally, the countdown started, and Livie pulled me over to where she and Eric stood, champagne in hand. And then, there came Nate.

The usual easy smile was gone. No doubt he worried he'd made me uncomfortable or maybe shouldn't have offered. I wished I could figure out what to say. I didn't make impulsive decisions, though, so I wouldn't give him an answer yet. Probably not for a while, until I'd considered every possible angle of the proposal and potential outcomes. I'd made the mistake of jumping in headfirst once, and I wouldn't again.

Even if pretty much every inch of me screamed, *"Yes!"* the minute he'd said it. The smarter part of me kept that in, locked behind a mask of shock because it wouldn't be safe to dive in like that.

"Three!"

Someone knocked into me, and I stumbled. A hand on my upper arm steadied me.

"Two!"

Of course, Nate had been the one to help. He always was, and now he wanted me to move in with him.

"One! Happy New Year!"

I mouthed the words as time froze and my stomach dropped. Nate looked directly at me with only a hint of the expression I'd seen last summer that had changed our dynamic so completely. That had torn away so much of what'd given me the first glimpses of joy I'd had in years, bringing in that dreaded fear of the unknown.

In a rush, I set a hand on his arm and kissed his cheek. When I pulled away, he gave me a thin smile. Before I could decipher it, Livie pulled me into her arms, and the moment ended.

After that, everyone chattered nonstop for a half hour, then fled. Ninety percent of the attendees left were over thirty, which meant none of us had any desire to stay up until dawn. I appreciated the rapid retreat of the partygoers because I needed a minute to myself. I couldn't think, especially not while in hostess mode. I didn't have to do as much this year now that Livie was an official host too, but I wanted to. I *liked* this part of things, even if it wore me out for a day or two after.

I gathered up the last of the champagne flutes and delivered them to the kitchen. At the sink, I found Nate chatting with Eric as they washed glasses—Eric scrubbing and rinsing, Nate drying and setting the now-clean items to the side.

"It was great, man. Another hit," Nate said.

As though he sensed me enter, he glanced over his shoulder, and our eyes met.

There was a familiar dip in my stomach again. Now that he'd suggested I move in with him, I knew I'd feel that until I decided. It was nothing more than the reminder that I had something dangling out there, unresolved. I hated that feeling, and so much of life had been that way lately. No wonder I felt nervous about this.

No wonder I'd so wanted—no, needed—to cling to the safety he had provided as my best friend. I'd needed that one quiet, safe place that didn't demand anything from me.

Until he'd opened that door.

"It was. People loved it," I added, breaking away from the upsetting memories.

Nate returned his attention to the job of drying. Good. We could move on.

I set the load of glasses on the counter. "That should be the last of them. Sorry."

Eric narrowed his eyes. "No apology needed. Thanks for grabbing them."

A little jab of embarrassment thrust into my chest. Of course I didn't need to apologize. I'd been working on that—not apologizing for everything I did or didn't do. I'd gotten a lot better over the last year. It was a surprisingly hard habit to break—this feeling that whenever something went wrong, it was my fault. The suspicion that if things went too right, it might still be wrong, or my reaction might be wrong, or my excitement might be, and so I should still offer up a verbal show of repentance to stave off criticism.

I exhaled slowly, breathing through the tight bands of tension that clutched at me just thinking about how hard I'd had to work to break this one stupid habit. *No, not going there tonight!*

"I'm going to round up the last of the trash and then head to bed," I said and left the kitchen before hearing their responses.

Five minutes later, the house looked remarkably good. It'd need a good vacuum in the morning, but that could wait. I had forced Livie upstairs a half hour before—she'd been up since five, too excited for the party to sleep in, and now she was completely exhausted.

Nate and Eric emerged from the kitchen. My eyes caught on the golden skin at Nate's wrist as he rolled down the cuffs of his shirt—he'd evidently rolled them up to help with the dishes. He had nice skin, strong wrists. Honestly, he was beautiful. I didn't often let myself think about my friend that way, but sometimes the thought crept in unbidden and I couldn't do much but agree with it.

Well, what I should've admitted to myself long ago—I tried not to let myself think of him that way. The moment we met, my attraction to Nate Reynolds had hit me right between the eyes. But more than a decade of knowing him and his preference for willowy blondes paired with his complete lack of interest in me? Message received. I'd told myself to lock it down in the beginning, and there it had stayed. The whole post-wedding-moment thing had come out of what felt like nowhere, especially after years of telling myself how *not* an option he was in the first place. That'd been painfully clear, since nearly every time I saw him, he name-dropped whomever he was currently seeing at the time. I couldn't recall a time he'd been single until maybe here in Germany. Though that, too, had been unclear.

So I'd kept myself from giving him a second thought other than friendship.

Rigggght.

"Thanks for your help," I said as he gathered his jacket and scarf.

"I love this party. Always glad to lend a hand."

I smiled, and Eric gave him a pat on the shoulder. "Drive safe and have a good trip. We'll see you soon."

My heart thumped at the realization that he'd be traveling the next few days. Somehow, I'd completely forgotten. I'd hoped I could sleep on his offer and then talk it out with Livie and Eric tomorrow and give him an answer soon after. "Oh, that's right. Have a good trip."

He knew me well enough to know I was unsettled. He dipped his head, holding my gaze. "We'll talk when I'm back."

I nodded in agreement, those eyes sending my stomach into a backflip. Without another word or touch, he was gone. I locked the door behind him, my mind crashing around in my skull. Last year, he'd hugged me tight. We'd spent the whole night tag-team hosting because Eric had been so preoccupied with Livie. We'd had so much fun, and I'd felt like myself for the first time in years.

Tonight, lead weighed heavy in my stomach and tightness gripped my chest. We still had fun together. But rarely had we joked and laughed and had those quiet moments next to each other that I loved. Ever since the wedding—no, the day *after* the wedding—the dynamic had shifted.

For one, we used to hug. We sat on the couch close

enough to touch—comfortable, friendly, caring. Not weird. Just... *good.*

Then, in that one moment, it changed. And I'd been angry. So, so angry. I'd tried not to show it, and since I'd become an expert at burying strong emotions over the last few years, I did it well. But by myself, I raged at him. He'd taken all that sweet, safe loveliness and tossed it out into the rest of the world. He'd ruined everything.

A conversation with Jane, my therapist, had helped me move away from that feeling a few days after I'd returned to Kugelfels from the wedding.

"Tell me about your reaction. Why do you think you're having this response?" Her voice had been smooth and calm over the line. I'd been so thankful she was willing to meet remotely after I'd moved overseas.

I'd taken a deep inhale and lunged in. "He's a key part of my support system. We were friends before, and we picked right back up when I got here. He doesn't treat me like I'm this wounded bird who needs to be coddled. I like our closeness, and I feel like—I just feel like that's changed."

I credited him with a great deal of the success I'd had in just *breathing* without feeling anxious and fearful every day, and he'd had to go destroy it.

"Is it wrong that he has developed feelings for you?"

"Yes."

"How is it wrong?"

"It changes things."

She'd stayed quiet, and the pause had told me whatever came next would be wise and maybe hurt a little.

"It may change your relationship. But is it *wrong* for him to have feelings like this?"

I'd sighed and leaned back on the soft pillows of my bed

in Eric's guestroom. "No. I guess *wrong* isn't the right word. But I wish he hadn't."

She'd chuckled softly. "Understandable. I want to encourage you to think about this as a new dimension of your friendship. It's something that will necessitate changes, as you've mentioned, but it's not something he has done *to* you."

It'd taken me months to stop blaming myself for being in an abusive marriage. The tendency to blame Nate instead of myself felt foreign and ill fitting, but in a weird way, it also felt like progress.

Or it would've, except the whole idea of blaming him for having feelings was stupid and a lot like what Jim constantly got angry about with me. My emotions were inconvenient to him unless they could be used to get something from me. I didn't want to be like that—not ever. And I only wanted good things for Nate. If I wanted anything from him, it was just... just... what we'd had before the wedding. Simple. Safe. Something easy and purely good.

I'd grudgingly accepted the truth months ago, but it'd taken time for the disappointment and sense of indignation to calm.

Eventually, I'd accepted that he hadn't done anything wrong. And neither had I. But a boundary had been erected that day, and we hadn't crossed it. We'd only touched like we had tonight—a hand steadying me, a kiss to the cheek when it seemed obligatory. Nothing friendly or fun or comforting.

Nate hadn't been around quite as much, but he was still a good friend. Fortunately, I'd gotten to know a few women here thanks to Livie, so I did have friends beyond just her and Eric. Sometimes, you needed someone to talk to who didn't live with you, and having Summer, Emily, Katie, and

Bec gave me that. Granted, outside of family and Nate, and even with them, I didn't share a lot of the hardest things. But I knew I could, and that gave me important mental and emotional space.

As I readied for bed, I decided I'd give myself the full duration of Nate's absence, and then some, to analyze this from every angle. I'd talk to Livie and Eric, even though I honestly had no idea what they'd say. And I'd be ready to give him an answer... eventually.

My mom would arrive in eight weeks. I still had time to figure it all out and maybe even find another option in the meantime. That might've seemed like a lot of time, but to find housing as a person without any real income, especially if I wasn't going to officially nanny for Eric and Livie anymore? Eight weeks was nothing.

As I lay my head on the pillow, exhaling relief that the party had gone off well, I knew. I already knew I'd move in with him. In truth, I'd known from the minute he'd suggested it. Because beyond my mom, Eric, and Livie, Nate Reynolds was the person I trusted most in this world.

CHAPTER THREE

Nate

Eight and a half agonizing weeks since New Year's Eve, I plodded along.

Normally, I thought of myself as a man who liked a fresh start. New year, same you, but an opportunity to do better. I liked Mondays for the same reason—fresh week, clean slate, time to make it happen.

But between a short trip before the holiday leave ended, then diving back into work, then a TDY to Afghanistan, and then a rotation that threatened to freeze my balls off and ended in the worst possible way, I felt tired. And that was only January. By the end of February, we'd had another bitterly cold, but fortunately less perilous, rotation, and I'd taken ski trips on the two weekends that hadn't been occupied with work. Yes, I felt tired more than anything else.

Ah, now see? That was an outright lie. I felt disappointed, first and foremost. With whom? Myself. And, because my skull was unaccountably thick, with Ariel.

She hadn't responded. Granted, I'd hardly seen her—truly, I'd not said more than a passing hello, and then weeks ago at Eric's, I'd shoved my car keys in her hand. He and I had rushed to the hospital, though *rushed* had actually been more like *drove painfully slowly despite the German plows doing their best*. Ariel and Livie had gone to get their friend Bec Jones and drive her to the hospital to see her boyfriend, Thatcher Wild. He'd been one of six men injured in a crash during the fateful rotation that, mercifully, had not resulted in any deaths.

Now that one had been a cluster from day one. The countries cooperating with the training event had come unprepared. The railways were slow, and not shockingly, their machinery had been a week late. Headache after headache, and I didn't even really have to deal with all that since my job as Executive Officer of the OPFOR Battalion meant I focused on facilitating my soldiers playing bad guy. But what that had meant during the first rotation of the year had been a collection of frost bite, and then this accident that had sidelined six excellent soldiers.

Thank God it hadn't been worse. It should've been, but somehow, only three trucks flipped, and all of their gear had been tied down. Three days later, we'd had everyone nestled back home. Thatcher, Masters, and two others had been discharged the same day. The last two had spent a few days in the hospital after needing to be sewn up. It was truly wild how quickly things had deteriorated.

Even after several weeks and another rotation, the dust was still settling.

It shouldn't have gone that way. Seeing Masters limping around, Wild still recovering... it killed me.

I might've sounded like a broken record, but I kept that internal. Despite suppressing the thoughts, Eric called me out.

"You realize this is not your fault in any way, don't you?" He leaned back in his office chair and eyed me where I sat across from him.

"Course."

His eyes narrowed. "Don't lie."

I checked my watch, adjusted my position in the chair, and avoided his gaze. "I'm not."

"You are. I know this because you're a bad liar when you're stressed."

I clenched my jaw but gave in. "Fine. I bear some blame, and I'm feeling that. I was the approval authority on—"

"See, now that's the problem. I'm Battalion Commander. And beyond that, every other team out there has an LTC at the helm, making the call, let alone the Garrison Commander and however many others. It should've been called days before it got so bad, and they know that. *You*, my friend, couldn't have stopped it any more than you could control the weather."

I exhaled through my nose. He was right. Of course. And he knew I knew he was right. Even though I'd worked for years with Greg, my counselor, on my impulse to feel guilty whenever something went wrong, it always hit at times like this. When something was truly wrong, it hit hard.

"You're a good man, Nate," Eric said softly, pulling my attention.

The tone struck me. "Where'd that come from?"

He shook his head, just once. "It's fact. Always been there. But just now, it came from me having a moment in which I admire your soft, squishy insides on those rare occasions you let them show."

I chuckled and pinned him with a stare as I rose to my feet. With a hand over my heart, I said in a mock emotional voice, "I've been seen."

He laughed, then waved me away. "See you tomorrow."

I returned the thought, then collected my things at my desk. Eric had promised Livie he'd be home before six tonight, which he'd told me no fewer than three times in the last two hours, so I left him to it. He also knew me well enough to know I wouldn't want to hang around and discuss my stupid tendency to feel guilty. It proved exhausting enough for me—like hell did I want to foist that on him.

This February rotation had wrapped up quickly, but paperwork had kept us working for days after thanks to a few smaller issues—nothing compared to the January mess. One thing they don't tell you when you commission into the Army as an officer? Most of what you do, after a point, is manage spreadsheets and PowerPoints. Forgive me for saying that—if it ruins the glamor, my sincerest apologies. Nevertheless, the shine of being an infantryman had faded a bit with age and rank. After coming up on seventeen years in, I felt old.

I hunched against the gust of chilly air that hit as I pushed out the battalion building's doors and ducked my chin. March would bring some reprieve from the wintry cold, depending on the usual factors. Punxsutawney Phil's sightings probably didn't apply in Bavaria, but here I was, hoping he didn't see his shadow. Though I did want to ski a bit more, so if it stayed chilly, I could handle it.

Just as I got to my car and opened it—the faintest waft of Ariel's sweet, clean scent still lingering inside—I realized this was the last weekend in February. Eric's mom would be arriving any day now, and we hadn't talked about that. Maybe he'd avoided it because he knew I'd told Ariel she could move in with me. Maybe he'd avoided it because, obviously enough, her answer was no.

We'd seen each other less in the last eight weeks than we had in any other stretch during her living here in Germany. Possible exception: the weeks after the wedding last summer. I'd taken every bit of leave I could, and somehow, it'd worked out that when I wasn't on leave, she was traveling.

I'd planned to order takeout and gorge myself on Indian food, beer, and something stupid on Netflix. But I'd have to get up early and go work out with Masters, so I amended the plan. Maybe not gorge. Maybe only two beers.

This brilliant debate played out on my twenty-minute drive home. The fields that flanked the road were frozen, though the crystalline look of the pine trees had melted off during the sunny afternoon. I'd welcome the spring and time change since it meant a little more light in the mornings, though I'd be sad to part with the little bit of light that remained now that I drove home. A few more weeks—another month, maybe—and I'd get to start and end my day with daylight.

After parking in my garage and hauling all my crap into the house, my phone buzzed in my pocket. Probably Eric with one last brilliant thought for me, or my sister, Maddie. She'd be meeting me in Garmisch for a ski weekend soon, so she'd been chattier than usual lately.

When I pulled out the device, my heart skipped. Not Eric, or Maddie, or anyone I would've expected. I'd conditioned myself *not* to expect to hear from Ariel, and I'd trained hard not to feel a little leap of possibility every time I got a message. I'd heard exactly nothing from her, other than updates about the accident during that time, and nothing since.

Until now.

I stared at the message, read it, and read it again. My heart thundered. This had to be it.

Ariel: *Can I come over and talk with you? Preferably tonight, but if you have plans, anytime this weekend if you're home.*

The sinking sensation pulled me down, down to the stool at the bar next to me. I slumped onto the seat and stared at the screen. Finally, I typed back. Might as well get it over with. I'd waited long enough to hear the words.

Tonight, we'd get past this.

CHAPTER FOUR

Ariel

I'd put it off as long as I could.

My mom had pushed her arrival date back by a week, so she wouldn't be here until Thursday. But she was originally supposed to arrive today, and I'd avoided talking to Nate, then avoided some more when she bumped her arrival.

I'd looked into other options and found none. I couldn't afford to rent a place, nor would I even technically qualify to through the Kugelfels housing office, and though Livie offered to help me navigate what that looked like outside the military situation if that was what I wanted, it just didn't make sense. Not when I had another offer I wanted to take.

Anytime I thought about actually living with Nate, what it'd be like to be near him all the time, flutters of anticipation and dread winged through me. I'd wanted to say yes, but that same voice that'd shut me down initially had kept me from answering before I exhausted every other possibility. On one hand, moving in with Nate couldn't be safer. I knew him and trusted him.

On the other hand, living with a man I'd found perilously attractive and completely unavailable for more than a decade? Someone I'd often thought of as the kind of man I'd want in a husband, who'd proven time and again he'd be an amazing father, who'd known me long enough to embrace my awkward quiet in some circumstances and my outgoing hostess in others... living with *that* man might just be downright idiotic.

I thought back to the conversation with Eric and Livie when I'd finally brought it up a little over a month ago.

We'd sat down to a family dinner, but the kids had raced through their food, then dashed upstairs to play before bed. Just the three of us remained, forks occasionally clinking against plates, all of us quiet after a long week.

"So... I have a possible solution to the living situation thing." *Eloquent, as always.*

Eric perked right up. "Oh?"

I nodded, eyes flickering to Livie, then back to Eric. "Nate offered one of his spare rooms."

Eric swallowed the bite in his mouth, and Livie's face brightened.

She spoke first. "That was so nice of him."

It was. It really was. Generous to a fault, considering if I took him up on it, he'd be saddled with a roommate. A female roommate, who may or may not impinge on his dating life. And the man definitely had a busy one, just like he always had. If his general charisma and friendship with Eric hadn't intimidated me so much, his social calendar definitely put the brakes on any true wishful thinking I might've entertained over the years.

"How do you feel about that option?" Eric asked, some amount of caution in his voice.

I exhaled. They didn't know about the odd moment the day after their wedding, but they knew something between us had changed. With the physical distance, the decreased time spent together, and the missing ease between us, they knew.

The words came like I'd recited them in front of a mirror—a paltry acceptance speech for a prize I never realized how much I wanted to win. "It's incredibly generous. I'm not sure I can say yes—it just seems like too much. But I'm glad to have the option. And if I can't figure out something else, I may take him up on it."

If I kept at it, I might just convince myself I wasn't going to say yes immediately.

Eric nodded but said nothing, since he'd already stuffed a piece of chicken into his mouth, and Livie patted my wrist. "That sounds like a good compromise."

I'd sworn them to silence—forbidden them to speak of it to Nate. I didn't want anyone but me discussing it. I honestly didn't know what Eric would say to him, though he seemed accepting enough of the offer. He knew his best friend well enough to know if he'd said it, he meant it. And he also knew I needed to deal with this on my own. One of the things that'd wounded me most deeply with Jim had been the sense that my autonomy had been stripped away. Making decisions like this for myself was more important than ever now.

So tonight, four weeks after the conversation with Livie and Eric, and almost two full months since he'd made the offer, I arrived at Nate's doorstep, my stomach a writhing knot of nerves. I blew out a big gust of air, steeled myself, and knocked.

Seconds later, there he stood, looking both adorable and ridiculously attractive. Shifting my eyes from his body, I held my breath like it might calm me.

"Hi, come in." He swung the door wide open, stepping aside so I could enter.

I'd been to his house a handful of times over the year and a half I'd lived here. Mostly, he came to Eric's, or we all went out to do something together. But come to think of it, it'd been probably eight months since I'd been here.

"Thanks for letting me swing by tonight."

"Of course. You're always welcome here."

He wandered into the kitchen, and I studied him, unable to keep my hungry eyes off him.

Hungry eyes? Seriously?

I had no time for that internal snark—not when he was here in front of me after what felt like so long, longer than the last few months. He looked perfectly at home and yet stylish, as always. Dark gray sweatpants, a hunter green waffle knit Henley shirt, and bare feet. His dark gray hair stood up at angles, like he'd run his hands through it and was the only part of him less than perfectly composed.

"Feels like forever since I've been here." I tried for cheery, but nerves strangled any attempt at normal, and my voice came out in a weird garble. Nate didn't seem to notice, though, so maybe it was all in my head.

"It has been a while. Beer?" He held up a bottle and didn't look even remotely ruffled by my being there.

That was good. If he wasn't uneasy, then I should relax too. We were friends, and he'd made an offer that provided the perfect solution to my problem. "No, thanks."

He nodded, poured himself one, then rounded the counter to stand next to it, drink resting in his hand. His relaxed posture, the casual way he smiled like he had nothing else to do, made an image flash through my mind. I could see him, standing at a bar with a date, charming her with his humor and gleaming smile. I blinked the picture and the accompanying spike of discomfort away and refocused on the moment.

"So..."

His smile widened. "So..."

Curse him, he didn't finish the thought. He simply smiled and took a sip. Part of me had hoped he'd make it easy on me, but to be fair, I'd left him hanging for nearly two months, so I couldn't blame him for leaving the ball so completely in my court.

A tension halfway between anxiety and giddiness coiled in my belly. "So I'd like to take you up on your offer."

The easy smile slipped from his face for a second, two, then returned, though his eyes dipped to the beer with purpose, and he took another long drink. "Tell me what that means."

My stomach—no, my entire body—threatened to drop through the floor. Had I somehow hallucinated that conversation on New Year's Eve? "You said I could live with you? I know it's been a while, but—"

"I did. Yes, I said that. I meant it," he rushed.

Relief washed through me. "Okay. Good. I'm hoping the offer hasn't expired."

"No expiration. Of course. Absolutely. Yes."

A hysterical giggle built in my chest, and I coughed to relieve it.

"Great. Then... yes, Nate, I'd like to move in with you." I smiled, feeling triumphant for voicing that so clearly, then panicked, realizing how it sounded. "To your spare bedroom. Because you offered. Because we're friends."

He nodded decisively, and our gazes locked. "Good. I'm glad."

"Me too."

Now that it was done, I genuinely felt glad. Relieved. I'd sensed it was the right choice almost immediately after he'd said it months ago, but I'd resisted. The Ariel who'd been through counseling twice a week just to be able to speak without apologizing demanded it. The person who'd jumped without looking—who'd been so desperate for a family and a future that she'd moved across the country with a man she hardly knew and then *stayed* with him. The woman who'd hated herself every day she stayed, but couldn't leave... *that* woman promised herself she'd check every angle before she said yes. What if this turned into a mistake—yet another one?

I'd worked to find other options, but none of them felt right—of course they didn't. At the heart of me, I didn't want them to. And also, logistically, they just didn't make sense with my income. This did. Plus, it was only for a few months.

Nate cleared his throat. "Want a tour?"

"Of course!" I said, maybe a little too loudly, but what's a little lack of volume control between friends?

He picked up his beer and gestured to the living room.

"Living room." He turned and pointed with the hand holding his drink. "Kitchen."

The look in his eye was a familiar one—the one that said he thought he was being clever. That high-strung, too-loud me relaxed an inch.

"Mind-blowing, Major Reynolds. Thanks so much."

He snickered. "All right, come along then, Wolfe."

Down a hallway, I remembered the half bath. Then up a spiral staircase, and now we'd entered new territory, and with it, the nerves had instantly doubled.

"A bathroom on this floor and two bedrooms—you can choose either, but I'd vote the one that doesn't masquerade as an office because then you won't have all my *yay me* Army stuff haunting you at night." He flicked his hand toward the door at the far end of the short hallway. "Have a look."

I passed the room he must've been referring to as his office. It had fancy-looking framed plaques and guide-ons, also known as flags. I didn't go in because the pull toward the room that would be mine came too strong.

A queen-sized bed with a fluffy white comforter and pillows sat in the middle of the space. A rug covered the bare floor—it looked soft. White painted side tables flanked the bed, each decked with a lamp. A white waist-high dresser nestled against the wall where the ceiling slanted up sharply.

"It's beautiful," I said, not sure why it surprised me so much. Who had slept here before me? Maybe his sister had come to stay? I'd never managed to meet her in real life. And, at least before last summer, he would've introduced her if she had been in town.

"Thanks. I hope you'll be comfortable. But we can get anything else you need. And you can change anything. I'm guessing the bed at Eric's will stay there, but if there's other furniture you want to bring or anything, just say the word."

He spoke from the doorway, leaning against the frame. His eyes skated over me, then bounced away to survey the room. He nearly glared at it, like he could suss out any potential issues I might have simply by staring hard enough.

Little did he know, I needed a moment. Stepping close

to the window and gazing out at the neighbor's place across the street, I gave myself a minute. The sight of the pristine, almost feminine room had made my throat tighten.

I'd had my own apartment before Jim. Light pink and super girly—I tended to like things airy. Jim's décor had been so masculine. I'd liked it at first, enjoyed the deep gray and brown fabrics and espresso-colored wood he favored. But one day, I'd brought home bright teal throw pillows to liven things up, and he'd laughed. I'd laughed too, joining in on a joke I hadn't known was about me. And then, he'd said I better take them back because I had no sense of style and didn't need to change anything.

I'd been embarrassed. We'd only been together a few months at that point, and I'd thought maybe I *had* overstepped. Maybe he thought I didn't like his stuff. In retrospect, it'd been a sign I'd excused. Maybe on its own, it would've been awkward and something to revisit, but in the end, it'd been the beginning of ways he'd controlled everything about our lives, right down to the throw pillows.

I snapped back to the present, running a hand over the duvet. *"But we can get anything else you need. And you can change anything."* Nate had said this so casually. He had no idea what those deceptively simple phrases meant to me.

Clearing my throat, I found my voice. "I don't have much. If it's okay with you, I'll bring a load over this weekend, and then maybe another drop later in the week? I do want to be out by the time Mom arrives on Thursday. I'm doing some stuff with Delia's class on Monday and Robby's on Wednesday. Maybe I can drop by on Tuesday?"

I pressed a hand to my belly, like it might help the nerves shooting through me. Putting dates on things made this real.

"Whenever you want. This is going to be your home, so you come and go whenever you want. Like I said when we first talked about it, I have a ton going on the next few months—rotations, TDYs, travel. So you'll have the place to yourself fairly often."

We walked back down the hall, then down the stairs to the living room, and he leaned against the counter. He pulled out his phone and studied it, then nodded. "So if you need any help, I'm good tomorrow or Sunday. I have Summer's feast thing on Sunday night. Are you going to that?"

"Yes. I didn't realize you were going." I'd been looking forward to attending another one of Summer's famous feast nights. Having Nate there would be that much better.

Or that much more awkward. It all depended on how things went the next few days. Would we really live like this? Tiptoeing around what happened last year, me fighting myself, my own draw to him, all the while?

"Yeah, she invited me after a workout thing at Sergeant Masters' house—he lives a few doors down from her."

"Oh, I'm aware." I didn't even try to hide the smile that came then. I was fully aware of the beautiful, quiet, odd man that lived just a few doors down from my friend, and I also knew that he'd thrown her for a loop, and I couldn't wait to see what happened between them. Because I would put money on *something*.

Nate narrowed his eyes, but his mouth curved up. It felt like a moment from before. "Aha. Well. Why don't you have Eric or Livie drop you with a load that afternoon, and then you can work on getting a little settled in before the dinner. We can go together, and then I can drop you back at their place if you aren't ready to stay here."

"Sounds perfect."

I grabbed my purse and jacket and moved to the door. My list of questions for him could wait until Sunday. I'd probably have more to add by then anyway. And it let me put off the most awkward ones, which I would have to address. Just not yet. Sunday.

CHAPTER FIVE

Nate

The look on Eric's face told me everything I needed to know. The time had come.

Frankly, I was shocked it hadn't come sooner. I'd figured as soon as Ariel told him, he'd be stomping over here ready to tear my head off. But nothing. He didn't even hint at knowing about my offer, which made me think Ariel had waited a while before telling him.

But now? Jig was up.

"All right. Lay it on me."

I waved my hands like I welcomed it. In a way, I did. We needed to get to the other side of this, because as much as I wanted to help Ariel, I didn't want it to mess things up with Eric. Not when I knew damn well my friendship with him would outlast Ariel being my roommate. That line I'd drawn was still there, and when she left in a few months, I'd force myself to move past the old hang up.

His eyes flickered to the hallway. No movement. Ariel was unpacking her suitcases.

"Tell me I don't have to worry about this."

That was his Commander Eric voice. *Noted.*

"You don't have to worry about this."

He squinted, reading whatever my body language said. I didn't think it'd tell him anything but the truth—he didn't need to worry about this. I hadn't lured his sister here to make a move on her. I really would be gone a lot, and she needed a place. And hell, I hadn't planned on making the offer, but once it had slipped out there, I'd had no desire to take it back. I'd been certain she was going to say no, so when the yes came a few days ago, I'd had a momentary meltdown. I'd already talked through all the reasons it was better she *not* stay with me to make her impending *no* more palatable. So her yes?

It was pop rocks and Coke to my brain.

I'd kept my crap together while giving her the tour, but by the time she'd left, I'd been borderline anxious, and God forgive me, excited. But dread also tagged along—so much freaking dread. Because of all those little reasons I'd told myself.

You won't have to share your space.

You won't have to see her all the time.

You won't have to control the overwhelming urge to touch her.

You won't have to stand inches from that freaking line you both drew and gaze starry-eyed at the possibilities of what crossing it would look like.

Damn, did that make me sound like such a creep, but I was looking for every possible reason to make myself feel better. With one word, she'd sent all those reasons running back into my mind, but now I would have to do those things.

Eric's stare stayed on me, like he might be reading every one of those thoughts. As much as I loved his sister's identical eyes, having his blue inspection pass over me was more than unnerving. Maybe because of those thick manbrows.

"I better not have to worry about this."

I laughed. "I'd never do anything to hurt her. You know my schedule coming up—she'll practically be living alone."

That was a big part of why I didn't feel as guilty as I otherwise might've. She really would have the place to herself most of the next few months.

He pursed his lips, but then nodded. Case closed.

That'd gone about how I expected, honestly. Maybe even a little better.

"Ari, I'm going. I'll see you later," he hollered.

Ariel popped into the hallway and leaned over the railing from the next floor up. My stomach dipped at the sight of her dark hair peeking down at us.

"Okay. See you tonight."

With that, Eric left us.

Me. And his sister. At my house.

Where we were going to live together.

My head swam. I needed to eat something. The lunch I'd had hours ago had burned off, probably within minutes of eating it. My watch told me I'd used six hundred calories during Masters' workout this morning. Before I stopped being able to think, I inhaled a banana and guzzled down some water.

"What time did you want to head to Summer's?"

I startled, then wiped my chin. I'd dumped water down my shirt, too. *Super.* Luckily, I hadn't changed for the dinner yet.

"An hour? It'll only take a few minutes to get there from here. Do you need help?"

"No, I'm good. At some point, we should talk about expectations or rules, or a roommate contract. Whatever you want to call it." Her eyes darted to the side, then back to me.

Roommate contract? Hadn't thought of that. But laying some ground rules made sense. "Of course. I'd thought we'd do that Tuesday night. It'll be later that night, but we can fit it in."

And that would give me a few days to come up with something.

"Sounds good. Okay, I'm going to get back to it. See you in a bit." She spun on her heel and disappeared down the hall.

I made my first rule for myself right then.

Don't watch her walk away. Ever.

Good. See? Already one rule down. I'd figure out the rules, then stick to them, and it'd be fine. I couldn't tell her that one, obviously, but I'd come up with something by Tuesday.

"Masters, do you know Ariel Wolfe?" I asked as we all entered Summer's house.

"We haven't met."

Masters took her hand and shook it, his eyes coasting over her. Not in a hungry way like men often looked at her, though, so points to him for that. He may or may not have gone up a notch in my estimation right then.

"Ariel, this is Nick Masters. He's the beast who runs the workouts for the battalion and who's training Rob. He's also an excellent NCO and a man of few words." That was putting it mildly. I turned to my pseudo-date, though I didn't look right at her face because she was too damn pretty tonight. My chest had been tight since the moment she'd stepped out of her bedroom fifteen minutes ago. "And this is Ariel Wolfe, as I said. She's Eric's sister and nanny to his two kids. She's also put up with me as a friend for over a decade, so feel free to cast her pitying looks all evening."

"Pleasure," Masters said.

I felt Ariel's eyes on me but didn't glance at her. For some reason, knowing her things—her clothes and shoes and whatever else she'd brought—were nestled into the room at *my* house made looking at her overwhelming.

Before we knew it, Summer presented the feast. Every bite was delicious, and the conversation and atmosphere were all delightful. If my gut twisted in longing when I watched the two couples at the table holding hands or smiling at each other in *that* way, like they had plans for each other once they left—well, I punched that sad little twinge back down to where it belonged. Hidden and ignored.

Since Summer refused help cleaning up, I wandered into the living room to grab our coats while Ariel ventured into the kitchen to offer help one last time. Though it felt odd to leave without doing anything, I was more than ready to go. I'd not sat next to Ariel for a meal like this in a long time. I'd eaten at Eric's and out with them a small handful of times since last summer but had managed to avoid sitting close to her.

The impulse to rest a hand on the back of her chair or even on her leg practically screamed at me. But both of those gestures were proprietary in a way that would be notable and problematic. We weren't there on a date. We were there as all I'd ever get from her, and it was time I got it through my thick head.

No. I had gotten it through. And I'd made my rules. I had my line.

Friends. Just friends.

Ariel emerged from the kitchen with bright cheeks. When our eyes met, she chuckled and shook her head. "No luck. She refused me, too."

"Stubborn one, that Summer Applegate," I said, holding out her jacket.

"That she is. And then she said—" She practically swallowed the words to stop speaking. When she turned to me, she'd pressed her lips together like she'd zipped them shut.

"She said what?"

Something about me? I wouldn't ask that outright. This kind of thing was total catnip to me. You let on you have a secret, and I want to know it. You tell me I can't have something, and I want it. You let slip a little something, then snatch it back, and I'm going to work to pry out the rest.

The only time this didn't apply was with the woman herself. Finding out I couldn't have her didn't make me want her any more than I already did, because once you're at max capacity, there isn't any more. It just never goes away.

"Nothing. She was just teasing me. Oh, wow, it's really coming down."

We hustled out the door once the thick flakes caught our attention. My chest did a little excited jump—I loved snow. Plus, this would get me in the mood for my upcoming ski weekend. Ariel slipped about ten feet from the car, but I grabbed her, one arm around her waist, the other at her elbow nearest me.

"You okay?" I asked, looking down at her to find our faces closer than they had been in a long, long time.

She nodded but didn't speak, so we turned and

continued the trek to the car. I opened her door and released her, firmly pushing away any feelings trying to creep in at being that close or catching the scent of her perfume I'd never tire of.

In the car, the silence was too much. My car could handle snow, but we had a bit of a drive ahead of us since we'd need to move more slowly. And I couldn't bear the quiet, especially since my idiot brain kept circling the way it felt to have my arm around her, even though she wore a heavy coat.

"So, what'd Summer say to tease you?"

I could see her look at me, but I kept my eyes glued to the road. I needed to focus and get her home safe. Plus, I was pretty sure her dress was riding up a few inches above her knee, and I did not need to be looking at her legs, even if they were covered in thick black tights.

"She was deflecting—trying to get me out of there so I wouldn't start helping her and break her rules."

"Okay. What'd she say?" The blush Ariel had worn when she left the kitchen would've intrigued me if her dangling the bait hadn't.

"She was being silly."

"Just tell me."

"It's nothing."

"Then tell me."

Her head whipped to the side, and I could picture her face. I didn't need to look. She'd have that irritated look she gave her brother, and oftentimes me. Her lips would be pressed together, flattening out the lush curves just a touch. If I looked at her, I'd still want to kiss her just as badly, but that stupid little part of me would also want to ruffle her hair or do something else to provoke her.

There'd be none of that tonight, nor had there been for ages.

"She said she thought you were *more than ready* to get me home."

I swallowed, a slipping feeling in my gut. If she only knew all the ways that was true. "Ha. Good one."

A sorry effort, but I had to say something.

"Yeah. She knows we're friends."

Ariel's voice didn't sound playful at all. She almost sounded a little sad. Which I hated and didn't entirely understand.

"Of course she does."

A far worse kind of quiet descended then—something awkward and uncomfortable. The kilometers ticked by slowly, and soon, we'd made it to the edge of the small town where Eric lived.

Just when I thought we'd be silent right up until she jumped out of the car, she spoke.

"What will we do about that, though?"

"That?"

She cleared her throat. "You know. Women who aren't necessarily your friends. Dates and... whatever. I don't want to get in your way."

I pulled up in front of Eric and Livie's just as she finished her sentence. I could've laughed for how ridiculous the question was, but I needed to make sure I understood. "You want to know how we'll handle me bringing women back to my place while you live there?"

She nodded, but I couldn't see much of her expression. She was backlit by the porch lights, her face thus cast in shadow.

"That won't be an issue."

"Really?"

That stabbed me in the gut. Did she really think I was so much of a ladies' man? True, I'd always dated and made a point to be sure I had someone to spend time with whenever Ariel was a more active part of my life. One might argue I'd created a persona around being out and about with people all the time, but some stupid part of me had hoped she'd know. That she, of all people, would see through it.

"I'm certain."

A beat, then she spoke. "Okay then. Thanks for the ride. I guess I'll see you Tuesday."

With that, she left, slowly plodding her way up the walk to Eric's door. I should've gotten out and walked with her, but that would've been date-like, and she probably would've looked at me like I had two heads if I'd done that. One last wave from the door, and then she was gone.

And only after I pulled away, on the road home to my house that would be empty of her only another two nights, did I realize that maybe she hadn't brought up the idea of bringing women back to the house for my sake.

Maybe she wanted to be able to bring someone home for hers.

CHAPTER SIX

Ariel

I'd slept at Nate's house since Tuesday night. I'd been exhausted and passed out early, and he'd gotten back so late, we hadn't even seen each other. He'd been gone when I got up, and I'd left to get to the school for my volunteering time before he got home from PT.

All in all, I could see how we might go quite a while without interacting. We'd seen each other in passing Wednesday night as I was cleaning up from the dinner I'd made. I hadn't made him any, and guilt had weighed heavy in my belly all evening because of it. He'd said he was leaving the next evening and would be back Sunday. We'd talk about the rules and expectations then.

Honestly? It'd been weird. Not *bad* weird, but just weird. On one hand, I felt like I was living alone. On the other, signs of Nate were, of course, everywhere. His style—classic, rich, and appealing, I'd call it—oozed from every inch of the space. There weren't a lot of flourishes, but the ones he did have were nice—a bar cart filled with every kind of luxury liquor available, for example. It made sense for his life—bachelor, entertainer, sophisticated man about town. Or whatever.

We'd need to talk more about the expectations. He'd mentioned a cleaning lady came once a week, which made that whole issue easier. And we had separate bathrooms, thank goodness. But would we share groceries? Would we ever eat together?

I'd gone from a bustling house with three adults and two kids to practically living alone. I had strength now I didn't have when I'd left the US to move here—so much more—and yet I didn't know if I wanted to be alone. Not all the time.

I'd felt alone for all but a few fleeting moments while I had been with Jim. That crushing loneliness had absolutely contributed to feeling so stuck, to staying with a man who controlled me, and eventually marrying him because it all ran away from me. I had Eric and Mom, but we'd all been through so much already with my dad's death and Eric's divorce so fresh.

Those were excuses I should've ignored—I knew that now. But moving in to the bright, clamorous life Eric had here In Germany had been part of what'd patched me up.

That said, I was an introvert and couldn't deny my innate need for quiet and solitude. And though I'd thought being alone here at Nate's would be a relief, both from the busy pace of Eric's and from the tension that slipped through nearly every interaction Nate and I had, I'd missed him this week.

Stupid thought. I'd missed him for months now, in truth. I'd looked forward to rebuilding the friendship we'd had, and he wouldn't have offered his home if he wasn't over whatever weirdness had infiltrated our dynamic since the summer.

A half-hearted laugh escaped then. I'd blocked out *the look* and that flood of frustration and fear that came with it. I'd felt like a dog scrabbling across wood flooring, unable to find purchase. That look had threatened one of the most valuable things in my life. Nate and I had both decided to ignore it, but in the end, we'd failed miserably because it *had* changed us. These months apart must've helped him... change back. At the same time, I feared it'd potentially cracked me open a bit wider.

Whatever the case, I looked forward to him getting home Sunday. I'd seen my mom, and she'd given me the biggest, sweetest hug ever. I hadn't seen her since the wedding, and I'd missed her. As much as her moving back to Germany for these last few months had caused a little ruffle in my feathers, I was settled now—or settling in, at least—and it was so good to have her here.

Plus, I didn't know what would happen when Eric and Livie moved. Our mom would go with them, but would I? I didn't really have a reason to, not with Mom managing the kids. And legally, I didn't have a way to stay in Germany. I'd move back Stateside but wouldn't necessarily move to where they went. But then, where else would I go?

I swatted away those worries. *One thing at a time.* I'd made it through the weekend, mostly spending time at Eric and Livie's and enjoying my mom, only popping home to sleep, and this Sunday morning, we were meeting at an adorable café in town for brunch.

Livie and my mom were already seated when I arrived —exactly on time, mind you. Evidently, they'd both adjusted to Eric's clock, set to *show up ten minutes early or you're late*. And thus, I was the slacker this morning.

"Sorry I'm late," I said, sliding into the waiting empty chair.

"It's okay," Livie said, then glanced at my mom. She swallowed, then smiled at me. "I was going to wait, but I just need to tell you. I don't know why I'm nervous."

I smiled at her, then sipped the water they'd already ordered me. *Ohna Gas*—without carbonation, because I never could get used to sparkling water. "Tell me. What's up?"

My mom patted Livie's hand, and something about that action made my stomach drop.

Livie took a deep breath, then caught my eyes and stared into them. "I'm pregnant."

At that word, that one spectacularly heavy and beautiful and awful word, my whole body stiffened.

"Oh." The sound issued from me, more like a breath than anything. I pulled it together though, pushing away that crushing sensation, like my insides were a sheet of tinfoil crumpling into a ball. "That's wonderful!"

Livie's eyes brimmed, and she sniffled. "I'm sorry."

That ball dropped like a leaden weight on my chest and pressed down, down, down. "No, no, no. This is wonderful news. *Wonderful.* You're making me an aunt, again! And it's going to be a little Livie-Eric baby! It's amazing."

I lunged for her, hugging her to me and sob-laughing. She made a similar sound.

She spoke gently into my ear. "I know it's not... simple. It's—"

I pinned her with a look that I hoped conveyed how important my next words were. "Thank you for sharing this news. Thank you for letting me be a part of the excitement. I'm honored, and I'm so excited."

She smiled, lips pressed together and trembling—to stay another sob, most likely. "Sorry. I'm a basket case."

My mom patted her hand again. "You're just fine. Pregnancy throws everything out of whack. I'm crying, and I definitely don't have that excuse."

She sent me a tender look, knowing my heart well enough to know this wasn't simple, indeed. Both of them did, or Livie wouldn't feel upset telling me. And she shouldn't feel upset. Though I'd need to face this when I had a moment alone, I felt loved and cared for in this one— even as I walked the tightrope of emotion. They'd been as gentle as possible with something that would cut deep.

We all chuckled at Mom, and the waitress arrived to take our orders. I used the distraction to settle myself, breathing in and out through my nose and promising myself I could have a good old-fashioned sob later. For now, supporting Livie and celebrating would be the focus.

We chatted a while longer, and the more she shared, the less I could believe I hadn't made the connection sooner. She'd known for two weeks and had suspected for about a month. She'd been feeling terrible, and now it made sense. Morning sickness, which she confirmed had nothing to do with morning.

I left the brunch feeling far better than I had during those first moments but bowed out of coming over for the afternoon. I needed to get ready for tonight, and I wanted to get organized for the week. And I didn't know how much longer I could summon happiness.

I slumped onto the couch and stared at the blank TV. I should cue up a movie. I should sink into a book. I should do anything other than sit here and let my mind fall down the hole waiting for me.

I'd learned to lock up my more emotional responses during my time with Jim. Not just the marriage, because I'd had to face the fact that his abuse had started long before we got married. I'd tricked myself into believing it'd get better if we were married. After years of therapy, I'd been able to accept that negative feelings weren't bad. They could even be good. But right now, I didn't want to feel sad.

I wanted to feel only happy for Eric and Livie. And I was genuinely happy they'd get to have a child together, and that Delia and Robby would get to have a little baby to love. They'd be precious big siblings to a baby. And my mom would get to help raise this baby in a way she hadn't gotten to with the big kids.

And me: I got to be an aunt again. I loved being an aunt.

But, oh, my heart ached. It hurt in a way I hadn't felt in quite a while. It was kind of surprising, once I stepped back from that. I'd been mired in so much hurt for so long that I hardly realized how far from it I'd come. But right now, I needed to let myself feel the full spectrum of emotions. Not just happy for my family. Not just eager for the new life.

I shut my eyes and let the other swing of feelings settle in. Sadness, and emptiness, and a bone-deep longing that rooted so forcefully in my stomach, it felt like it anchored into my soul.

I want that.

I wanted to be a mother so much. It was what I'd always wanted. I'd been wandering around, trying to figure out what was next for me, but *that* was what I wanted more than anything. Mom and Livie knew it, Eric knew it, and they'd hesitated to tell me. I hated that, but I understood it—appreciated it even. I didn't want them to feel anything but deliriously happy, even if it came like a punch in the stomach for me.

I could point to so many decisions made with that longing to have my own child, my own family, in mind. Almost everything with Jim after the first few months fell to that—to a desperate need not to have wasted time with him. To get to the next part, the good part where I was a wife and mom. Hurtful, stupid decisions, and thanks to that history, I'd trudged a long road back to trusting myself.

Jim had known too. He'd used that desire more than once after blowing up at me or belittling me, especially early on. It was the promise he made every time he needed to reel me back in. *Let's get married, and then we can start our family. Let's get through this month, and then we'll start trying.*

I'd never expected to be someone who cried every time I got my period, but I'd pinned my hopes of happiness on a new baby. I'd convinced myself it would solve our problems—soften Jim, make him happy with me, help me be content with him. I'd pour all my love and care into the baby, and I'd have purpose.

And even though I cried every month without fail, it turned to relief as the months wore on and his meanness worsened. Relief, and heart-rending loneliness, and the shredded ribbons of hope for what I might have someday. Somehow. With someone else. Because I'd realized a child with Jim would tether me to him forever, and more to the point, that he'd be the same person. Maybe worse, with the stress of a new baby.

It'd been over two years since I'd left Jim. Two years of healing and freedom and grieving so many things. Two years of placing one foot in front of the other, wondering what all of this meant for my life. I'd felt it coming, but since the new year, I'd known the time of my shuttling around Delia and Robby needed to come to an end. The time had come to pass the baton back to Mom and figure out me.

At thirty-three, I needed my own direction. I needed my own *life*. Even if it looked so completely opposite of what I imagined—divorced instead of married, childless instead of snuggling my own kids, essentially jobless instead of blissfully staying home to care for my family.

The difference between me now and me two years ago was clear, though. Because as the brutal swing of loss and gut-level wanting swept over me in waves, I didn't feel like I stood in sinking sand. I didn't question whether I even deserved to be standing. I *knew* I did, and I knew I'd walk out of this and keep breathing.

Nate

The faint scent of Ariel's perfume as I entered the house made my pulse perk up. After three hours in the car driving back from Garmisch, my body and mind were twin slugs. But that little tease of her presence here reminded me she might be home—as though I could've forgotten. Like I hadn't spent the last four days in some of the most glorious mountains, cutting down slopes and gulping down the beauty of the place like the more runs I made, the more deep breaths I took, the less I'd feel her grip on me.

Maddie hadn't made it—she'd gotten hung up with work, and so I'd been solo for the entire weekend. Not ideal, especially with Ariel on my mind even more than usual.

I'd managed to stay away all except the first two nights after she'd moved in. Thanks to the ski trip, she'd had time to settle without me awkwardly milling around asking her if she needed anything. *Good.* She needed it, and soon enough, I'd start into another rotation and she'd have even more time to herself. And I wouldn't feel like I needed to physically restrain myself in order to stop just trying to *talk* to her. I'd done okay so far, but again, the credit there was due primarily to not actually being here.

I dumped everything but my bag inside the door—I'd deal with putting away the skis and boots another time. Tossing the keys on the counter, I promised myself a tall glass of water with ice in just a minute and took care of business. After using the facilities, I left my bag on the stairs, and heard a gasp.

"Ariel?" I heard her but didn't see her.

Then she popped up in the living room, looking around a little wild-eyed. And *whoa,* she looked rough. Alarm shot up my spine and I rushed to her, around the couch, and sat next to her. "What's wrong? What happened?"

She blinked rapidly, then rubbed her eyes. "I fell asleep. I'm sorry."

Her voice sounded raspy and unusually rough. Dark circles hung under her eyes—not just sleepless or sad dark, but like racoon-style, gritty mascara; she must've been crying at some point, and not just delicate little tears. I wanted to take her hand, something, but instead just sat there, leaning as close as I could without touching her.

"Don't be sorry. What happened?"

Her beautiful, ridiculous blue eyes flickered back and forth between mine, and her chest rose and fell like she could hardly breathe. And then she launched at me, wrapping her arms around my shoulders and pressing her face into my neck as she cried.

I froze for only a moment before gathering her to me, giving her the full measure of comfort I could offer with my arms around her. I hugged her close, firmly, matching the pressure of her embrace. The only sounds were her breath and the small, agonized sounds she must've been trying to hold back.

What the hell happened? Was she remembering something with Jim? Had she gotten bad news? I shut my eyes and gave myself over to the moment, holding her, my heart breaking with her, though it didn't know why. "Shhh, Ariel, love. You're all right. You're safe. You're all right."

At that, she froze, then pulled away. My words broke the moment wide open, and though selfishly I regretted having to let her go, my concern and need to know what had happened overrode the feeling.

"It's not bad. I mean, I know I'm safe. It's not anything like that."

"Good. That's good."

"I probably shouldn't tell you this—Eric's going to, I'm sure. But Livie told me today she's—" she sucked in a sharp breath and held it for a few seconds, before releasing it, "—pregnant."

"Oh, damn." That response came only because even I knew Ariel wanted kids, and badly. I could rejoice with them later. But now, just now, seeing her undone like this, I felt what might be a sliver of the sadness she felt.

She smiled then—of course this woman, weighed down by her own feelings, still smiled for her brother and friend. "It's good news. It really is."

"It is."

I couldn't help it. I ran a hand over her hair, needing to comfort her. We sat close, spoke with faces inches away from each other, and now that she'd broken the seal on touching with that hug, I wasn't going to stop. Not if it helped in some small way.

"It's just—" Another quick inhale, hold, then slow exhale through her nose. She swallowed and breathed, then gave me those crazy-ass blue raccoon eyes again. "I am so happy for them. But I am so, so sad for me."

Her eyes welled, and I pulled her to me. She came with me as I leaned back against the couch, arms around her, her weight against my chest. I stroked one hand down her soft, tangled hair and her back, then closed my eyes, willing peace and comfort to filter in through the pain. I prayed in a begging, needy way that this sadness, one day, would be eased.

Minutes later, she pulled away and sat up.

"I'm sorry." They were useless words, but true.

"Thanks. I hope you don't think less of me for this."

I shook my head. "No. Never. I know you're happy for them. Your feelings for *you* don't negate that. But it isn't simple."

Though not to this degree, I'd felt something like this at Eric and Livie's wedding last summer. I was genuinely elated for my friends, but I wanted it for myself, and I'd had moments where that wanting had nearly gutted me.

"Thank you," she said again, then ran her hands under her eyes in an automatic move to check her makeup but stilled. A laugh punched out of her. "Oh, boy. I look like a creepy clown, don't I?"

She popped up and shuffled to the bathroom as I said, "Not creepy. Maybe a tragedy clown? A mime?"

She came back out, toilet paper in one hand as she wiped at the arcs of black under her eyes. "I look like a member of KISS."

I laughed outright at that. Her hair was a little crazy and big, especially because she tended to be so polished, so it did seem particularly wild in contrast. And of course, the makeup. "You kind of do. Give me a little 'Rock and Roll All Night.'"

She cackled and shook her head, a smile lighting up her face. KISS member or not, she still killed me. Her raw beauty in that simple moment felt like a full-on assault.

"I don't think we want to hear me sing right now."

"I always want to hear you sing. We've got to capitalize on this look. If you won't, then I will." I hopped up and sauntered toward her. At about three feet from her, I broke out into a pose, pointing at her and singing in a hideous, shrieking wail, "I was made—"

"No! No."

"For loving you—"

"No, that's good." She giggled and ran for the stairs. "I'm good. You're good. I'll get this off, and then you won't be compelled anymore."

I continued the song as she disappeared onto the second floor and smiled, cutting off my horrid singing. I had an awful singing voice. Before she got married, she'd discovered this during a ride in my car when I sang along with Springsteen. She never let me live it down.

Bringing it back in this moment felt natural and good. I hated that she'd had such a rough afternoon, but I had to admit I loved being the one to cheer her up. Not that she had to buck up and be happy—not at all. I was also glad that she would let me hold her as she cried.

I would do that. Always. If she'd let me.

Don't go there, fool.

I blew out a slow breath and grabbed my bag, then jogged up the stairs. "I'm going to start the laundry, and then maybe we can order in some dinner and talk roommate rule stuff, yeah?"

I didn't stop on her floor, just kept right on up to my

bedroom at the top of the house. It was a long way up today after a weekend of skiing. My quads burned, but not as much as they might've if I hadn't been training with Masters.

"Sounds perfect," she said, her voice floating up from below.

A few minutes later, with laundry started and takeout ordered, we sat back on the couch. Before we dove into roommate stuff, I wanted to make sure she felt up to it. "You okay?"

"I am. I just needed to let myself feel all that mess. I'm sure it'll crop up again here and there, but not so much, I don't think. I've noticed how hard it is to let myself do that—really feel everything. But once I do, I feel lighter and better."

I nodded, fully understanding. "My therapist says that ignoring negative emotions can harm us psychologically. That our culture of ignoring the hard, messy things is actually dangerous."

She blinked. "You see someone?"

"Have for years. You think all this sturdy magnificence comes naturally?" I joked.

She chuckled. "I guess not. Silly me."

Her warm smile made it feel like my heart was glowing. She had no idea what an easy target I was. "I'm glad you're letting yourself feel everything—every bit of it. And I'm really glad you're here. You can do your KISS impression anytime you need to."

"Very kind of you. Now, down to business."

I took the cue and we launched into discussing grocery shopping and dishes protocol and TV rights. I'd never enjoyed such a mundane conversation more. If it was dangerous, sitting close to her and delighting in the way she'd recovered thanks to my help, I ignored it. If it made me a fool to relish her attention and the way she nudged my shoulder like she used to when I made a joke, so be it.

If this was all I'd have of Ariel Wolfe, then I'd take every second while it lasted.

CHAPTER EIGHT

Ariel

I finagled a job!

I said *finagled* because I felt bad about being hired for a position I knew I couldn't keep for very long. Eric would PCS in four months, and my command sponsorship, the legal status I held that allowed me to be in Germany for more than ninety days at a time and come on post, would be null and void.

I didn't tell them when exactly I'd be leaving, but they knew it wouldn't be long. I'd been working with the ladies at the Red Cross almost the entire time I'd lived here, so it wouldn't be a shock. The job wouldn't pay much, but it was something to keep me busy three days a week. The other two, I'd volunteer with Livie's class or pop into Delia's or Robby's.

This helped. That restless, *What am I doing with my life?* itch had become unbearable within a week of Mom arriving. I was technically still the kids' nanny, and I'd still do most of the shuttling around. Mom would take over some of the meals I usually cooked, and we'd trade off helping with homework and other stuff while Eric and Livie were at work. As nice as it was to have Mom here, it made me feel useless. And though I knew I still had a role to play, I hated that feeling.

I'd become so familiar with it. I could see Jim's face, sneering in a way I would never have imagined when I met him, *telling* me I was useless.

At first, he was all charm. Completely swept me off my feet, and after having been in a relationship for three years that I thought would end in marriage but didn't, I had panicked. I'd thought, *Here's a guy who is charming, likes me a whole lot, and wants me in a way that feels a little dangerous, a little exciting.* I'd felt like I'd lost time, spending my first few years at the end of college and just after with a guy who just didn't fit—we'd both known it, but I'd plodded along, thinking something would magically change.

Then came Jim. We started dating, and within a month, he got orders to PCS. I'd been having so much fun, been so ready for something new that held some passion, that when he asked me to go with him, I did.

If I could go back and slap that woman, shake some sense into her, I would. I left a decent teaching job, all my friends, and a place I loved, and I followed him. I took a lower-paying position because he wanted to make sure we had time together. We'd known each other less than five weeks when I moved in with him. At first, I thought his irritability and anger were due to the move and job change, and I excused it. Any time I'd get really concerned, he'd do something sweet to apologize. Flowers or a fancy night out, or what I'd come to realize as the primary way he manipulated me: talking about our future together.

I'd spent months grappling with that one. I'd been uneasy about him, about our dynamic, and yet he had this way of pushing all that away by making me the center of his attention. He'd talk about the future—marriage, kids, him becoming a battalion commander and how great I'd be by his side. It all appealed to me so much, and I'd come into the relationship feeling like I was behind where I wanted to be —older than I'd planned on being when I started a family and had kids. As the months ticked by, I grew more isolated, lost all my friends, and couldn't imagine having to start over yet again. Especially because I'd jumped in with him so quickly.

My mom had urged me every way she knew how *not* to do that. I wasn't that young, but I didn't know him, and moving for a guy after a month? Insane. Except that so many women did this, and I'd heard the stories—met a soldier, married him a month later, or something that sounded crazy until the marriage lasts thirty years. My silly, romantic heart loved the idea.

Instead, Jim kept me on a leash for two years before we married. I'd acknowledged soon after it ended that when we did marry, I'd known it was wrong. But by then, I had been so isolated from everyone, I didn't know how to stop it. Instead, I tricked myself into believing it'd get better once we got married. He'd be happier with me, maybe treat me a little nicer. And I'd be happier being his wife, having a real role where I could more easily volunteer in his unit and maybe even get pregnant right away. He'd said he wanted that.

The first few months after I left, I whipped myself over

how it had gone. For how long I'd stayed. It took three months after our wedding for him to hurt me physically. He'd never touched me in anger before—only words up to that point. It was never hitting, though, just smaller things that I excused away. He'd held my wrist too tight because he was upset. He'd gripped my shoulder that hard because I'd scared him when I got home late. *Whatever.*

It was Eric who broke things open. While prepping to move to Europe, he'd asked if I wanted to come visit before they left since it'd be a much longer trip once they did. We chatted about where we might travel if I came and visited them in Germany. And at that, I started bawling. I'd never get to Germany. Jim hadn't let me go out for lunch with a girlfriend two weekends before—he'd never let me go to Tennessee to see them off or to Europe for a visit.

I'd said that—*He'll never let me go*—and Eric had taken note. I would never forget how quiet, how gentle his voice got when he pleaded, "Just come stay with me, Ari, and we'll figure this out."

How I wish I'd done it right then. It had taken me another few months before I talked to a lawyer. Eric had insisted on sending me money for that, for anything I'd take, and once I did, he helped me make a plan.

My wedding anniversary—what would've been three years—would be coming up in a few months. Sometimes thinking about that, how recent it was and how far away from it I felt, brought me so low, I couldn't breathe. Other times, I felt only relief to be here, far from all that mess, and having taken back so much of myself.

I had. I was so proud of myself, and grateful. I'd shown up in Germany a few months after the divorce, which Jim had given me far more quickly than I'd ever imagined, until I found out he'd been sleeping with someone else and wanted to marry *her*, so my getting out of the way worked well for him. When I arrived, I'd been hollowed out. Emptied of anything that made me. The months between the divorce and move had been those deep trenches, the ones I'd slogged through just to look myself in the mirror.

I'd still felt like half a person. Except when I was playing with Robby or reading with Delia. Except when Eric ribbed me or Mom hugged me. Then I remembered who I was, at least a little, and took a step back toward myself.

And Nate had helped too. The first time I'd seen him here, it'd been four years since we'd been around each other. We'd always kept in touch, but the minute I started up with Jim, that had stopped. Jim hadn't wanted me keeping up with male friends, and I understood that. Fool me thought that meant he'd also stop keeping up with women, but whatever.

Eric had told Nate to give me a few days to settle in, but once I did, he was there. I'd opened the door, nerves bursting through my belly, and there he stood. His eyes had skated over me, then met mine, and then we'd been plastered together in a hug that lasted minutes. He'd whispered in my ear, "I'm glad you're here. I'm so glad you're okay."

"Me too," I'd eked out, relief and misery and safety mixing in my belly. Here was a man who I knew down into my bones wouldn't do and say the things Jim had. Like Eric and like my father, Nate was a man who could be trusted.

And after last weekend, things were back to normal with him. Whatever distance had been thrust between us after the wedding was gone. He'd broken it with the hug, the tenderness, and the ridiculous singing, and it felt like we were finally back. I hadn't realized how deeply I'd missed having fun with him, though if I thought about how angry

I'd been with him for the changed dynamic, I guess it wasn't a surprise.

The week since I'd sobbed into his shirt looking like a sad clown had gone quickly thanks to the new job during school hours, plus Nate had worked late, and I'd been helping with dinnertimes since Livie was still so sick and the smell of food made things worse. I'd bowed out of girls' night because my mom wasn't feeling great, Livie was under the weather, and Eric haggard from work, and *this* was why I'd come. Well, other than to piece myself back together.

But when I saw a way I could help and do it joyfully? I was so there. Livie apologized about twenty times, and I told her to stop that nonsense. I'd sent all the grown-ups to bed after the kids went to sleep, and then I'd cleaned a little. The cleaning lady came on Fridays at Eric's, and yet somehow by Saturday afternoon, only a day later, the house would usually look like a bomb had gone off.

I stumbled into Nate's house—my house now, *odd*—and immediately knew he wasn't home. I'd been hoping maybe he would be, finally. We'd been ships in the night, only a few words here or there on our way to do other things. I wanted to see him, maybe even hang out. Then it hit me.

He was probably on a date. Saturday night, not traveling, no work—yep. Definitely on a date. The tired feeling slipped into something heavier—disappointment tinged with longing.

As though I'd summoned him, Nate walked through the door and confirmed my suspicion. He wore dark jeans with a white, blue, and gray plaid shirt. Nice shoes, of course, and his hair was styled with a little more product than on days he wore his uniform.

He looks so good. So good.

I startled, the thought hitting me low in the belly and

flustering me more than the man himself, which then also flustered me more. "Oh, hey. Did you have a—how's it going?"

"Good. Just had dinner with a friend. You?"

He busied himself with unloading pockets and tucking away keys—he was systematic with things like this, I'd noticed. I liked it. It didn't exactly surprise me, but he so often seemed relaxed, like he might not actually care about stuff like that. I liked knowing this small thing about him— he liked his wallet, keys, phone, spare change, all in certain places.

"Helping out at Eric's. Livie's still feeling terrible, my mom wasn't feeling great, and Eric kept trying to send me home even though the bags under his eyes had their own set of luggage."

He snickered and stepped farther into the room, about a foot from me. "It was nice of you to help."

A twinge of... *something* whooshed through me. His voice sounded low and smooth. His eyes looked particularly focused on me. He must not've shaved because he had this slightly more than five o'clock shadow thing going on that really suited him.

"Well, I'm off to bed," I said, taking a step away from him and all his weirdly sexy post-date vibes.

"Sleep well." His eyes dropped away from mine and swept over me, then jumped away when he turned and strode into the kitchen.

I shuffled up the stairs, my breath oddly short. It had been a weird day, and a busy week. That must be why he looked so good. Or, *no*.

I mean, he looked good because he'd always been good-looking. That wasn't new. I'd thought he was gorgeous the first time I'd seen him—I'd even had a little crush. But now?

We were finally back to being friends—actual functioning, non-weird friends. This was absolutely *not* the time to start noticing the cut of his jaw or thinking about how much I wanted him to hug me again.

Not. The. Time.

Nate

Up, up, up the hill I pushed, until the whole little city lay before me from the top of the castle, or *burg*. Most Bavarian towns were built around either a surviving castle or the ruins of one. My small town had redone their castle, shored up the grounds, and now hosted local fests and other events at the top. It had also been placed at the strategic advantage for battle at the highest point, and thus provided my excellent view.

I spotted my house, only a half mile away. I'd done my best to sprint up here after a loop of five miles. Today was a distance run since I'd worked with Masters yesterday and done sprints, but I liked to push up this hill. It was short, sharp, and brutal. I needed that.

But why, Nate? Why do you need that, one might ask? Simply put, I'd let my natural sunny side up disposition get the damn better of me. The interactions with Ariel, though brief, had all been positive. And apparently, that was all it took to send my mind skipping down the flowery lane of wanting her again. Not just like I always did, but like actively hoping, wondering, and examining everything that happened between us, waiting for her to give me any sign.

I'd put my hopes to bed since last summer in some ways, and all over again on New Year's. I had. I'd drawn the line with myself and resolved that I wouldn't keep living my life, at least my romantic one, on pause and waiting for her.

And then I'd opened my damn mouth and asked her to live with me, which created the ultimate two-month pause. But also ended up with her saying yes. And moving in. And crying on my shoulder. And hugging me. And talking to me.

And so, what should have been a simple long run ended with me sprinting up a hill and huffing so hard at the top, I nearly lost my breakfast. A breeze swirled dried leaves on the cobblestone-paved plaza, and I attempted to exhale all that anxiety and angst building inside me. On the way home, I felt better, less like I had no control.

By the time I reached my house, I had overheated. I stumbled up the walk and ripped off my sweatshirt. With it came my shirt, and the chilly air on my bare skin created a welcome shock.

I would support her. Love her as a friend. Do whatever I could do to make sure her last few months here were good, even if the thought of her leaving killed me. The guilt that crept in at feeling like I'd manipulated her to get her here didn't help matters—but logically, I tried to brush that aside.

The offer had come from a place of wanting to help. Secondary to that was the opportunity to have her close. But had I planned on putting the moves on her when we lived together? No. I could honestly say never, and because of that, I shouldn't have the guilt.

This didn't need to be complicated or fraught with emotions because I was the only one having them, and I could control them. Like I had since I'd known her, I could and I would.

Our time together had a ticking clock. The renewed friendship would be a nice way to go out. When her time here ended, we'd have some new, more positive memories together. I'd make the most of them, and when she left, we could both move on.

This time, I'd finally actually move on.

That thought buoyed me as I stepped inside, reattached the lone key I took with me to the ring where the bunch of them sat, and began stretching. At almost thirty-eight, I'd be in serious trouble if I didn't stretch thoroughly. One of the first things Masters had insisted on when I'd asked for help with an at-home training program to bolster what I was doing at PT in the mornings was stretching. I didn't see that coming, but the more I learned, the more it made sense.

I pulled one foot up behind me and leaned back slightly to increase the pull on my quad while my other hand scrolled through my phone where it rested on the countertop next to me.

"Hey, how was your r—"

Ariel's voice cut off, and when I looked up to see her standing about five feet away, she stood frozen, eyes pinned to my chest.

I dropped my foot as a blast of adrenaline and awareness hit me. "What was that?"

Her eye bounced up to mine and blinked. "Um, I was asking how—how your run was."

Just as I was becoming pleasantly smug about the blush at her cheeks and how her eyes dropped down again, she whipped around and walked back into the kitchen. Wearing what I now registered was a soft-looking baby blue robe that hit no lower than midthigh.

Banishing all more reasonable thoughts, all oaths to remain detached beyond basic care for her fleeing, I moved after her. I followed into the kitchen, catching up to her, my eyes gliding over the shape of her legs and the way the belt tucked around her waist.

"It was good. Hard."

She turned, her gaze sweeping up my torso like a caress, then met my eyes for a fraction of a second before she began cracking eggs into a bowl. "Good."

"Can I help you?"

She started to turn her head, but jerked it back, focusing on her work. "No, that's fine. Do you want eggs? You can go, uh, go shower. Or whatever. If you want. And I'll have these ready."

Glee slithered up over my shoulder and circled my neck, nearly squeezing out the laugh that threatened. But I couldn't laugh now, even if her being flustered by me, *for once*, made me want to take another victory lap up to the castle. Though not really, because I didn't want to leave this room until I saw that blush at least once more.

"Sounds good. Thank you."

She nodded to the eggs. "No problem."

"Hey, Ariel?"

Her hands stopped, and her chest rose like she might be inhaling strength. I wouldn't pretend the sight of her needing to prepare herself to look at me didn't give me a sick amount of satisfaction.

Finally, she gave me her eyes—right in mine, no roaming —and there it was, that beautiful burning red blush. "Yes?"

"Everything okay?"

She nodded again. "Perfect. See you in a minute."

She'd shut down any question of more discussion with the shower suggestion and now the clear dismissal, so I sauntered out, taking my time to get my phone, then slowly plodding up the stairs. This smugness might seem unbecoming, but listen—the woman had never so much as given me a second glance. Forgive me if the sight of her tripping over herself a bit all because of my naked chest gave me a thrill.

I'd been a scrawny kid and a gangly teen. I naturally tended toward the wiry side, but as an adult, I'd worked on strength and speed so PT tests were never an issue. But since the summer, I'd needed another outlet for all this pent-up tension and anxiety, and since Masters was an actual expert right at my fingertips, I'd started working out harder. Eating a bit more purposefully. And I'd packed on muscle.

So when she looked at me like that, it felt good. Damn good. And I wouldn't apologize for it. That I felt her eyes on me again as I walked up the stairs only added to the pleasure.

And what did it mean? I wasn't fool enough to hope.

Actually, no, scratch that. I absolutely was. I'd been hoping. But the whole point of the mental flogging I'd given myself not a half hour ago was to remind myself why I'd invited her here and what could happen. And that was nothing. Not even for these few months she had left. Because I wouldn't be another man in her life to turn out to be a bastard. Her ex had done enough damage, and I wouldn't do anything to take advantage of her, not that I believed I actually could.

But wasn't that what I'd just done? Acted like an idiot, all smug and satisfied?

By the time I reached the shower, shame had knotted

around my neck. I shouldn't have been preening under her watch or taking my time to make sure she got an eyeful of me. I scrubbed the shampoo through my hair with punishing pressure, attempting to wash away the frustration and the very real sense I'd behaved badly.

There was no thrusting that aside, though. Because the more I thought of it, the more I realized the truth. And then true horror struck at the realization that maybe I'd made a mistake in assuming it'd been admiration in her eyes. *Oh, no*—maybe the blush wasn't a sign of attraction but of embarrassment or discomfort.

Heart in my throat, I finished up, dried off, dressed quickly in sweatpants and a T-shirt, and rushed down the stairs. She was spooning the eggs onto plates as I entered the kitchen. I didn't wait for the mortification over my idiocy to grow even more unwieldy—I just leaned a hip against the counter about two feet from where she stood and dove in.

"So, hey. I'm sorry. I didn't mean to make you uncomfortable, and I don't want you to feel like you need to worry about me prancing around shirtless. I was being an idiot—so, you know, what's new?"

I forced a chuckle, then turned to grab a glass for water before I could see her face. I filled the glass from a pitcher in the fridge, then gulped down the whole thing. She still hadn't spoken, and edgy energy twisted in my gut.

I set the glass down and took a breath, steeling myself for the awkward haze to descend on us once again. But what I found was Ariel, holding out the plate of eggs, a hint of a smile on her beautiful lips. My pulse skittered, and I took the plate, careful not to touch her where she held it. Like the coward I was, I moved to the table and took a seat, attention on my phone to block out the uncomfortable quiet.

But then she sat down across from me instead of… what? Who knew what I expected, but it wasn't her sitting down at the same table.

"You don't need to apologize," she said, then took a bite.

"I do. I did. It won't happen again." Nice of her to try to make me feel better. Not a surprise—she was, at heart, a peacemaker.

She made a sound like *hmm*, and we ate quietly for a few minutes before she spoke again.

"Kind of a shame, don't you think?"

"I don't follow. What's a shame?"

She set down her fork and took a drink of coffee from a Polish pottery mug she'd brought with her. I'd seen her use it at Eric's—maybe she'd bought it on a trip with friends since moving here.

"I mean, you've worked so hard. It seems a shame for you to never be shirtless again."

I swallowed the food in my mouth rather than cough it up onto the plate in front of me. Her words shocked me, to say the least. "What?"

She flashed her eyebrows up and down. "You're extremely fit, Nate. You work hard for it. Why not prance around when you feel like it?"

I covered my mouth to cough again, as something warm and slippery seeped into my belly. Oh, the temptation to really dig in here—to nail down if she was joking or genuinely telling me she found me attractive.

But the tone was so mild, no heat or anything, and she had that shimmery little look in her eye that she got when we joked around sometimes. Maybe this was her way of smoothing things over—helping me not feel bad about making her uncomfortable. Not at all her responsibility, but I could play along, help us get past this. So I joined in.

"I am an exceptional prancer."

The smile curved her lips on one side. "You really are. Almost professional level."

"What you don't realize is that half the reason I invited you to live here is so that I can prance with an audience. But I will be more respectful and do it with a shirt on from here on out."

She swiped a hand dramatically across her forehead. "Thank goodness. I'm not sure I could handle topless prancing on the regular."

I laughed outright at that while also silently thanking God for this quick recovery.

Lesson learned: no more shirtless wandering around. Even if her eyes on me did create the kind of thrill only she had ever given me.

"Duly noted, Wolfe. Duly noted."

CHAPTER TEN

Ariel

I'd been feeling... *things.*

Hard to ignore things.

Thinking about Nate in new ways *things.*

Not. Ideal.

We'd finally banished the weirdness of the last eight or nine months, but the whole me seeing him shirtless flipped a mental switch I did *not* need flipped.

I'd felt it before—the attraction. The draw to Nate. I'd felt it the first time I met him and almost any time I went a while without seeing him. But we never dated, and he'd never expressed a bit of interest. Honestly, I'd always assumed he'd viewed me as *Eric's Little Sister*, which I'd gathered from Eric's friends when I was younger meant they wouldn't touch me with a ten-foot pole.

I'd had a crush on one of Eric's friends when he was a senior and I was in eighth grade. Of course, in retrospect, no eighteen-year-old is going to date his friend's much-younger little sister, but it'd still driven home the message that dating his friends wasn't going to happen.

I'd taken the lesson, learned it well, and never had trouble with it again. Especially since Eric got married young, and he and Renee only hung out with other married people, or honestly, not at all. It was weird with them—most of the time, she'd disappear when I came to town, off to do her own thing or have a girls' weekend.

We all knew how that turned out, so whatever. I didn't mourn my ex-sister-in-law's exit from the family, even if I did hate that the kids had been through the divorce. Seeing Eric and Livie together, I couldn't regret it for him either. I was already closer to Livie after eighteen months than I had been with Renee for more than a decade.

The one person who'd made me look twice? Nate Reynolds. *Goodness*, he was cute. He'd been a young lieutenant when I'd met him and, *oh my*, the swaggering confidence just about made me gag, it was so off-putting. I didn't like cocky guys—didn't appreciate the over-confidence or alpha thing. I was shy—even more so then—and it wouldn't have done it for me. I could appreciate he was gorgeous, and he definitely was, but the attitude? Nope.

Until he came up to me and said words I never would've imagined coming from those perfectly shaped lips. "So, I hear you're a reader. Who's your favorite author?"

I'd expected a cheesy pick-up line or maybe awkward small talk. Then this guy goes straight for the goods. *Books*. Lovely, perfect, beautiful, safe books. We'd talked for twenty minutes straight, not even noticing the people around us, until Eric finally interrupted and glared at Nate. He didn't normally do the mean big brother thing, so it looked completely ridiculous on him. Once I assured him

Nate and I were destined to be great friends and nerd out on books, he'd relaxed.

If butterflies flapped around in my belly every time I saw Nate after that, or if my chest warmed when he asked Eric for my number so he could text me about a new series he'd started, I never let on. And if he ever felt anything for me, he never said or did anything either. Plus, the guy always seemed to have a girl—dates, parties, *stuff* going on, from what Eric said. That held true whenever I talked to him—heading out on a date, spending time with a friend, and so on. I didn't ever know whether it was the same person or different people, but he was always unavailable to me.

So I never let myself think of him like that. Not for long, anyway.

Fast forward years of us chatting, texting, and reuniting when I'd visit Eric the few times they overlapped at a duty station—of course, minus the years I was with Jim—and here I was, feeling seriously conflicted about Nate.

But *was* it conflicted? More like *attracted*, pure and simple, but very conflicted about what that meant. As I said, Nate had always been gorgeous. He must've packed on pounds of pure muscle since I'd seen him at the beach at the wedding last year, and even then, he'd been appealingly fit.

That look he'd given me last summer, though... I could still remember the heart-sink, the fear when I realized everything had to change. He'd slipped and showed me something I shouldn't have seen—it'd sent too many ideas clamoring for first place in my attention. Hope, insane thoughts of being with Nate, and sticky, suffocating fear.

More than anything, it had been a *feeling*. An intuitive sense that he wanted things from me I couldn't give him, and because of that, things had to change between us. We'd gotten too close since I'd moved here—he'd become my primary support beyond Eric. The change between us had been a loss of safety—something I'd been clinging to since the day I'd grabbed hold of it by leaving Jim. Last summer had blown the safety of Nate to smithereens.

And that look had flipped the magnets. Now, getting close was effort, awkwardness, and discomfort.

Or it had been. Until the night I'd bawled in his arms, and then we'd joked about his terrible singing. Then it became like everything was better between us, and we could truly be friends. Though this awareness of him physically proved more than a little inconvenient. I couldn't live with him and maintain our friendship and have those kinds of feelings running around. He'd gotten past whatever his deal was months ago, and I would too. I had to, because the elation of having him back, of being with my friend again, was indescribable. Relief and joy and, yes, that simple, powerful word—safe.

After all, lots of men were fit. And good-looking. And charming. And sweet. And secretly book nerdy. And athletic, but in a practical way. And capable—*okay*. Probably better to stop listing his qualities and start thinking of Nate, my friend, who would walk in the door any minute ready for a movie marathon and takeout from Karla's.

We had just these two days before he left on his Spring Break trip to Morocco, and I left with the family for one last big hurrah at what Eric had called a *kinderhotel*. Apparently, it was geared toward families with kids, and he and Livie were footing the bill for me and Mom to stay with them, so I wasn't about to complain.

Speak of the devil, there he was. "I am so ready to sit on the couch and not move for the next twenty-four hours."

Nate banged through the entryway with hands full of

stuff and stopped just inside as the door swung shut behind him.

My heart sped up at the sight of him. I'd always liked a man in uniform—I'd married one once, after all—but Nate looked really good in his. Even after a super long day.

"A full day? I think you'd go insane."

"Not with a steady supply of food and drinks. Possibly a companion to channel surf with me." He flashed a smile but didn't move. He just stood there, like he couldn't decide what to do.

I shuffled to him and reached for the coffee mug and water bottle he had looped around one finger. His eyes tracked me as I held his hand up, supporting the weight while I transferred the vessels to my grip. His skin was warm, as usual, though I hadn't touched him often. Not hardly at all except the hugs a few weeks ago.

Just the quick graze against his fingers sent heat thrumming through me and a flash of those hands holding mine.

"Thank you," he said, his voice rough and low.

A thrill shot up my spine. I swallowed back that feeling and smiled brightly. "You look a little lost. Can I take anything else?"

His brows raised, then he looked down in confusion, like he'd completely forgotten he was still holding a gym bag, a lunch box, and a backpack likely weighed down with gear.

"Uh, this?" He held up the lunchbox.

I took it, then tilted my head. "I think your brain shut down. Drop the stuff and come inside. We'll deal with all that later."

He blinked, then dropped his stuff, which crashed to the floor. He winced at the sound. "Whoops. Maybe shouldn't have actually dropped it."

I chuckled. "Let's get you something to eat. Then you can go change and get into your *lounge* pants."

His eyes narrowed. "Yes, I will get into my *lounge* pants, thank you. You can keep your gross *sweat*pants."

I laughed loudly at that, a bit of the awareness that fluttered through me dissipating. *Thank goodness.* I focused back on his statement.

This was a frequent fake argument we had. He maintained that sweatpants were only used for working out, and that calling pants one wore when *not* working out sweatpants was gross. I told him that lounge pants sounded uppity and like he thought he was too fancy for regular people sweatpants.

Potato, potahto.

I settled his things on the counter and reached into the fridge, opened a beer, poured it into a stein, and handed him the drink. He still appeared to be mostly dazed as he accepted it. Poor man, he must've been dead on his feet.

"Did something happen? Are you okay?"

His eyes snapped to me. "What? No. Thank you for this."

He put it to his lips, and I looked away for fear I might end up watching a little too closely.

"If you're too tired, we can save the movies. You can totally head to bed—"

"Not a chance. I've been looking forward to this. I just need a minute to... reinhabit myself."

"*Reinhabit?*"

He did a little frowny-smile.

"Not a great word. I just feel kind of wrung out this week. Definitely ready for the break." He took a slug of the beer, then set it down with a *clink.* "But first, I'm going to change into *lounge* pants and hang with you for the night."

"Living the dream, my friend. Living the dream," I said, heading back into the kitchen to get my own drink.

The insane amount of pleasure his insisting on sticking to our plan gave me should've alarmed me, but I couldn't be bothered. I wanted this time with Nate, and he wanted it right back. The sparkle of attraction I felt every time I looked at him lately didn't mean we couldn't curl up on the couch and relax together.

If anything, it was one more reason why I needed to get over it. Appreciate the man, sure, but then put it behind me and enjoy the return of our friendship. Of his support, and his willingness to share a little bit of himself with me.

I didn't watch him go but could've sworn I heard him mutter, "You have no idea," as he headed up the stairs.

CHAPTER ELEVEN

Nate

She truly had no idea.

I trudged up the stairs, the surreal, foggy feeling dragging at my heels as I went.

I'd literally had this dream. It was part of the reason I'd been so dumbstruck when I walked in. She'd been standing at the bar, reading something, and had looked up when I came in. She hit me with what I liked to call the Ariel Wolfe Special, which was a smile that basically took my heart and tied a knot with the arteries.

The weight of the week and the relief of finally being home had stopped me, but her being right there when I arrived froze me to the spot. I couldn't remember what to do first. Set the keys down? Drop my bags? Just sit down and surrender?

She'd approached, and in my dream, she'd kissed me to welcome me home. Today, in reality, our hands had brushed when she took my mugs, and the subtle warm scent of her perfume swirled as she walked back into the kitchen.

Then she'd given me a beer. She'd already ordered our takeout. I'd go back down there and sit next to her, this woman I now lived with, and I'd have a great night. Granted, I'd have to suppress the large part of me that wanted to touch her, hold her, finally tell her what a fool I was for her, but that was nothing new. This night might be a bit more challenging thanks to my general exhaustion, but that was fine. I'd handle it and soak up the time before I headed off to make yet another trip alone on Sunday.

I pressed my palms into my eyes. Damn, was I tired of that. Sometimes, I went with friends, and I'd even traveled with Eric, his mom, and the kids a few times the first year or so I was here. But most of the time, I traveled solo. Occasionally, Maddie joined me, sometimes my buddy JJ came along, but generally, it was just me.

I used to love it. Even two years ago, I relished it. But the shine had worn off lately, and though I looked forward to being away from work, I felt a tug of regret. I didn't look forward to being alone.

After ditching the uniform and getting into the aforementioned pants and a T-shirt, I splashed water on my face, then looked in the mirror. *Damn.* I looked old and tired. Droplets of water tracked down my face and dripped off my chin. "Get yourself together. *Now.*"

The combination of a weirdly hard work week and being so ready for a break but hardly wanting the break I had planned made me feel small. Walking in to find my actual dream girl here to help me, take care of me, and spend time with me threatened to flatten me.

"Shut the hell up and go enjoy your friend."

Yes, I spoke aloud to myself. Again. Living alone had

made me a person who talked to himself, and I didn't feel bad about it, nor did it signal a loss of sanity. Sometimes, a man needed to knock some sense into himself, and the only way to do it was audibly.

I patted my cheeks a few times, dried my face, and made the long haul down the stairs. My legs still had the leaden quality they'd had all day—I was burnt out. Tomorrow, I'd do a long, slow workout and an easy jog, and then I'd have a full week off. I'd still run and do body-weight workouts while I was gone, but I'd be away from the heavy-weight circuits. Part of me dreaded breaking my training schedule, but the other part knew that my body and mind were ready for a change up, and this time would serve me well.

By the time I reached the kitchen, I'd shaken off some of the malaise of the week. Seeing Ariel with her feet up on the ottoman while sipping wine sent a little burst of anticipation through me, and I felt like I stepped back into my own feet. Finally.

"So did you order me the cheeseburger?"

She turned, eyes wide. "No. I ordered you mango chicken and spring rolls. Did you want the cheeseburger?"

I chuckled, and she rolled her eyes as I grabbed my beer and brought it with me to find my seat on the couch. Oh, to live a life where I could slide into the space right next to her and kiss her neck and just breathe her in for a moment. Alas, I sat a cushion away and settled the beer on a tray next to me. Since I used an ottoman rather than a coffee table, I had trays to provide beverage placement options. This was the phraseology my sister had used a few years back when she'd sent me the links to this setup, and I'd gone with it. I liked it.

"Of course I wanted a cheeseburger from the local

Indian food takeout place. And ideally, crinkle-cut fries that will be thoroughly steamed inside the container so they're just a mushy, formerly fried yellow substance. If you could work out a way to get some of that sham guacamole that comes frozen? Double helpings of that, too."

She shook her head but didn't hide her smile. "You're a pest."

"Prince. I think you meant to say 'prince.'"

She looked up at the ceiling, squinting and tapping a finger at her chin, then pointed at me. "Pestilent, I think."

"Paragon of charm and humor."

She pressed her lips together, and my stomach flipped. *Got her.* She hid the laugh, but I knew I got her.

"No, no, no. I meant pedantic."

"Priceless."

"Perturbing."

"Pleasing."

"Pretentious."

"*Precious.*"

A laugh escaped, but then she sobered. "Pugnacious."

Unadulterated delight washed through me.

"Pretty." I brushed my fingers along the sides of my head as though to style my hair.

She bit her lip and studied my face, but the doorbell rang and drew her attention away.

"Well, you are that. I can't deny it." She then launched off the couch to get the door.

It only took me a few seconds to follow her and accept the bag as she thanked the delivery person. I banished the glee that zipped through me from her saying I was pretty. She didn't really mean that, only said it to play along and be funny, but still. I'd stockpile these little moments, take them and hoard them to myself. And when she left, I'd let them, and her, go.

Also, maybe I was hungrier than I realized, because this was some sentimental drivel.

"This smells so good. It looks so good." My eyes shut as I inhaled, then it hit me. "Wait, you shouldn't have paid. I was supposed to pay."

She raised a brow as she removed the lids of the takeout containers. "How do you figure?"

"You ordered. I pay. It's science."

She laughed. "What? No. That's not a thing."

"It's the way of the world, Wolfe."

"In your universe of one, maybe, but in the larger world, no." She dished rice and a few heaping spoonsful of steaming chicken korma onto a plate, then slid to the side, presumably to make room for me.

"How else do you determine who pays?" I almost said *on a date* but of course didn't, because this wasn't a date, and that would've been idiotic.

She turned and leaned her side against the counter so she faced me. I faced the countertop so I could only see her out of the corner of my eye.

"Well, when someone lives in a house the other someone owns and doesn't pay rent, the first someone gets to buy dinner from time to time."

I shot her a dirty look. "I don't own this house."

"Rent, whatever."

"Not *whatever*. It'd be illegal for me to charge you rent. Don't think it's me doing you a favor—I rent this place with my government housing allowance. If I charged you rent, I'd be subletting a military housing unit, which is against regulation and could technically get me drawn up for UCMJ." Fat chance, of course, but she didn't need to know that.

"Fine. You're only a partial saint, not a full one."

She took two forks from the utensil drawer and handed me one but didn't look me in the face. As soon as I took the fork, she walked out of the kitchen, leaving me standing there like an idiot.

As much as I was joking, that last retort, and the refusal to meet my eye, raised a flag. I joined her on the couch and settled in, plate on my lap and beer still on the tray next to me, before speaking. "Hey."

She turned her head and raised her brows.

"You know I'm glad you're here, and I don't feel like you owe me anything?"

"That's nice, Nate. But it's too nice. I do owe you, and so at least every once in a while, I'm going to buy your dinner and you're going to have to deal with it."

Her immediate return to eating made me stay quiet. Different thoughts slipped through my mind, one after another. I fiddled with the remote, calling up the movie we'd agreed on but paused it only seconds after starting it.

"Listen, seriously."

She heaved a big sigh but gave me her attention.

"You don't owe me. That's not the kind of relationship we have, nor do I want it that way."

She blinked once, twice. "I appreciate that."

"It's great having you here. If I thought you'd moved in here with a big sense of guilt or something, I'd be pissed."

One brow raised. "Oh, you would be?"

"Yep. And you know how bad my temper is."

She chuckled. "A notorious screamer."

"*Screecher*, really. Banshee-level screeching when my panties get in a twist."

She laughed but pushed my shoulder. "Don't say 'panties.' Now, start the movie, you ridiculous man."

With more than a little warmth and relief in my chest from the exchange, I hit play. We focused on the food during the first few minutes, each shoveling our portions into our mouths and occasionally commenting on how delicious it was as we watched Tom Cruise running from place to place in his latest franchise action film.

But soon enough, we took a break, cleaned up our dishes, and settled in. I kicked my feet up, leaned back, and spread my arms along the back of the couch. A deep, satisfied sigh escaped. She glanced over at me and smiled, and my heart dipped.

As much as I wanted things to be different between us, I relished even this time. Relaxing on the couch next to my good friend, a woman I respected and liked, a person who made me laugh and feel good. Especially with the clarification that she didn't owe me anything behind us. I'd hoped it was clear from the beginning, but perhaps not. I didn't want her feeling indebted to me. I just wanted her to feel at home and safe.

A belly full of great food and no obligations for a week. This was exactly what I'd needed.

CHAPTER TWELVE

Ariel

The credits of the first movie rolled, and we both moved to the kitchen. I grabbed a bag of popcorn, and he refreshed our waters. Somehow, we didn't need to talk much, but we both moved through the action without issue. We'd done movie nights in the past, before last summer, so maybe that was why.

"So, how's the whole job search, life path thing going?" he asked, legs crossed in front of him where he stood leaning against the counter as we waited for the popcorn.

"Still pretty clueless. I mean, I am doing the Red Cross thing, which is great. And I love volunteering in the classrooms. I just... that's only for a few months, and I have no idea what to do about the move." *Understatement.* I had to answer not only *"What do you want to be when you grow up?"* but also *"Where do you want to be?"*

My heart knew the answer to both in that moment, with

just that thought. The *what* I couldn't have, but where? I wanted to stay here. I loved it here in Germany and didn't want to leave with the rest of the family in a matter of months.

He crossed his arms and leaned more fully against the counter, nestling into the position like he could stay there all night. That was something that'd always struck me about Nate—he had this odd, alluring combo of having energy pulsing just under the surface, and yet the ability to look completely at ease in any given moment. Like now—I could believe he'd stay leaning against the countertop all night, long after I went to bed.

"It's not a bad thing to have the job for a few months—builds your experience. And maybe it'll spark ideas for what else you want to do. What's the deal with the move?"

The popcorn began popping like crazy, so I kept an eye on it as I spoke—burned popcorn smell was the worst. "Obviously, I'll be moving when Eric leaves. I can't stay since my nannying job is technically the reason I'm allowed to be here. But the thought of being back in the States..."

The rawest edges of panic had subsided when I thought of the move back. For the most part. But I still felt completely adrift. Eric would be moving to Fort Bragg, North Carolina, so at least not back to Texas—I didn't want to be anywhere near the place I'd lived with Jim. But did I want to live in North Carolina? Not particularly. No offense against the place, I just had no idea what I *did* want, except that I didn't really want to leave Germany. I'd be so sad without my family, but—

"Whatever you do, you're going to do great."

I rolled my eyes while pulling open the microwave. "You can't know that."

"I can."

I dropped the piping-hot bag on the stove and set the bowl down. "You really can't."

I busied myself slowly pulling the edges of the bag, avoiding the fake buttery steam and making a mental note to buy regular kernels, not bags, for our next movie night. No need to be feeding him this artificial stuff.

"Hey."

His low, quiet voice startled me, though it'd been seconds since he'd spoken last. He stood next to me, and his large, warm hand brushed against my wrist.

"I know you'll do great because *you're* great. You're awesome, Ariel, whether you find your career path when you move, or in ten years, or don't end up deciding on one thing. I realize this is ridiculous advice coming from someone who is mildly obsessed with performance as a metric for personal worth, but you are innately valuable. The pieces of your life you have to decide in the next few months will come together, and if you hate the way they do, you'll change them."

I swallowed, my heart aching to believe the words. "I've messed up, though. Maybe *I'm* messed up, and my ability to make choices is broken."

His face hardened. "You're not perfect, Wolfe, but no one is. You made mistakes, and I hate the way they turned out, but you know what that makes you?"

We hadn't spoken about my past much at all since I'd moved here. I'd opened up a few times in those first months of being here while I decompressed from everything, gotten into counseling, and learned to do more than put one foot in front of the other. But not much since then. Mostly because I knew this was the stuff he'd say—things too good, too generous and kind to be real, except I knew him well enough to know he meant every word.

I pulled in a watery breath. "What?"

"Human, love. It makes you human."

I nodded and held up the bowl full of popcorn, and he grabbed our waters. We moved together to the living room as I spoke.

"Yeah. I get that. For the most part, I think I'm done guilting myself, though I still have to work on not listening to the voices berating me for being a thirty-three-year-old woman with nothing to show for her life other than a divorce and a lot of therapy. But I have realized I don't think I trust myself very much anymore. I haven't *had* to for the last few years—I got the divorce, moved to Florida of all places, and then finally out here, and I've been on autopilot since. Just focusing on the kids, travel when it worked out, enjoying life here. Now that I have to look ahead..."

I'd only just stopped looking behind me. I'd worked every day to focus on being mentally present here and now. To begin looking ahead again had hurt, but knowing that the future would arrive so soon—the move, the need for a new job, new apartment, another reinvention of myself—it made the newly blooming shoots in me threaten to wither.

"It's a big transition. It'd be daunting for anyone, but it's your first big one on the other side of a lot of healing and work you've done for yourself. It makes sense you'd be nervous. Hell, I would be. In fact, I always get nervous for moves, even though I love it."

"Really? You? Nervous?"

He chuckled, and something about the little half-smile he gave me as he settled further into the couch and spread his arms across the back made my stomach dip.

"I get nervous."

"I find that hard to believe."

"Why?"

"You're always so calm. You look like a duck in water in any situation."

"You haven't seen me in that many situations."

"Well, Eric has told me enough stories, so I know it's true. He has always admired your ability to adapt quickly." Not at all the way my brother tended to be, though he did well enough, obviously, or he wouldn't have made it very far in the Army.

"You and Eric have been talking about me?" He flashed his brows up and down.

I shook my head at him and grabbed the remote. "Yes. All the time. I'm surprised we manage to talk about anything else, we talk about you so much."

"Ah, that's what I like to hear."

I clicked through various screens to get to the next movie while we chatted, in no real hurry to end the conversation. "So, what about you?"

"Me?"

"Yeah. What's on deck for you? Job? Future Mrs. Reynolds prospects?" The words jumped out of my mouth before I gave them a closer look. I definitely didn't inspect the twist in my chest.

He cleared his throat. "Well, I'll have my promotion ceremony in a few months."

"Crazy! So, you'll be Lieutenant Colonel Reynolds?"

He nodded. "Yep. And I'll PCS next summer—we'll see whether I'm selected for a battalion command here in the next few months, and that'll determine where I go."

"So exciting."

It really was. I couldn't imagine a scenario where they didn't select him for a command, but I also knew it could be a bit of a crapshoot after hearing Eric talk about friends who had or hadn't gotten them.

I'd always loved that part of the Army—the new assignments and jobs and bases. With Jim, I got so excited thinking about where we'd move, what we'd do. Granted, with retrospect, I could see some of that was my mind finding any version of an escape or an excuse for change it could, but still. We hadn't been together long enough to live through a change other than his move right after we started dating. *The worst decision of my life,* as I sometimes thought of it, but I'd worked not to dwell there.

Enough of that. *Be here now!* I wanted to know everything Nate had to say. Especially if there was a response to my awkward Mrs. Reynolds comments.

"And... other stuff?"

On second thought, why was I prodding him about this? Did I want to hear him tell me about whomever he was dating? No. Definitively no. I watched him out of the corner of my eye, not sure what to do with myself other than try to focus on the screen in front of me.

"Uh, ha. You know me. Still just... dating." He folded in on himself, those long arms crossing over his chest again.

"No one who stands out?"

His eyes found mine, and a beat passed. "No one who's available."

My throat worked, but I couldn't swallow, and the air locked up in my lungs. I grabbed my water and took a sip.

"Ah. Well." I held up the remote. "Ready?"

He nodded, then his eyes hit the screen and didn't move. Not once for the next hour and forty minutes. And the entire time, I sat there, mind circling his words.

Somehow, I knew, in the same way I had last summer, he was talking about me. My chest had constricted before he even spoke the words, the intensity in his eyes pinning me down. But did he really mean *me*? Could he possibly?

The insinuation was that whoever did stand out wasn't available. And I was single.

But I hadn't been *available*. I hadn't even considered dating until the last few months, but there wasn't anyone, not really. Because Nate was pretty much my closest friend here. I loved my girlfriends, but Nate and I had history. We cared about each other. He'd supported me so fully, without reservation, from the moment we met. He even took the news I couldn't talk to him anymore when I started dating Jim with grace.

I couldn't imagine being with someone I didn't know. I'd leapt with Jim, and how'd that turn out? The lesson had been learned, and I couldn't imagine wanting to go out on a blind date or get set up by a mutual friend. Even someone close to me vetting the potential date. And yet, here I sat by a man who'd just hinted that he'd be interested. In me.

And I'd always been interested in him.

Was he not dating anyone else? I honestly didn't know, but that statement was so pointed. And I knew Nate. I didn't know everything, but I knew he could be trusted. I knew, with him, I'd be safe. At least in some of the most fundamental ways.

It would change everything, though. That had kept me away, full stop, the last time we'd gotten anywhere near admitting something like this.

I didn't see the movie. My eyes stared at the screen, but I couldn't focus on anything other than the quiet words I felt my heart wanting to say. These words never came out, but they whispered through me the rest of the night.

I'm free. I'm free.

CHAPTER THIRTEEN

Nate

All plans to take it easy on myself in my Saturday morning workout went out the window the minute I spoke the words to her.

"No one who stands out?" she'd asked.

"No one who's available," I'd corrected, staring into her wide, blue eyes, feeling the earth crumble away under me.

I hadn't planned the words, but out they'd come. And by the way she'd stayed quiet—both of us had—she knew I meant her. I wondered if she saw right through me or if this was a surprise to her. She'd seemed contemplative but not upset. When the movie ended, we'd moved around each other in silence, though it wasn't exactly strained. Just... full. And then we'd said good night, parting ways on the second floor when she slipped into her room and I continued up the spiral staircase to mine.

I'd worked out in the basement, pushing hard on reps,

and then did sprints outside. I'd planned a few long, scenic runs for the upcoming travel, so I didn't want to risk burning out my legs today, but the sprints helped exhaust some of the anxious energy. Despite a late bedtime, I'd woken at six.

By the time I made it back to the house, my nerves were looser, my body exhausted. But mentally, somehow, I'd wound myself tighter around the anxious anticipation of seeing her again. I'd never been so clear with her. The moment at the wedding last year—that had been close, but it'd only happened thanks to my general miserable condition. And she knew it had to do with her. Just like last night—though I hadn't said anything specific, she had to know.

The quiet between us, the way we said good night, I had no doubt she knew I meant her. And this morning, I'd know a lot more. If she avoided me—bad news. If she seemed standoffish—could go either way. And I couldn't actually imagine another response.

I started the coffee maker on the way to my shower, noting that Ariel's tendency to wake early, and her absence in the kitchen thus far, did not bode well for me. As I took the stairs two at a time, alternating thoughts of self-condemnation and hope fought for prime placement. On one hand, I cursed myself and my stupid big mouth for saying what I did—something unmistakably forward. Now she knew I was interested—I snorted while pushing through my bedroom door. As though *interested* was even close to an accurate word choice for how I felt about Ariel.

Making a more accurate list wouldn't help my mental state, so I skipped over that futile exercise and moved to the less upsetting side of the discussion. Yes, I'd put myself way out there, and that was probably dumb. Probably. But the foolishly hopeful man who often kept me going when the rest of me faltered—he said maybe there was a chance.

Maybe we could have something in these last few months of her time here.

And if it crashed and burned, then I hadn't outright said I wanted her. I'd kept it vague, even if we both knew exactly who I meant, so we could just... ignore it had happened.

On that other, hopeful, mildly reckless side, I hardly dared think of what might happen. What if she only needed a little hint? I didn't imagine she'd suddenly jump me next time she found me in the kitchen, but what if she just needed to have it on her radar for a minute? In a way, other than my sad-sack, hung-over look of desperation that launched a thousand awkward moments between us.

"Seriously, man, you are pathetic."

I said it aloud, pulling on jeans and a long-sleeved gray T-shirt. I'd need to pack today, and I had some bills to pay. I could send Maddie an e-mail and see what she was doing. JJ was already gone, so I couldn't use him as an excuse to get out of the house, and Ariel would likely be hanging with Eric and his crew today, so that was a no-go if things were off.

I padded quietly down the stairs, noting Ariel's door was open and the bathroom door on her level was closed. No kidding, an entire flock of butterflies let loose in my chest. I smiled to myself—scratch that. Not a flock. A *kaleidoscope.* One of the words for a group of butterflies was "kaleidoscope," and I knew that thanks to the woman in question. She'd read it in something and couldn't wait to tell me. It'd been about two months after she'd moved here, and it was the first real hint of the woman I'd known before.

Ariel before had been pure joy. Imperfections and anxieties and sometimes so shy around new people, I'd miss her voice in a group. The shy factor had seemed to deepen at first, though by that first New Year's party about three months after she'd arrived in Germany, she'd taken on the title of co-hostess and had come alive a bit more.

I didn't know the full details of what Jim had done to her. Part of me didn't want to, but if she ever wanted to tell me, I'd listen. She'd given hints, and so had Eric, and it was all enough for me to put together that he'd harmed her.

My teeth grated against each other as my jaw clenched at the thought. Ariel had lived near a military base where Jim was stationed. The one where I lived had been only about an hour from her, so we got together once a month or so. But at that time, I still felt she was off-limits to me. Trust me, I'd spent plenty of time examining why I felt that way, especially after she started dating Jim and moved across the country to be with him without much more than a mild apology and quick goodbye. She'd already cut off communication between us, and Eric had been concerned. I had too, but I feared it was jealousy, of which there was plenty.

I wished, so often, that I'd... said something. Done something. I didn't know Jim, but all the signs of a controlling sketchball had been there. Could I have done something to help her? Could I have talked her out of moving to Texas?

"You look very serious."

Ariel's voice drew my attention from the black depths of the coffee I'd been staring into, and immediately, my pulse spiked.

"Deep thoughts over here. You know me."

Her eyes narrowed as she approached. "Everything okay?"

"Yep. Just spacing out." I took a drink of coffee, not breaking the eye contact she'd given me but needing some way to hide my rioting pulse.

"Did you sleep last night?" she asked, slipping into the kitchen.

I turned fully and looked down. I did. The short blue robe pulled tight around her, draping over each glorious curve, held me rapt. "Pretty well. You?"

So far, she seemed normal. Maybe too normal, which might mean we were doing the *let's ignore you said you were interested, and I knew exactly what you were saying* thing. Fine. I could live with that far better than I could with the version of things we'd been stuck with before she moved in.

She filled a mug with coffee as she spoke. "As tired as I was, I had trouble falling asleep."

"Did you?"

She nodded as she blew into the mug, steam rising in front of her face. Her gaze locked with mine. "Had a lot on my mind."

Any calm I'd managed to unearth in the last few minutes disintegrated. My stomach dropped, pulse sprinting again.

"Huh," was all I managed.

She smiled. "Yeah. *Huh.*"

She left the kitchen and walked to the stairs, leaving me speechless and breathless and more than a little stunned.

Was she saying... *wait.* What was she saying?

"Where are you going?" I said, tripping after her to the bottom of the staircase she was already halfway up.

"I've got to run to get ready. I'm helping get the kids packed. Since we're driving, Eric is prepping the cars and we're doing everything else."

"Oh, okay. Will you—I mean, will I see you before you leave?"

Did I sound particularly pathetic right now, or was it just me? I internally rolled my eyes, praying it didn't sound as whiney and affected to her.

Her face split into a wide smile. "If I'm not back before

you go to bed tonight, I'll make sure I'm up before you leave. Six, right?"

I nodded.

"It's a date, then." Then she turned and left.

And I stood there, frozen in place, mind whirling around what she meant. People said that—*it's a date*—all the time. They meant it platonically, like they'd say, "It's a meeting." Still. *Still.* She'd hinted hardcore at my comment last night. She'd been preoccupied by it. And she wouldn't have done it in such a cute, open-ended way if what she felt was awkward or frustrated—right?

I thought of nothing else.

CHAPTER FOURTEEN

Ariel

Nate had already started the coffee, bless him. I'd stayed at Eric's fairly late, chatting with him, Livie, and my mom. Had I been avoiding Nate? Maybe.

I wasn't proud of that, but at least I'd told him I likely wouldn't be back. I couldn't blame myself too much, though. I'd traveled a huge emotional distance in the last few days. I'd gone from my own little world, eschewing even the thought of a relationship to... thinking about Nate.

Not just thinking about him, but opening myself to a possibility I'd never truly entertained. Before, it'd seemed impossible. And since last summer, it'd seemed... scary. Terrifying, really, except what resulted from all of that felt pretty close to losing him completely anyway. But now?

I'd hinted yesterday morning at that, somehow finding it easy to almost flirt with him. I didn't plan it, nor did I premeditate the whole "it's a date," thing. But some part of me had wanted him to know I wasn't ignoring that heavily dropped insinuation Friday night. I wasn't running away from things between us like I had after the wedding. Like we both had.

But did I want to date Nate?

Yes.

No.

Both answers rang out in equal measure. Well, maybe not *equal*, but clear enough. Yes, I did. I loved him as one of my dearest friends. He was kind and silly and a little cocky with a side of nerd. And he was gorgeous.

But also no. Because I'd proven, oh so clearly, I couldn't be trusted to make decisions like this. When you stay in a relationship like the one I'd had with Jim, you walk away questioning everything. Had it all been in my mind? Was I the one who made everything go wrong? Couldn't I have seen the signs before? Why had I stayed as long as I had?

Trusting myself, even with the simplest things, had taken time. Moving to Germany had been the first, and a huge, leap. The fact that I was coming to live with Eric and the kids made it easier, but I'd hardly taken a full breath those first few weeks here, so scared I'd wake up and realize I'd hurt myself again by jumping into something.

But I hadn't done that. It'd been the right decision, and an important one. And so had moving in here with Nate.

Dating Nate? Potentially ruining everything between us if things got awkward or went wrong? Losing the little ground we'd gained in the last few weeks and watching whatever was left of our friendship, of his support, crumbling beneath us? That, I couldn't stomach.

As the evening hours slipped into night and night into dawn, that little spark of energy, that *hope* that something good could grow between us, had been stamped out. The threat of losing him after losing so much had nearly swallowed me whole. I should've been braver, but I just didn't have it in me. I didn't know how to trust that the anxious twinge in my belly was just nerves and not something more insidious. Not a warning I should heed—one I might've missed before.

It wasn't Nate I didn't trust. It was me.

Speaking of the man himself, he thundered down the stairs, backpack and suitcase in hand, looking polished and ready to travel in jeans and an olive-green lightweight jacket. He'd styled his hair—it was a little longer on top these days, but he'd gotten it trimmed at the sides recently, so it looked clean and handsome.

My heart fluttered when our eyes met.

"Morning," he said, clearly his first word of the day. He didn't look remotely sleepy, likely thanks to honing the early morning wake up process from years in the military.

"Morning. You all ready?"

"Yes—" he cut himself off, then swallowed. "I wish I was going with someone. I like traveling alone, but this time..." His gaze hit me, heavy with meaning.

"I've always wanted to see Chefchaouen, the blue village."

He smiled. "I won't make it there this time—I'll be in the mountains most of the trip, other than arriving and leaving from Marrakech. Maybe next time."

"Good plan," I said, reining in that ridiculous impulse shouting, *I'll go with you!*

His eyes slid over me, then bounced away. He grabbed a water bottle, his keys, wallet, and passport, all of which waited in a neat pile on the bar where he must've set them earlier.

"Well..."

My heart raced and my stomach twisted. Why did I feel so sad, so desperate for him to stay? I was leaving tomorrow too, and we'd both be back by next Sunday. This was nonsense.

I pushed past these weird, heavy feelings and pulled him into a hug. He tripped forward, and our bodies pressed together as I held him to me. Only a second later, his arms wrapped around me, tight.

"Have fun. Be safe. Be smart," I said into his shoulder.

I felt the laugh in his chest.

"I always am."

This was the point at which a hug would end.

We didn't move.

He was so strong and solid. The last time he'd hugged me, I'd been a mess. I couldn't appreciate the strength of him, the hardness of his shoulder where I'd rested my head, or the firm muscles in his back where my hands pressed against him.

He smelled like coffee, minty toothpaste, and a clean, fresh scent that might be his soap. I dipped my head, just a little, and inhaled. My mouth was a fraction of an inch from his neck, and I saw it in my mind—pressing my lips to the smooth curve under his jaw he must've shaved minutes ago.

Maybe his breath would hitch. Maybe his hands on my back would move to my waist, lower.

Okay, killer, hold up.

I'd flustered myself, but instead of pulling away, I leaned up and kissed his cheek. Less sensual, more... friendly?

As I pulled back, he studied me, his eyes stormy and full.

I stepped away and picked up the coffee mug I'd abandoned on the counter. "Have a great trip. I'll see you next week."

He cleared his throat. "You too. Tell Robby and Delia I expect to hear every detail of the trip next time I'm over."

And seconds later, he was gone, and I was left to think about how long the week ahead stretched out for miles now that he'd gone.

We'd arrived at the *kinderhotel* late Sunday afternoon, and I hadn't been thinking of Nate. Not constantly, anyway. Instead, I'd been worrying about Summer. Something was going on with her and Nick Masters, who seemed very definitely interested in her. They'd started dating, I thought, but she'd sent a few texts in the last day or so that'd raised some concerns.

She'd said, "I'm broken."

The words struck, a jab to the still-tender part of me that felt very much that I'd been broken, too. Jim had broken me. I'd broken myself. My plans, my life, my dreams —I'd felt so utterly broken in the end. But the gift, the triumphant little reminder sang out—I had healed.

Not everything. There were still pieces I needed to glue back in. But I saw myself less as broken and more as... weathered.

What Summer now struggled so mightily against— asking for and receiving help—had been something I'd dreaded and even refused to do. I'd felt strongly that I'd made a commitment to Jim, and I had to live with the consequences. That was a good way to live—you make a choice, you live with the consequences. But when that choice leads you into possible harm and you need help getting out of it, it is okay to look beyond yourself for help. The idea of abuse being a consequence anyone chooses was resoundingly false, and I thanked God I'd been able to hear that, believe it, and clutch the truth to me not long after I began therapy.

What I'd said to Summer about loving someone swished around in my mind. *"Loving someone isn't quite the same as needing them... it could be a really wonderful and freeing thing, instead of something that ties you up."*

I'd said it so confidently, and yet did I believe it? For my own situation, did I believe that maybe not loving Nate, but at least dating him, could be freeing? That it could be something that let me breathe and enjoy life rather than fear its brutal consequences and tied me to misery?

I wanted to. Oh, how I wanted to.

"This place is so nice. I'm glad I could be here for this," my mom said as she wrapped her arms around me from where she stood at my side. She was just an inch or two shorter than me, and she smelled like Mom. Like home. "I wish your dad were here."

The familiar ache of missing my dad pulsed in my chest. "Me too."

He'd died not long before I'd met Jim. His loss had deeply affected all of us, and it had absolutely played a part in my ignoring the warning signs I'd seen with Jim, even early on.

It'd made it hard for my mom to see them too. It'd felt nearly impossible to let on that anything was less than perfect—I didn't want her to worry. And Eric was fast approaching the end of his marriage—they'd separated when I first started dating Jim. It'd felt wrong to talk about it, or even raise a concern, when he was so overwhelmed with all of that.

They'd both begged my forgiveness, as if they had any

blame for my choices. But I loved them for that—for wishing they'd seen through my thin, shaky assurances, especially after we were married.

Enough of that. Enough of Jim. I didn't like that I was thinking about him so much lately. It had to be living with Nate and these emerging feelings for him. That Jim had been the last person to get that response from me made me want to spit, and yet the feelings themselves, the ones for Nate, were like slipping into a warm bath after a chilly walk or sliding into clean sheets with shaved legs. They felt like simple joys, and I didn't want to stamp them out.

"Are you okay, honey? Are you liking living with Nate? If not, we can arrange—"

"Yes. It's great. Truly."

She studied me, concern and love in her dark blue eyes. "You're sure?"

I pulled her into a hug. "I promise. I'm safe with him, Mom."

That truth snapped through me. I'd always been safe with Nate. And maybe knowing that made the difference. And believing the words I said to Summer—that being with someone could be freeing, not confining—maybe that was the answer for my question about whether I could try with him.

Nate

Morocco was amazing. I had a better time than I thought I would after all that whining about going alone. I hiked, I ate, I thought of Ariel too much. But the biggest accompanying feeling was *hope*.

That kiss on my cheek before I left had made me want to grab her and kiss her properly. I hadn't, thank goodness, but it'd packed a punch. She'd probably kissed my cheek a few dozen other times—in greeting after not seeing each other over the years, or whatever. But definitely not since the wedding last year.

I'd promised myself to enjoy the trip, but I let the thoughts, the hope, run wild. As a natural optimist, that came easily—it was the forbidding of such thoughts that took so much energy.

Somehow, with Ariel, I didn't face all that sense of doom I did with anyone else. I'd always felt like that was because they weren't her. Even with the women I'd dated while Ariel was not an option, I couldn't fully commit to them mentally because I just saw it crashing and burning.

My parents had laid out the example long ago. Marriage in the Reynolds house was nothing more than a cooperation of assets. When they had to be together, they were antagonistic at worst and purely fake at best. After growing up with that and seeing friend after friend face nasty divorces, I could admit that I held in tension the desperate desire for, and genuine fear of, marriage. Because committing to someone, giving myself to her, and then waking up to disdain and resentment one day sounded like a kind of death.

It had occurred to me that Ariel had served as an excuse to avoid something more—and by *occurred to me*, I meant Maddie tossed that one out about two years ago not long after I broke things off with her best friend. But I had tried once or twice over the years, and Ariel always hung there like the ideal. She wasn't perfect, but maybe I'd convinced myself she was just to avoid the downfall I saw others experiencing. Except deep down, I wanted the whole deal. Of course I did. I wanted a family—wife, kids, maybe even a dog. So it wasn't just that I wouldn't settle down. It hadn't happened yet because I hadn't been with the right person.

If the fear of what my parents had loomed in my mind, I couldn't help it. There was no way to ignore what'd been the primary example of dysfunctional persistence in my life. And I wasn't alone in it.

Maddie was a mess with relationships too. If I was perpetually single and keeping it casual, Maddie was a serial dater. She went from relationship to relationship. Finally, a year ago, she'd called it quits and sworn off dating altogether. She'd stuck to it, but she'd thrown herself so far into work, I worried she didn't know how to crawl back out.

She'd confirmed as much when we'd texted back and forth toward the end of my trip.

I was supposed to fly in Sunday night, the very end of spring break. Normally, I didn't see a reason to come back early—I didn't have all that much to do to prepare for the week, and there was little incentive to get home and lay around solo. I liked my house, and again, didn't mind being alone, but I tried to make the most of my time here in Europe, and trimming off days for creature comforts of routine wasn't me.

But, oh, how I wished I'd planned that better. I'd booked the Morocco trip in February, before I knew Ariel would be living with me, and long before I knew there was even the smallest chance she'd... well, what? What was it she was doing or thinking?

That question had occurred to me more than once, trust me. She had made no declarations, no full-on acknowledgements of what I'd said or clearly wanted, or more importantly, what *she* wanted. But I'd decided to hope, and until she closed the door, I wasn't going to stop.

Who was I kidding? I'd held on this long, hadn't I?

So, I should've gotten back home Sunday night, on the late side but with enough time to catch up and see if that warmth and openness still simmered between us.

Did that work? Of course not.

A strike in Marrakech of some kind or another meant no flights left the airport for a full forty-eight hours after I should've departed. I'd managed to find a room at a place in the city and wait it out, because after a dozen phone calls, it became clear that was the only option. I should've known better than to be surprised—transportation strikes were not uncommon in the EU and surrounding countries. But, damn, did it ruin my plans.

I got back to the house in the middle of the night Tuesday. The next rotation had started, and I'd be working my butt off to catch up, but I needed sleep. Eric knew my plan and had approved it, because there was really no choice, but this meant I slept until nine the next morning so I could function, then headed in. This also meant that by the time I rolled out of bed, I'd missed Ariel, who'd left to volunteer at the school already.

I could smell the fruity scent of her shampoo when I stepped onto her floor on the way downstairs to the kitchen. I could see she'd had coffee and breakfast by the plate and mug in the dishwasher. The fridge was stocked—I'd need to thank her for that. Repay her, too. We generally shopped for our own food, but she'd texted on Monday to ask if she could get me anything, and I'd taken her up on that.

It was four more days until I even caught sight of her. I'd come home to shower, change, eat, and get as much sleep as I could before I rolled out at 0430 the next morning. The X days—the most intense days of training—started soon. That meant I wouldn't be home except for a shower, maybe, for at least the next six days. There would be no deep conversations, no revelations about our relationship, and that killed me, but I was in no shape to wade through whatever unspoken signals might appear. It'd just have to wait.

Mercifully, Ariel seemed to know this. I came through the door loaded down with stuff. She hustled over from the couch and grabbed my water bottle and coffee mug.

"You're alive! I've seen signs of life these last few days, but I'm glad to actually see *you*."

"I live, indeed." I plunked the other stuff down and followed her into the kitchen.

"I had dinner over at Eric's with Livie and my mom, but I brought some leftovers if you want them."

"Yes please," I said, almost too tired to be hungry, but I knew better than to skip eating.

"Is it going well?"

She pulled a glass container from the fridge and dished food onto a plate. My eyes skated over her hair piled onto her head, baggy T-shirt, and sweats. I wanted to wrap my arms around her waist and press my face into the smooth skin of her neck. She looked warm and cozy and so at home, it made my chest tighten.

I refocused on the task at hand—unloaded my lunch box, rinsed my water bottle and coffee thermos, made a quick mental promise to myself that I could be asleep within the hour. It was a bad idea to go into the X-days already exhausted, so I had to get some rest.

"Here you go. Hope it reheated well." She pulled out a chair at the table where she'd set the plate and a glass full of water.

The pleasure of having her here and having her so willingly make me some food... I must've been even more tired than I realized because I nearly choked up. "Thank you."

I sat, eating quietly, my mind a gelatinous blob full of nonsense.

"Are you okay?"

Her voice stirred me from the staring contest I was having with nothing. "Yes. Super tired, but I'm fine. Thank you for dinner. I'm sorry I'm not better company."

She shook her head. "No, don't apologize. You're fine. Get up to bed, and I'll take care of your plate."

"You don't have to—"

Her hand on my shoulder stopped me. "I know. I want to."

Warm, gooey *feelings* coated my insides. "Thank you."

"All right, Major Reynolds. Get thee to bed."

She took my plate and moved into the kitchen, leaving me to my feelings and exhaustion. After a few minutes, I rallied, stood, and refilled my water.

"Thank you, again. It's X-days so I won't be home much at all until next weekend." I searched her face now, hoping for something. Who knew what.

"Okay. Then I'll see you next weekend. Will you be home for meals and stuff or just swinging through to shower?"

She knew the drill by now, after living with Eric for so long. "Mostly done Friday. I'll probably have to go in Saturday at least, but I'll be around in the evenings for sure."

"Good. Saturday movie night?"

"Yes, it's—yes." I almost said *it's a date* but stopped short of that, unwilling to tread in that direction. She'd suggested a movie night—that was hanging out, and it was a good start. Maybe that night, we could...

"Sleep well, Nate."

I said good night and let the good feelings of the exchange, of her taking care of me, and of her even being here in my house, carry me up to bed.

The busiest days of the rotation ended without too much insanity, thankfully. I actually got a full night's sleep on Friday night. I woke a little later than usual and missed Ariel. She'd been asleep when I got in at ten, and it must've been because she'd rolled out early this morning. I hated not knowing how she was doing, but at least I knew we'd spend the evening together.

I exhaled and scrubbed my hands down my face, unable

to do much other than sip coffee and think for these few minutes before I headed back into work for a while.

Was it bad that I'd already started a countdown to my next big trip? It wouldn't be all that exciting—just heading to see family in Italy—but it'd be a break from work. I hated this sense of exhaustion lately and needed to rediscover my joy, or something. Generally, I really liked my job. I loved working with Eric, even as maddening as he could be, and that time was quickly coming to a close. They'd release the CSL—Command Select List—in a few months. That'd tell me whether I was selected for a battalion command. If I was, I'd have about a year from now before the biggest responsibility of my life started.

I could say that as a man who wasn't married and didn't have kids. I firmly believed that the care and keeping of one's family superseded all work obligations, but that was easy for me to say, right? I didn't have the pull between two good things. I didn't have to tuck my kids in one night and then not see them again for weeks, or months, at a time.

I intended to feel that tension someday, though. I wouldn't just disappear into the ethereal "office" like my father had time and again, conveniently coinciding with arguments or particularly sharp disagreements with my mother. He chose to miss out. I wouldn't do the same if I ever had the chance.

Usually, I avoided thinking about that lack. My mother was quick to remind me and Maddie that we hadn't provided her any grandchildren. Without a doubt, the first question Annette Reynolds asked upon connecting with her son would be, "Who are you dating and when is the wedding?"

No pressure, right? She used a twinge of humor there,

but in the last few years, it'd worn thin. So, so, thin. Especially after The Disappointment.

Oh, have we not talked about that? So, let's get it out there. About nine months before Ariel's divorce—and that is pertinent here—I started dating Juliet Christensen. Longtime family friend, and a woman whom I wouldn't be surprised to find my mother had betrothed me to at a young age. We got along well, and she didn't mind the fact that I moved across the world in the middle of dating her since she had money out the eyeballs and loved to travel. I think Mom always liked that the Christensen family fortune notoriously started with a *b* rather than an *m*.

Anyway, she's a great woman. We had fun together, and I think if we'd kept at it, we might've ended up somewhere together. Maybe. I always thought she might be looking for someone more stable, less tied to the Army, even though she'd seemed happy to come hunt me down to get together.

Because I genuinely cared for her, when Ariel divorced, we broke up. That may seem like a non-sequitur, but to me, it added up. Once Ariel was *free*—not free to date, but free of that crap-heap of a marriage, I didn't have the ability to be with someone else. Not that she suddenly became an option. In fact, as had been shown quite clearly right up until maybe just the last week or so, she simply wasn't one.

I'd gotten the call from Eric, told him how deeply sorry I was, since the word of the divorce also came with some ugly truths about what'd happened to her, which had been more than difficult to hear, and then I'd called Juliet. No question, no doubt, just clarity of purpose. And Juliet had taken it with her usual grace and generosity.

The good thing was, I'd been honest with her from the beginning. I'd told her I'd been hung up on someone for years, and that was why I'd never gotten serious with someone. She'd had her own reasons for being single at the time. And our parting ways was more than amicable. It was also right.

Maddie had been furious. She hadn't said anything, which spoke loudly in Maddie language. She'd hinted at me being hung up on Ariel through the years after I'd admitted it to Maddie one stupid night after seeing Ariel with her boyfriend at her twenty-fifth birthday. If Maddie had known I'd broken up with Juliet for Ariel, she would've lost her mind. But she'd never understood how I could hold out hope for this one person. But I did.

Because my heart had been hung up on Ariel Wolfe since the day I met her. It might sound ridiculous. It made me a few shades of pathetic, though I could honestly say it wasn't for lack of trying, at least in recent years. But at this point, I wouldn't deny it, and I wondered if maybe, *maybe*, our time had finally come. We were late to this party—so late. But we could have a few last dances, so to speak. We might just have our turn.

CHAPTER SIXTEEN

Ariel

I'd spent the day with my friends doing something good for the community, and it had filled me up. You know that feeling? When you're so full of positive feelings and happy memories and laughter it feels like it'll bubble over?

That was me as I bustled into the house at four-thirty Saturday afternoon. I'd managed to keep my excitement for tonight under control, thanks in part to a crazy busy week at the school, my volunteer job, and helping with prepping for Summer's swap event this weekend. It'd gone insanely well, and I could tell she felt it was a success. It had been, and I was so proud of her for asking her friends and community for help, especially because it only made the event stronger.

I'd spent the evening sorting through things at Eric's because once he heard about the swap, he'd decided he wanted to clean out kid clothes. I'd gotten home and basically passed out, then got up early to help with whatever Summer needed. And this meant I hadn't seen Nate.

But when I pulled into the driveway, his car was already there. He'd beaten me home, and the sensation rolling through me was a crazy mix. Definitely jumpy. Between the time apart over spring break and then the rotation, we'd truly not even seen each other in passing except four days ago when we'd made the plan to hang out tonight.

So, walking in the door, my whole body vibrated from happiness and anticipation, and yes, a few nerves. The scent of something delicious reached me as I set my keys on the counter and hung my purse on a hook. My eyes immediately found Nate, who glanced over his shoulder to hit me with a quick smile before he returned to stirring a pot on the stove.

"I hope you're hungry and willing to eat early. For some reason, I was craving Bolognese sauce, and I have no intention of waiting much longer to eat it."

My heart swelled. He'd made dinner. Homemade. I knew he could cook, and liked to, when he had time.

But this wasn't about me. He'd just said he'd been craving the sauce, probably due to living off camping food during the rotation. Still...

"I'll eat whenever you want. I had an early lunch, so early dinner would be great."

His back still to me since he faced the stove, I took in the sight of him. A thin T-shirt clung to his shoulders and upper back, then hugged along his trim waist. The ends of an apron knotted behind his neck and around said waist. He wore his lounge pants, no shoes or socks, and already, my pulse had picked up.

"How was your day?" he asked, turning to catch my eye.

The minute our gazes connected, a little *zip!* snaked through me.

"Good. Really good. Yours?"

I sounded weird. Could he tell? Did he know that was my nervous voice, kind of shaky and weak?

"Blessedly short, and now I'm on to the good part." He winked, then turned back to adjust a timer on the oven.

"I'm going to run get changed, if that's okay?"

He gave me a look like what I'd said was odd.

"Of course it's okay. Take all the time you need. Everything will be ready in about ten minutes, but if you need more time, take it. It'll all keep."

Unable to find words to respond, I nodded, then ascended the stairs and closed my bedroom door gently. For some insane reason, I felt like I might cry.

I sat on the end of the bed, bouncing on the mattress a few times out of habit before unlacing my shoes. While going through the motions of changing, I mined myself for how I'd gone from so happy to nearly in tears.

But the tears weren't truly sadness. Not quite. More like a bittersweet pain. Because seeing Nate in his apron, cooking a meal he was ready to share with me... it was something no one but family and Summer Applegate had ever done for me. Certainly not a man I was—well, whatever this whole thing was. Nothing yet beyond friendship and roommates, but part of my nerves stemmed from what I planned to tell him tonight.

Cooking for me wasn't a big deal. It wasn't. I knew that. He didn't mean it to be some grand gesture, but wow, did it hit me squarely in the chest. Jim had literally never cooked. Not once. And I'd never seen that as a problem. He'd explained he was raised by traditional parents, and I didn't mind cooking.

He worked long hours in the Army, and I didn't have much else to do in Texas without friends or much of a career to speak of. I didn't mind the laundry and cleaning and cooking —those were all things I could do for him, for us. But I never realized it was just one more way he took. Because he never said thank you for any of it. He never acknowledged the time or energy it required, and he never returned the favor.

If that was all that had been wrong between us, it would've been a problem that needed discussing, but not a dealbreaker. Not something you leave a marriage over, in itself. But I'd come to terms with that move being a way to isolate me. I'd confronted the fact that I'd lost my support system when I'd relocated with him, and his refusal to let me work under the auspices of being traditional and wanting to *take care* of me had quite effectively chipped away at my self-confidence on top of further alienating me from people.

It wasn't fair to compare Nate to Jim, and yet this wasn't the first time I'd done it, and it wouldn't be the last. Especially if we dated. I hadn't been with anyone since Jim, and honestly, I'd only really had one other boyfriend before him in my early twenties, so Jim was my biggest reference point. My spectral barometer against which most men would easily succeed.

Nate was so far above and beyond him, it didn't make sense to try to put them side by side. I didn't need to date him to know that. I'd known it all along, ever since we met and he showed me his fellow book nerd card.

So tonight, I'd spend the evening with someone great. And I'd push away all the comparisons and the surreal feeling that watching a man boil water for pasta he planned to feed me brought on, and work to experience tonight as a woman spending time with a man she liked. A man she more than liked.

~

"Where did you get this recipe?" I asked, wiping my mouth after the last delectable bite.

"Chiara Contelli. She's the chef at my parents' place in Rome. She grew up in Bologna, though, so this is pretty close to an authentic Bolognese." He leaned back in his chair and rested his hands on his flat stomach. "I love that stuff."

He was adorable, eyes closed in bliss as he slunk down enough to relax his head against the back of the chair. But the information didn't quite compute.

"Your parents' place in Rome?"

One eye opened. "Yeah, you know they're kind of ridiculous. We've talked about this."

"Maybe? I mean, I guess I remember you come from money, as they say, but I didn't realize you came from *my parents have a house in Rome* type of money." Crap. What?

He chuckled and sat up straight. "Well, now you know."

"Do they have... other houses?"

He squinted, appearing to register the odd tone in my voice. "Maybe."

"Where?"

He tossed his napkin onto the plate and shoved the utensils closer to the middle. "Here and there."

My eyes widened. "Where?"

"Does it matter?"

And then *I* heard it. The twinge of vulnerability in his voice. He'd never once indicated to me that he came from a family with that kind of wealth. Eric hadn't said anything either.

Did it matter? Kind of. Because it was part of him. But in the way he meant—in the way that would influence my feelings for him? "No. Not at all. It just seems like I've known you for a really long time not to know this kind of thing."

He shrugged, took my plate and stacked it on his, and stood. "It's not something I advertise."

"I gathered that."

He shot me a look. "People have different reactions to it. Some are unfazed. Some feel weird. Some get oddly interested in being my best friend and meeting my family."

My heart sank for him, wondering what kind of things had happened to make him feel cagey. "I'm sorry."

"You haven't done anything wrong, and you don't need to be sorry." He flashed a quick smile, then returned his focus to rinsing the dishes.

We worked together to clean up, and all the while, my mind pulled details from our past that clicked into place with this news. He'd always traveled extensively. Even while here, he'd been far and wide. I'd always assumed it was because he'd been single, so he didn't have the same household responsibilities someone like Eric did. It wasn't like Army paychecks were extravagant, but at his rank and with no major debts, anyone would be doing really well if they only had themselves to consider. But that'd probably been a little naïve.

He settled into the couch, that same position with his arm running along the back. I took up my usual post, a cushion away, resisting the little flash of a vision that had me sitting right next to him and resting my head on his shoulder.

I wanted to go ahead and tell him what I'd decided I was going to, but I felt so crazy nervous just thinking about saying the words, I stayed quiet. He cued up a movie and pressed play, but immediately paused it and looked over at me.

"Sorry I'm weird."

I raised a brow.

"About the family thing. It's honestly not because I expect *you* to be a jerk about it. I know you wouldn't be. I have just always kept that part of my life close. Not long ago, my sister was in a relationship and the guy ended up admitting he was only with her for her money."

I gasped. Not normally a response I had, but that was just too cruel.

"Yeah. It sucked. And it reinforced why I don't mention it or even hint at it. Obviously, I have nice stuff, but I live off my own income—my Army income. Always have."

His eyes flickered back and forth between mine, like he might be able to figure out how I really felt about all this if he just looked closely enough.

"That's great. I—I'm not sure what to say except this isn't something that influences how I think of you or anything. I'm sorry you felt like you didn't want us to know, but I can see you had your reasons."

"Well, Eric does know. But yeah. Thanks."

"Ah."

Interesting my brother had never said anything, but he must've known Nate didn't like people knowing. Or had Nate asked him not to? And why did this make me feel weird—this ultimately had nothing to do with me. So Nate was filthy rich—good for him. Great.

"Hey."

His hand brushing over mine startled me from those thoughts. I looked over at him.

"Don't overthink it. I'm still me. The money belongs to my parents for the most part. It's—it shouldn't change a thing."

Did he really think I was going to think differently of him? Though, I was over here mentally running around all over this revelation, still stunned by it. The news was less disconcerting than my reaction to it, and that didn't make sense. "Am I acting weird or something? I'm sorry. I don't mean to. I'm feeling silly for not realizing, but I also get that it doesn't matter. You can be billionaire Nate or pauper Nate, and I'd still be on your team."

His answering smile spread slowly, then lit his entire face. My stomach fluttered—he really was quite handsome, especially when he smiled like that.

He clicked play, and the strains of the soundtrack began. All the while, my mind jumped around, thinking of this discovery about him, his clear reluctance for anyone to know, and that smile.

CHAPTER SEVENTEEN

Nate

She fell asleep, head on the back of the couch angled toward me, about an hour into the movie. She'd been busy all weekend—I couldn't blame her. And soon after staring at her beautiful face for a few minutes, I fell asleep too.

I jolted awake hours later, some unknown sound shaking me from sleep. It was only nine, but it might as well have been two in the morning. I'd already stiffened up and had to stretch my neck gingerly before I could slide toward Ariel. I'd said her name twice while dealing with the state of my twisted spinal column, but no dice.

So, I set a hand on her arm. "Ariel."

Nothing.

I squeezed her wrist, gently but firm. "Ariel. Wake up."

She sighed and her eyes fluttered open, and that cerulean blue gaze hit me. She looked right at me. Being the object of her focus made me weak. I wanted to lean over the last eight inches and kiss her until those eyes shut again. And something in her eye made me feel like maybe she was thinking the same thing.

Heat flooded my chest, and that low, winding *want* I all too easily felt around her twisted in my gut.

Warning! Warning! Back away, idiot!

I stood up. "Glad you're up. I'm heading to bed. It's only nine-something, but I'm beat."

"Oh, okay. Yeah, I'll do the same."

I didn't stick around to watch her, afraid of what my barely awake brain might try. I wouldn't dare actually kiss her, but I might touch her again, and that would be unwise. We plodded up the stairs, me first and her just behind. I wanted to say something but had no idea what. So, when she stepped onto the second floor, I turned, only to say, "'Night."

I expected the same in response, so I kept slowly plodding up the next flight to my room. But only three steps up, her voice stopped me.

"Nate, wait."

I turned to see her on the landing, arms crossed and tucked close, her lips pressed together. Was she... nervous? Concern shot through me. Damn. Had she gotten weird over the whole—

"I want to say that..." She cleared her throat, shifted foot to foot, then pinned me with that gaze again. "I'm available."

I blinked. Was she really saying what I desperately hoped she was saying?

Like a genius, I didn't say a word.

She nodded. "Okay then. Good night."

She then slipped inside her room and shut the door.

Wait... did that just happen? Did the woman I'd been veritably pining after for years just give me a green light to ask her out?

I stayed frozen on the stairs for probably a full minute, my mind an absolute blank. Finally, I shook that off and let myself review what she'd said. *I'm available.* Yep. That was what she'd said.

Sure, it could've been something like, *I'm available to talk if you ever need to*, or *I'm here for you*-style availability. But that word choice had been so specific, much like mine had been when I'd told her there was no one special who was *available*.

Which meant only one thing, and that was why my feet carried me to her threshold, and I knocked.

The door swung open part way, and she held the frame and the panel, head tilted.

"Hey," she said, a little wrinkle at the center of her brow.

"Hey. So. Would you want to go out with me sometime?" And because I was the prince of cool, I added, "Sooner rather than later, preferably."

A grin smoothed away the confused look, and she let out a little disbelieving laugh. "Yes. Yes, I would."

My hands clasped behind me to keep from making a stupid victory gesture, or grabbing her and kissing her, or any number of other moves I was only just controlled enough not to make. "Good. Okay then. Sleep well, and we'll figure out the plan tomorrow."

"Sounds good. Sweet dreams."

I took the stairs two at a time, certain I needed as much space between us as possible in the wake of the last three minutes. Arguably three of the best minutes of my life.

I had no idea what would come next. A date, obviously,

but how would that go? Did she like me, or did she feel like she needed to try this? Like it *should* work because we'd been friends? Like she'd said yes because I was a safe choice, not someone who'd push her or hurt her.

Well, in truth, none of those were terrible reasons if they did factor in. But man, I wanted it to be because she found me as irresistible as I did her. It was way too soon to expect that, or anything, from her. I would keep it at that— no expectations. Just enjoy whatever we could have for now. She'd be gone soon, and I'd finally move on.

For now, I'd take this victory and run. So, I forced my way through the bedtime routine, mind wandering through every possible date idea, and finally passed out around midnight.

I liked that she woke up early. I naturally did too, or maybe it wasn't so much natural as it was beaten into me by years of early morning PT. But at this point in life, I hated sleeping in unless I would otherwise face a terrible sleep deficit. Ariel seemed to be the same.

She beat me downstairs, so I woke to the scent of coffee and bacon. As though I could adore her any more than I already did.

"Hey. I'm heading out, but I'll be back by five today." She looped her purse over a shoulder and slipped her keys into the front pocket. "I left you some food—sorry I can't stick around to eat with you."

She looked so pretty today. I wanted to smooth her hair behind her ear and kiss her just below it in that soft hollow. She'd be warm and smell so sweet. And I'd be *close* to her.

"Nate?"

Whoops. Morning brain not functioning on all cylinders. "Sorry. Still waking up, I guess. Thank you for making me food, which was unnecessary but not unwelcomed. Where are you going—if you don't mind my asking?"

I added that last bit because I never wanted to be in the same league as her ex, and the bit I did know included him doing nothing short of putting a LoJack on her car so he knew exactly where she was at all times.

"Finishing up Summer's swap event. It's only until one today, but then we'll be packing it all up which will take a while, depending on how much is left. There was quite a bit still yesterday, even though people had taken a ton compared to what we started with in the morning."

She dipped her head to her phone and smiled at it— must've gotten a message.

"Sounds good. Do you need any help with the packing up?"

She smiled one of those smiles that made my heart twist. It was this particular look. Her eyes got soft and she looked happy, and for lack of a better term, *pleased*. And I wasn't scared to admit I loved getting that smile.

"That's so sweet. I think Summer has extra volunteers lined up for the afternoon, but I can text you if it looks like we need more hands?"

"Absolutely. I'll just be home, being a bum today." *Thinking about you*, which was nothing shy of pathetic, but she'd said yes to going out, so it was maybe marginally less so now.

"Nice."

She walked to the door but turned, hesitating. She glanced up at me, then quickly back at her purse, like there was something essential she needed in there. Her cheeks looked slightly darker—tinged pink. Was she blushing?

"So hey. Is tonight too soon to take you out?" My stomach took a flying leap.

Her eyes shot to me. "Uh, no. It's not. That sounds good."

"Good. We'll just go somewhere in town, keep it simple this time." Because if I had any say, it'd be the first of many. We could cram weeks' worth of dates into the time before she left. If this is all I'd ever get, I wasn't about to waste time.

"Okay. Well. I'll see you later, then."

Our gazes hung, her bright eyes holding mine. I wouldn't be the one to look away. Eventually, she did, blinking down to the door handle and pulling to let herself out without another word.

I ran a hand over my head, needing a second to ground myself before I moved on. She made me shaky and fog-headed just from eye contact. I didn't actually know how I'd stand to finally be on a date with her after so long.

Moving into the kitchen, I set my determination. I'd wanted this for... too long. I wasn't about to wuss out now. I sat down with coffee and a plate of eggs and bacon and made plans.

CHAPTER EIGHTEEN

Ariel

I didn't mention the date to anyone. We were busy enough all day that I easily distracted myself from the impending plans with Nate.

Ha, right. That was a total lie.

After the divorce, I'd promised myself I wouldn't lie. To others, yes, but especially to myself. If I'd been more honest with myself about what was happening and how it made me feel—how scared and trapped I felt—I wouldn't have ever moved to Texas. I wouldn't have gotten married. I might've found someone else and avoided the whole mess completely.

I also tried my best not to what-if things like that. Mostly, I'd embraced the fact that I'd married a controlling, emotionally abusive jerk. Coming to terms with that had taken a long time—the entirety of my first and only year of marriage, in fact. And while I no longer viewed the abuse as my fault, I had to own up to some of the things that went wrong. Part of that was allowing myself to lie. I knew why I did it, and most of the time, I could forgive myself for it, even. But I had also stared myself in the mirror after one particularly rough session with my therapist and made myself promise I wouldn't lie again.

So, if I was being honest, I could admit it. I was more nervous to go out with Nate than I'd been since moving to Germany. I was also more excited than I could remember. Over the last few years, I'd had plenty of anxiety but hadn't been truly excited about something in so long. Too long.

I wished I was like Summer, who absolutely fed off volunteering and satisfying a need in the community. Or like Bec, who had her own unique professional drive. Or Katie, who had a career she'd dreamed of for years. Or even my new sister-in-law, who'd spent so long in career and travel mode and had just started what she called her *new adventure* with my brother. They all had so much to look forward to, and it wasn't just about the men they'd paired up with.

I'd learned what happened when I put all my relational and life-related eggs in a one-man basket. It wasn't healthy, or good, or right. But I also felt rather keenly that I didn't know what I wanted to do. I'd bounced around from one thing to the next over the last decade or so, never really finding and connecting with what vocation would fulfill me.

What if it's not going to be a career that fulfills you?

I huffed, frustrated to have that thought yet again. I'd changed my way of thinking in the last few years. Part of what had made me susceptible to Jim was my desire to settle down, have a family, and just... live. My mom had stayed home on and off through my childhood, and I'd always wanted to do that. My sense of urgency to get to the *married with kids* part of life was absolutely a factor in my ignoring the warning signs with Jim. After admitting that, I'd decided I needed to change the focus, find a career, and funnel my energy into that. Find a new dream.

But some little scrappy part of my soul held tight to the desire for a family of my own. Something like Eric and Livie were building. Something like I grew up in.

I had to stop thinking about families and marriage and all that, or I'd be a total freak on this date tonight. Already, I felt the flutters in my belly and couldn't swallow quite right. By the time I arrived back at home—at Nate's—I needed a minute to myself before we did this thing.

"How was it today?" he asked from the vicinity of the couch.

I set my purse down and glanced over to find him stretched out, head on a pillow, book in hand, but he popped up to sitting when I walked farther into the room. My heart thumped.

"Good. Pretty good crowd for the first few hours, and then Summer had like eight additional volunteers to help the cleanup, and she's got people delivering all the donations tomorrow."

She made me so proud—she'd organized everything so well, and she'd clearly asked friends and coworkers for help. Knowing what a challenge that was for her, or at least having some idea, I hoped she felt the sense of triumph she deserved to. Based on the way she choked up saying thank you to everyone today, she did.

"That's great."

"Yeah." I swallowed. *Oh*, the nerves. I could hardly think.

"I can be ready in ten minutes, whenever you want to go. I made a seven o'clock reservation, but if we want to leave sooner, we totally can. I wasn't sure how you'd feel after working all day." His eyes narrowed. "You okay?"

Here was a small test for all that reminding-myself-about-not-lying I'd just done. But should I really tell him the truth? A regular person going out on a date with a friend wouldn't say a word... would she?

His brow furrowed, and he moved to me, stopping about a foot away. "Ariel?"

Oh, crap. He sounded worried now.

"I'm fine. Or, I guess, I'm nervous." I flashed him an awkward, too-large smile. "But that's not bad. I just... being around people all day kind of has me worn out. So I wouldn't mind just sticking with the seven o'clock plan, and I'll take a couple hours to recharge and regenerate my words."

His head tilted to one side. He wasn't smiling, but for some strange reason, it *felt* like he was as he studied me. "Regenerate your words?"

"That's how I think of it sometimes. Like I've got a bucket full of words for the day, and if I pour them all out at a certain point, then I need some time alone to regenerate them. It's nothing to do with you, or how much I—"

He stepped closer and put a warm hand on my arm to stop me. "I'm not worried about that. It's a helpful analogy. If you've got a bucket, then so does Eric, where Livie and I have got wells."

I smiled. "That sounds accurate."

"And Robby has an ocean."

I chuckled. "Also accurate."

My nephew could speak without taking a breath for what felt like forever. He was the sweetest little person, but oh, my, could he talk. Delia was quieter by nature, but sometimes, I wondered if that happened simply because

Robby talked so much, she didn't see a point in speaking unless something really mattered to her. My heart warmed at his mention of my niece and nephew, the fact that he knew them well enough to know that about Robby, and that he had his own relationship with each of them.

"Well, go relax. I definitely want you to have time to regenerate." One side of his mouth rose into a charming little half-smile. "And don't be nervous. We're going to have fun, and there's no pressure. Not ever. I just want to spend time with you." He squeezed my arm, then padded back to the couch and dropped down into it. "And I'll be right here until about six-thirty, so let me know if you need anything."

Instead of standing there staring at him stretched out on the couch, I helped myself to some water and went to my room. Once there, I sat and just... sat. I truly was worn out. But the exhaustion was only a small part of the mix of thoughts and emotions swirling in me.

I just want to spend time with you.

He made me wind tight and relax all at once. My stomach knotted with nerves even as the pinch between my shoulders eased. I'd never felt such a confusing mix of attraction and comfort, nervous anticipation and peace.

Except with him. I'd felt safe with Nate from the beginning. I wondered if maybe I'd always felt all of this since the beginning and had shoved the reason for the excitement and nerves into the back of my mind to prioritize our friendship.

Whatever the case, I was no less nervous for the date, but it felt less *anxious* and more excited. I fell back on the bed and shut my eyes. I needed a nap, maybe some reading, and time to clean up. Then I'd be ready for my date with Nate Reynolds.

CHAPTER NINETEEN

Nate

The evening had a surreal softness around the edges. No, that wasn't quite right. I'd been trying to figure out what felt so... *something*... but couldn't put a finger on what exactly this felt like. Yes, surreal. Dream-like, maybe. Like a freaking long time coming, yes.

But something else too. Something soft-focused but not hazy. Or maybe I'd lost it. That was entirely possible, because when Ariel stepped off the stairs into the living room in a deep blue dress a shade or two darker than her eyes, I forgot how to breathe. Like literally, I'd sipped a drink of water just before I saw her, and in that moment, I couldn't figure out how to swallow and exhale at the same time.

She was stunning. As always. But seeing her like this made warmth crawl from my toes to my chest and expand out in ripples as I registered that the dress, the gorgeous hair, the makeup... it was all for this date.

For me.

And then, I had to get a damn grip because that was too much. I still didn't know exactly where we were here. She'd said she was available, and she'd said yes to tonight, but what that meant to her could be very different from what it meant to me. For me, it definitely meant *oh-thank-God-finally* and for her, it might be something more like *okay-I'll-show-up*. She looked amazing, but she might've just been in the mood to get dressed up.

I hoped some of her thoughts on the matter would be revealed. I also wanted to remain conscious of the fact that she'd had an exhausting day. We could do something more elaborate next time. Tonight, a simple dinner at one of my favorite little German spots in town would be perfect.

We sat down across from each other in a small wooden booth and the waiter handed us menus. And then it hit me.

That odd feeling? It was satisfaction. Pure pleasure at being here with *her*, going through all of this date night activity for *Ariel*. How many times had I done this with other women and wished, somewhere in me, it was her sitting across from me? And now, here she was, tucking her dark, spiraling hair behind her ear and perusing the menu. When she looked up, she must've sensed I'd been looking at her for more than a second, and a blush brightened her cheeks.

"Do you know what you like?"

I nearly laughed out loud. *Yeah, and she's sitting right in front of me.* But that would be too much for a first date, especially with this woman, and especially when I didn't know where she stood on *us*.

"I like the crispy duck. Or the jaegerschnitzel. You?"

She shared her favorite dish, which I would've guessed. She loved rice, and this place had mind-blowing veggie fried rice. It was a combination German, Italian, Asian place, specializing in Vietnamese food. And you might think that sounded impossible, but each of the cuisines was delicious. I'd never had anything that wasn't great, and some of their dishes were among my favorite I'd had, ever.

Our drinks arrived—a beer for me and a glass of red wine for her. I held up my stein. "To us."

She chuckled and clinked her glass with mine. "To us."

We each took a drink but held eye contact. As so often happened, looking in her brilliant blue eyes made me feel a little like someone had swept a leg and left me off-balance.

"It is pretty amazing we've been friends for so long," I said, needing to end this intense little staring contest.

"It is. I kind of love it."

"Just kind of? I wholeheartedly do. You're one of my favorite people."

"Well, likewise. I—" She stopped abruptly, gaze flicking around the room before they settled back on me. "I've always wanted to say I'm sorry. For the time when we didn't talk."

I scoffed. "You say that as though it was your choice."

I'd never forget the text. It'd come not long after they'd started dating. *"I'm sorry. I'm dating someone, and he's uncomfortable with me texting other men. I get it, but I am sorry. If he knew you, he wouldn't be concerned."*

I'd responded, something short and sweet. And then I'd sat back and wondered if the guy somehow knew what I felt for Ariel. That was stupid because we'd never met. But all he'd have to do was meet her, and then he'd know most people *would* be interested in her. She was quiet and thoughtful and generous and stubborn and sweet. She was a total nerd and used the wrong word for lounge pants. She was an insanely loving sister and aunt, a devoted daughter, and in that text, I also learned she was a faithful partner.

"I should've told him—I don't know. I should've fought for our friendship a little harder." She exhaled slowly. "But I didn't. And so, I'm sorry. Even though I'm not sure what I could have done differently, I wish I had, you know?"

She looked like she had something more to say, and since she rarely referenced this time in her life, I wanted her to keep talking if she wanted to. "Makes sense. I'm sorry you had to choose, and I'm sorry I didn't fight either. But honestly, if we were dating, I'm not sure I'd love you trading texts with some other guy all the time."

Her lashes fluttered. "A lot to unpack there."

"Really? What?"

"Well... I guess, first, I need to understand the last part. Does that mean you'd ask me to stop talking to other people?"

I could be a little slow on the uptake, but I knew where she was going and why her whole demeanor had sobered in the last few minutes.

"You should talk to and communicate with whomever you want, whenever you want. If we were in a relationship, it wouldn't be my job to make rules for you. That's your decision. But I'd also hope that you'd respect me enough to have boundaries with other people. So, for me, I wouldn't be speaking to other women I've dated. If I have people I work with I need to communicate with, I do that through e-mail or group messaging. I have some amazing female friends, but if I was in a relationship, the dynamic there might change a little—I'd probably ask you how you felt, and we could figure it out together."

She swallowed and nodded. "That sounds reasonable."

"Good. I mean, I admittedly have a lot to learn about relationships, too, so I'm not speaking as an authority. But I'm a one-woman kind of man, so there's not a real issue for me there. And frankly, other than you, all my close friends are men or are married to my male friends, so I wouldn't hang out with or talk to them individually anyway. Does that make sense?"

"Yes. Very clear. And... it makes sense."

"What else did you need to unpack?"

She took a sip of her wine, then leaned back as the waiter set her plate in front of her. I hadn't even noticed the food arrive. Once the waiter had deposited my plate and left again, I picked up a fork but spoke before I dove in. "So, what was it?"

"Ah. Um, I was just going to address the *if we were dating* portion there." Her gaze hit me, then returned to her plate.

My stomach flipped. *Okay, here we go.* "What about it?"

Those eyes pinned me as she chewed, then swallowed. "I guess I'm wondering if I missed something."

I raised a brow.

"We're on a date, no?" Her cheeks had stayed that reddish hue, but she didn't seem embarrassed. I didn't want her afraid or embarrassed to talk to me. About anything. Ever.

"We are on a date. But admittedly, I don't know what that means for you. As I said, there's no pressure here. I don't want to assume that since you said yes to coming tonight, that means we're—"

"We are. Dating." She smiled, then tucked her lips between her teeth to stifle it.

I didn't bother trying to hide my response. It probably

looked like someone had clicked on a lightbulb over here thanks to the bright blaze of my cheesy grin.

"Well. Good."

"Good."

After that, we relaxed into less charged conversation. She told me a bit more about the event this weekend she'd helped with, and I told her about the rotation in all its long, boring glory. I mentioned my upcoming trip to Italy and just barely resisted inviting her, which would've been insane and about as far as you could be into the *too soon, man* category.

Before we knew it, I'd paid and we were rustling out the door. As soon as we exited through the old, heavy wooden doors and out onto the street, my pulse ticked up. Now we'd have to navigate this part of the date. But rather than agonize over whether to hold her hand or kiss her, I'd decided after she'd declared we were dating that I'd just ask. That if I didn't know what was going on or what was right for her, I would simply *ask*.

Sounded simple but took a decent measure of my guts. Because on some level, I expected her to reject me, reject the possibility of this whole thing. I'd trained myself to expect that after so long, hoping for a different outcome felt foolish, even if I'd never been able to stop hoping.

I opened her door for her, and she slipped in with a simple thanks. The jog around the car went too quickly. Nerves made my throat dry, and I felt like I couldn't quite swallow. Instead of dwelling on all the ways my body wanted to make sure I knew I was nervous, I hauled into the car and got it going. Bayern Drei, the local radio station, played Olivia Newton-John's "Xanadu." We sat quietly for about two blocks before Ariel burst out laughing.

I joined her. "This song."

"It's ridiculous," she said, her voice strained from laughter.

"I feel comfortable saying I never once heard this on the radio in the US, and that I hear it at least once a week here. And honestly, I don't even listen to the radio that often here."

"Same! I've been trying to figure out what it is about the song that has made it so popular here. It's confusing. I mean, good for Olivia, but..." She faded off and rested her head against the seat.

I could feel her eyes on me but kept mine on the road.

Pulling into the driveway, everything grew quiet. Even the radio somehow sounded quieter. Each movement pounded through me, fully surreal and yet also blessedly real. This was all actually happening. We'd just been on a date, and she'd confirmed it.

Instead of pausing there and talking, we both got out and met in front of the car. I'd parked in the driveway, and for one of the first times, I was glad for the long walkway to the front door.

"Can I hold your hand?"

I should've felt stupid asking. I generally wasn't the kind to ask for permission—not that I didn't want consent. I could usually feel out a situation and sense whether my touch would be welcomed for small things.

But with Ariel, I didn't want anything to be miscon-strued, and frankly, I didn't trust my ability to gauge what she might want. I'd never been so hyperaware and yet muddied when it came to reading someone. If we kept at this, I hoped I'd chill out a bit and be able to read her better.

"Of course." She reached for mine and laced our fingers together.

The slide of her palm against mine felt so good—too

ridiculously good to be simple handholding. We walked up the path to the door and stopped. I said a silent prayer in hopes I wouldn't bungle the next few minutes and in a plea she wouldn't know what a nervous wreck I was.

"Want me to leave you here at the door and go drive around the block?"

She squeezed my hand and chuckled. "Only if you want to."

"Nah. I can drop you at your bedroom door."

We entered the house still holding hands. At some point, I'd have to man up and do this.

I exhaled, feeling eager and wild and not at all the image of a cool, charming date I'd envisioned being tonight. "This is stupid. I'm nervous."

She smiled up at me. "Don't be."

I huffed a little but smiled back at her, wanting so much to lay it all out. I wouldn't, but I suspected that impulse would be there until I finally did—if I finally did get to. The logical voice in my mind dove in then. *You're not going to because she's going to leave. You're going to take what she gives, and then you're going to get your crap together and move on.*

For now, I stuck with honesty, which I would give her in full measure whenever possible. With those blue eyes spearing me and her perfect lips still curved into a soft smile, my voice came out gruff.

"I can't help it."

CHAPTER TWENTY

Ariel

That grit in his voice... *oh, hello.* It turned my insides out. I squeezed his hand for what felt like the tenth time in the few minutes since he'd asked if he could hold mine. Just thinking of that made my stomach flip. This wasn't at all how I'd expected him to be on a date. Not that he'd disappointed me. More like he'd surprised me.

Nate carried around so much charm and playfulness, so seeing him serious, hearing him admit he was *nervous*...

"I know. I am too," I finally answered.

"You are?" he asked, inching closer.

"Of course."

"You don't have to be."

He looked so concerned, like my nerves meant something bad. But the low tone in his voice, the way he dipped his head so he spoke quietly and just to me, made my pulse race.

"Same goes for you."

He shook his head. "All right. Neither of us should be nervous, but we both are."

I bit my lip to tame the answering grin. "Sounds like it."

He cleared his throat. "Listen. I don't know how to do this with you in any way other than asking your opinion. So, this is me officially notifying you that I have no moves here. I don't know how we should go forward, so I'm just going to ask."

"Okay. Ask me, Nate."

Our bodies and faces were inches apart now. We'd both slowly moved closer, the pull to touch him, to tilt my chin up a little more and press my lips to the smooth curve of his jaw nearly irresistible.

"I need to know how you want this to go. How you want to go forward."

His gaze touched every part of my face, snagged on my lips, then found my eyes again.

"Slowly." I said the word, though it rang hollow in my mind, in this moment. But that flutter in my belly, a combination of desire and fear, reinforced it.

He nodded. "Okay. We'll go slowly."

"Okay."

We might've been moving slowly, might've just agreed upon it, but my breath came quickly. I was nearly light-headed with his proximity and more than a little overwhelmed by his words, his sweetness—*him.*

Then he leaned closer, his body not quite touching mine, and his lips brushed my cheek. My breath caught at the sensation and his nearness, but all too soon, he stepped back. He raised our hands and pressed a kiss to the back of my knuckles, then gently released me.

"Good night, Ariel. I had a great time."

And then he turned and left. No glass of water like usual, no... anything else. I watched his feet disappear up the stairs, and it took me a full minute after I heard his door shut all the way at the top of the house before I jolted into action and got my own glass of water, then headed to bed.

I hadn't expected him to leave. I'd thought we'd watch a movie, or have a cup of coffee and chat, or something. Did his leaving mean he didn't want that? Or did my saying I wanted to move slowly sound like I didn't want to continue the date?

I suspected Nate didn't normally move slowly with his dates, but I didn't actually know that. I only assumed. So maybe that would be too much for him, but I wouldn't apologize for it. Though he didn't seem upset. He didn't seem anything other than completely genuine.

As I readied for bed, I promised myself I wouldn't assume the worst about Nate's reaction. I wouldn't lay awake and dissect the evening, looking for warning signs or indicators my desire for a measured pace had ruined things. And of course, I completely broke my promise to myself and hardly slept a wink.

"'Morning, Wolfe. I made you waffles."

My heart leapt at his voice and the greeting, and obviously, the mention of waffles. "Thank you. That's sweet."

"I am, if not sweet, then at least a highly motivated suitor."

He tracked me as I entered the kitchen, taking a drink of

his coffee without looking away. He wore his uniform, and for some reason, that hit me as insanely attractive now, while also making me feel borderline indecent in my robe and slippers.

I snickered to cover the heat crawling up my chest. "*Suitor?*"

He smiled. "What's wrong with being a suitor?"

My focus on the very challenging activity of pouring myself some coffee, I summoned the courage. "Nothing, I guess. You've just always been more of a *play the field* kind of guy, right?"

The room went silent. Even though he hadn't been making noise, it was like the energy sucked into a black hole. When I dared turn around, he studied me, coffee in one hand resting against his chest.

"We decided we're dating last night, right? Or did I hallucinate that?"

Surprise and the urge to laugh jumped into my throat, but I nodded. "We did."

His brow furrowed, and my stomach twisted when something like hurt crossed his face. Before I could say anything, maybe shoot out an awkward apology for whatever unidentified misstep I'd made, he spoke.

"Did something change for you?"

"What?"

He approached me, stopping a foot from me. In his uniform and boots, he stood another inch or two taller than usual. "Did something change between last night and this morning I should know about? It's okay if it did, but please tell me now before I make any more a fool of myself."

I swallowed, nervous energy pinging around my body. "Nothing changed for me. But I was confused."

"About what?"

I exhaled through my nose, then just went for it. "I was surprised you left. Kind of thought we'd hang out a while after. But it's fine."

His face moved from concern to something like amused as I spoke, and then suddenly, he hit me with one of his heart-stopper smiles.

"Me kissing your cheek and saying good night confused you?"

I resisted the sinking, silly feeling. I didn't want to feel that way. I'd felt it so often with Jim, and having it now, with Nate, just made me...

He put a hand on my shoulder.

"Hey, don't—please don't be upset. Or... anything. I didn't mean to laugh or seem like I was laughing at you. I was smiling because..." He chuckled low and ducked his chin, then shook his head. "I don't want to overwhelm you, Wolfe. I've wanted this—something between us—for a long time."

A sparkly, gleaming sensation slipped through me. It wasn't entirely news that he'd liked me, at least in some way, for a while. The whole reason things got weird between us last summer was rooted in that—not just that he'd insinuated he had feelings for me, but that I'd known exactly what he meant when it happened. I couldn't pretend that moment away, and he'd failed at ignoring the feelings he had for me. But I hadn't known what it really meant, nor did I now. His saying that... well. I liked hearing it a lot. "Okay."

"And you said you wanted to move slow, which makes sense. And to be clear, I'm fully on board with that." He held up his free hand and the coffee mug. His expression was all honesty, with just a hint of a smile lingering at the corner of his mouth.

"I do. I am too."

Though part of me just wanted to kiss him. Right now. I wouldn't, but that little grin made me want to grab him. But I also needed to understand what he was talking about—what he meant last night and this morning.

"So..." he said, like I should be able to figure out what all that meant.

"So? I guess I'm slow here, sorry. Please, just tell me. We've been friends for years, and I know this is all new territory..." I trailed off at the intensity on his face.

He set his coffee mug on the counter next to me and stepped close. He took a few strands of hair between his fingers and let them slip out before tucking the hair behind my ear. His hand rested lightly on the slope of my neck, and his thumb arced a half circle over the thin skin of my throat.

Heat tracked where his fingerprint slid against me. My heart kicked just as my stomach swooped low.

Then, dipping his head so he did that thing where he spoke quietly and intimately, just to me, he said, "Ariel, I have enjoyed our friendship. I'm glad we've been close in that way. But the way I want you is not at all friendly. And last night, after spending the evening together on a date, getting to talk to you and laugh with you and know you were *with me*..." He broke off, those intense hazel eyes flickering between mine. "I didn't have all that much *slowly* left in me. I said good night so I could respect your desire for slow."

I opened my mouth, then closed it again. He had to feel my pulse racing under his thumb. He'd never touched me like this... this light, sensual way. It was just a hand, just resting there with one finger moving so slightly, but the placement was intimate. Paired with his words, my body had turned molten and so warm, I wanted to toss my robe to the side. Or maybe, I wanted him to do it.

"Nothing about the way I want you feels slow, or safe, or friendly. I'm doing my best to move at your pace, and I'm glad to do that. But sometimes, I'm going to have to take a breath."

His fingers slipped up to lift my chin. Holding my gaze, he slowly leaned down and kissed just millimeters from the corner of my mouth. His scent of coffee, mint, and fresh, clean laundry detergent filled my senses.

Then his watch beeped, and he straightened and stepped back. "Time for work."

"Oh, yeah," I said, mind still frozen on the intent in his eyes, that pure, lava-hot wanting racing through me at just the touch on my neck, my chin.

He rinsed his mug and put it in the dishwasher, then gathered his lunch box, travel mug, and water bottle. He didn't look at me again until he'd collected his keys and patrol cap. For my part, I hadn't had a single coherent thought since he'd started his explanation of why he'd left. I'd need hours, if not days, to dissect that, and I couldn't do it with him looking on. Though I hated that he had to work, I would be relieved to have some space to think.

"Ariel." His voice cut through my spiraling thoughts.

"Nate."

A smile flashed. "Do you want to go out with me again this Thursday?"

"Yes."

He chuckled. "You don't even know what we're going to do. What if I want to take you shopping?"

I recoiled, and he laughed. He was well-acquainted with my hatred of shopping for anything other than food. "You wouldn't be so cruel."

Goodness, his laugh, his smile, his whole *being* was so gorgeous in that moment, I could hardly breathe.

"I wouldn't, it's true. I want to go to the Volksfest. It starts Wednesday, but I've got a late meeting. I figured Thursday would be better. Plus, it's the country band, which is always awesome. I'm out of town Friday to Sunday, so Thursday's my best shot."

Annoyingly, my spirits sank at the mention he'd be gone. "That sounds fun. I'd love to go with you."

Oh, but Eric and Livie and lots of other people we knew would be there too.

"I can hear you thinking, Wolfe. Eric will be at the keg tapping and opening on Wednesday, and I'm pretty sure going back with the kids Saturday. But we can keep it between you and me that it's a date, if you're more comfortable with that."

He seemed entirely unfazed by the proposition of keeping it between us, so I said, "Okay."

He nodded. "Okay then. I have a weirdly insane week since I'm gone this weekend and then take off for Italy next week, so I'm not sure how much I'll see you, but I'll be back by four on Thursday."

"See you then. Have a good week. And... sorry."

I cringed, even as I said the word. I hated the impulse, hated the part of me that still felt I needed to apologize for asking questions, or challenging someone, or doing anything other than agree, agree, agree, and move on.

He'd moved toward the door, but at my voice, he stilled, then set everything he carried on the ground right where he stood. He turned around and his face was so fierce, I nearly gasped. He stomped back toward me, around the island of the kitchen, and ducked his head and cupped my cheeks in his warm hands.

"Don't apologize to me for asking questions or anything else. Ever. You don't have to do that with me, okay?"

My jaw pinched. I didn't want to cry. I desperately didn't want my past coming in to ruin things between us already. "Okay."

He inhaled slowly and shook his head. "You have no idea, Ariel. But I swear to you, you can just be yourself with me. I have no expectations for this. Don't get me wrong—I have a whole ton of ideas and things I want, but I have no expectations of you or what right looks like here. Ask me whatever you want, whenever you want. Let's promise each other right now that we'll be honest. Even if it hurts or seems hard, we'll be honest. And you don't have to be sorry if what you have to say doesn't agree with me or is something you're afraid I might not want to hear."

I let out a shaky breath, awed just shy of silent by his words. I'd heard the very opposite of that so often with my ex, it was hard to believe Nate hadn't taken these phrases from a playbook on how to speak to a woman coming out of an abusive relationship. Maybe he had, but every word came out genuine. "Okay."

One side of his mouth pulled up into a smile. "Seriously. I don't want to hear 'I'm sorry' again anytime soon."

His little smirk helped the heavy feeling in my chest lighten a bit, and I recovered my sense of humor. "Even if I step on your toes?"

He shook his head once. "Nah. I can take it."

"Even if I give you food poisoning accidentally?"

One brow raised. "Accidentally? Then nope. On purpose, we might be having a different conversation."

We both chuckled, and he pulled me close to kiss my forehead and wrapped his arms around me for a hug. His arms were firm and sure, no awkwardness, but no heat or coercion there either. The sweetness and care of the gesture fizzed through me, buoying whatever was left of that shadowy cold regret.

Just before I snuggled closer, he released me.

"All right. I have to get to work or my moody boss will have a conniption. But I'll see you Thursday, yeah?"

"Yes. See you then."

He hustled out the door with one last smile and a cheesy little wink that made me laugh. The moment the lock clicked, the silence of the place filled my heart with such longing, almost desperation, I felt winded. We hadn't even kissed, and yet watching him go to work felt practically painful. I'd never felt that way about Jim. I'd always had this sense of relief tinged with guilt when he left, especially after the first few weeks in Texas.

But I always missed Nate. When we were friends, I missed seeing him and chatting. I missed hearing from him when he was traveling or busy. I'd straight up cried over what felt like losing his friendship after I cut things off with him while with Jim. I'd felt it was right, but still just... missed him. And in this last year, up until I moved in, I'd missed *him*. He'd been part of my primary support, part of my healing, and so dear to me. And then, we'd had to step away.

So now... now I knew my feelings were ballooning. Probably unhealthily. And I needed to calm that down. Naturally, having a friendship with someone before dating meant there existed a connection far greater than when one started dating someone completely new.

At the same time, so much of interacting with Nate felt completely new to me. He wasn't the suave charmer I'd assumed he'd be in a dating situation. He was genuine and honest and so sweet, it almost made me uncomfortable.

Except he'd cut through those serious moments with humor and set me at ease again.

Basically, I was a wreck. But that meant nothing was new. I had three days to get my head on straight and figure out how to be around him without this needy *wanting* taking over and driving me to do something insane. I'd done far more stupid things for a man I liked half as much—now was no time to drop my guard.

CHAPTER TWENTY-ONE

Nate

Maddie eyed me through FaceTime. "That's what you're wearing?"

I looked down at the lederhosen, small black-and-white checkered plaid shirt with detailed stitching on the chest, and the feathered cap on the bed. "Yeah. Everyone dresses up."

"You guys are weird," she said with a little eye roll.

"You're weird."

"*You* are weird."

"Weirder."

"Weirdest."

We smiled at each other, mutually acknowledging our sibling idiocy.

On her end, she let out a big sigh.

"What's that for, superwoman?" I asked, plunking down on the bed to chat a while longer.

I needed to give Ariel space, and I figured trolling around, pacing the living room wouldn't really be doing that. I'd never considered the tricky logistics of dating someone you lived with... convenient, but also rather odd.

She scrunched her nose. "Nothing big. But... I'm really glad I'll see you next week. I need a hug from my big brother."

"You've got it. But it won't come free."

She nodded, then sighed dramatically. "I figured as much. I've had my lawyers liquidate some assets so I'll have enough on hand."

"Perfect."

I beamed at her, loving her quick comeback. We always had these kinds of conversations, and they made me miss her. I could also tell she really did need that hug. She'd bowed out of the ski trip months ago due to work, and that had raised the concern then. It'd only worsened since. Something seemed deflated about my ball-busting, name-taking sister, and that just didn't sit right. I also knew better than to prod her about it again in this conversation.

"So... how's it going with you know who?" She scribbled on something in front of her. Likely to avoid looking at me when she asked this.

"Ariel?"

Her lips pursed. "Yeah, Ariel."

I had no hope of hiding the smile, but I tried anyway. "Going well, from what I can tell."

Her eyes shot to me. "She won't just tell you? *Still?*"

"I didn't say that. We just barely had our first date less than a week ago. It was good."

Annoyance flashed through me. I knew this would happen with her, but I'd hoped maybe she wouldn't go this way.

"I'm just saying. You've sabotaged every other chance at happiness you've had for the last decade-plus, so I'm not going to be happy with her wishy-washy BS. I'm not okay with you scrounging for her scraps."

Ah, there it is. The version of Maddie that had gotten her where she is today—one of the richest women under forty. Also, my irritating little sister who knew just where to hit.

"I'm not taking scraps. She's been through a lot, and we're taking it slow. That's good. I do have *some* self-respect."

She squinted. "Do you?"

"Ouch, Maddie. Yes."

She frowned at me through the screen, and her shoulders dropped. "Sorry. I'm not trying to be a jerk. I want this woman to realize how lucky she is. You are basically the best person ever, definitely the best *man,* and I'm done with her stringing you along."

I forced a chuckle, though her words struck home. "I appreciate your overwhelming faith in me, but don't let it make you dislike her. Hopefully sometime in the not-too-distant future, you'll meet her. Hopefully more like get to know and love her too. We're moving slow and that's good for me too—it's keeping me from getting ahead of myself. Obviously, I've got a lot invested, and she's coming at this from a different place."

"Fine. Good. I'm happy for you."

I laughed at her then, because she sounded so dead-pan and her face was slack and free of any expression except maybe boredom. "Good. Thank you. And we'll talk more in like five days, right? You'll be there Tuesday too?"

She confirmed she'd be arriving before me, and we said our goodbyes.

I hated conversations like that. They left me unsettled. I'd learned to handle uncertainty better than I used to thanks to hours and hours of therapy, and probably a little maturity too, but I still found any strain between me and Maddie nearly unbearable. I'd tried for years to be a peacemaker for my parents, and sometime around when I graduated West Point, I gave up. Or gave up stressing about it. They'd never divorce because of the way the money was all tied together—they'd both lose too much. But they were people who should divorce. I'd spent a fair amount of time on that in therapy too.

It took me a few minutes to shake off the feeling that something was wrong. I couldn't do anything about whatever was happening with Maddie—she wouldn't talk about it until we were face to face. And as for things between me and Ariel?

I exhaled slowly, eyes closed, and searched myself. Did I feel upset about what Maddie had implied—that I was settling for scraps? Damn, what a harsh way to put it. But there had been times where I could see how that was true. Not in a long time, though. Not since she married, for sure.

Since she'd moved here, we'd had a real, working friendship. That wasn't scraps. It might not've been what I wanted—not everything I wanted—but it wasn't scraps. And what we were doing now? Not scraps either.

The mistake of revealing my feelings last summer had changed things, and part of that was because of me. I'd gotten to the place that night where it felt like something should happen, but for her, it'd been purely friendly dancing and fun. For me, it'd been a night in the arms of a woman I'd wanted for over a decade who couldn't see me. She didn't want me the way I did her. Cue my twelve-hour bender and letting my guard down enough for her to see through my *yes, I'm totally happy just being your friend* persona.

I'd drawn a line that night and stuck to it. I couldn't continue to fool myself into thinking she'd get to a place where she'd want me. And yes, I knew it might not have been long enough since her divorce, especially with all the baggage of her particular ex situation, but I had been out of my mind trying to keep so much feeling for her packed away. I missed her too much, but that distance between us led me to the next line. Not in the sand, but in the frosty night of New Year's Eve. It'd been six more months since the summer, since the distance, and she hadn't budged. Nothing had changed.

Part of me had hoped—had waited, even—for her to seek me out. To confront what she'd seen in me that day and salvage our friendship, at least. Or more. Or say she felt it too, but it was too soon. To say she loved me, even as just a friend. But no. Nothing.

So New Year's Eve on Eric's front stoop, I'd breathed in the frigid truth that she was never going to be with me like I wanted. I accepted it as best I could, using the chill winter air to buoy me. And then she'd stepped out, and no sooner had she shared a little piece of herself than I told her to live with me. To move in and solve a problem. Because, finally, I could do something for her. Finally, I could be of practical help to a woman I loved but was forbidden to love.

In the weeks that followed, I'd agonized over the weakness of that move. Was it the same as erasing my line and taking whatever she'd give like Maddie just accused me of doing? In the end, I didn't think so. Not completely, anyway. Because my motivation in that moment genuinely wasn't to try to woo her. It was to help her.

And now? Things had changed in what might be the

best possible way. Even if we were essentially out of time, this—dating, real conversations, a new step in the emotional intimacy we'd had as friends—this wasn't scraps.

My heart kicked at the memory of earlier this week. I'd said way more than I intended to, but her doubt, her insecurity over what was happening between us... I couldn't stand for it. That crap-heap of an ex had harmed her in so many ways. Moments like that, when she should only feel good and happy but instead felt unsure and self-doubting, made me want to punch the guy. To say the least.

I didn't let myself sink into the memory of touching her, hugging her, or that heat in her eyes and the way her chest rose and fell in her little robe when I told her how I wanted her, why I'd gone to bed after the date. Instead, I checked the mirror to make sure everything looked right and headed down to my second date with Ariel.

"They're just so... stoic," Ariel said, glancing at the line dancers on the wooden dance floor.

The twenty-by-twenty-foot square in front of the stage served as a dance floor. Under the massive red and white striped tent packed with fest tables, this space and the band playing just past it were the focal point.

The five-day fest brought in huge crowds from the American community associated with Kugelfels Army post and also from the surrounding area. The best part about this fest was that it also brought in a lot of the local Germans. The fest honored the cooperative relationship between Germans and Americans. The Army post hosted the event, but the food vendors, ride operators, funhouse people, and booths selling stuff came from the larger fest circuit—basically the German version of carnies.

But what held Ariel's attention was the group of more than twenty Germans line dancing an intricate, choreography-heavy number to a popular American country music song. They all wore embroidered leather vests with their country dance group's emblem. They seemed to genuinely enjoy it—they must. What made it a bit confusing and utterly delightful was that song after song, they danced in perfect unison, thumbs tucked into blue-jean pockets, nary a smile to be found.

That's right. Complete and total stone-faced glee. You'd think they were preparing to take a calculus test or maybe attend a long meeting without snacks. Or have dinner chez Reynolds when both Annette and Patrick were in attendance.

I focused on Ariel's face where she'd ducked it toward the plate holding her half-chicken and potatoes, made an effort not to notice the nice things her dirndl did for her—I'd been failing at that all night. "It's the best thing about this fest. I mean, aside from the whole Americans and Germans coming together to celebrate our friendly feelings through the years thing. But second? The German country line dancers."

She tucked her lips between her teeth to stifle a smile, then shook her head at me. "Some would think you're joking, but I'm pretty sure you mean that."

"I one hundred percent mean that. Now, are you going to go out there with me and join them? You have to be prepared to have all the fun and give no hint of it." I wiggled my eyebrows at her.

"That's a definite no for me. I have very little coordination." She took a bite of her dinner.

"I happen to know you dance just fine," I said before thinking better of it.

We'd danced at Eric's wedding. All night, even though I'd realized what a terrible, awful, no good, idiot thing it was to do the second I had her hand in mine and felt her shoulder blade under my palm. The warning lights had flashed, but rather than make up an excuse right then, I'd stayed. I'd danced a moderately slow song with her, something about perfection or love, and as true as the words felt to me, I'd also sensed doom.

I'd known I couldn't keep it up—not like that. Not any longer.

But after that, we'd danced more. Then took a turn or two with the other bridesmaids, with Mrs. Wolfe, then chatted with Eric. I'd always circled back to her.

I'd been only mildly inebriated by the time I got back to my room, and that's when I'd cracked open the small bottles in the minibar to drown out the desperate, aching feeling. The crushing realization that it just couldn't keep up like it had for the months since she'd moved to Germany, and frankly, the years and years leading up to that.

And that's what she no doubt saw in my eyes the next day when she came to check on me. Cue the months of awkwardness, distance, and more damned longing from me paired with resolving to be done with it all.

I shook all that off. I didn't have to wallow in that memory when I had her, right here, with me now.

She swallowed, her demeanor now a bit guarded somehow. "I guess you do."

"You danced just fine then," I said, my voice a little gruff.

"You're good at leading. But that dancing was slow or just fun. I couldn't do one of those line dances if my life depended on it." She nodded to the side where the dancers continued stomping and shuffling through their steps.

"Well, I'm going to take a turn here in a minute. Then I'll take you to ride the Ferris wheel."

I jumped up and joined in, sliding and heel-toeing my way around the floor. I made sure to keep a completely straight face, and I did not glance at Ariel once, or I would've lost it. I could tell she was laughing, probably not hiding it anymore since I was her target. There were a few hoots and hollers, a few "Get it, Reynolds!" called out, and I hammed it up, increasing my concentration. When the song ended, I shook a few hands of the surrounding dancers, who all broke that serious mien to smile at each other and enjoy their victory over the choreography.

Before the next song started, I slipped onto the bench next to Ariel. Sure enough, she was laughing. She wiped at the corners of her eyes and shook her head at me.

"You were magnificent, Nate. I just wish I could see it in some tight Wranglers. Though the lederhosen aren't bad."

Her eyes slipped down my chest, my whole body, then bounced back up to mine. The slight redness in her cheeks sent a crush of longing through me.

Instead of hooking a hand behind her head and pulling her to me, I gave her an exaggerated wink.

"I'll wear Wranglers if you do, baby. Let's go take our ride in the sky."

CHAPTER TWENTY-TWO

Ariel

Nate's easy smile disappeared about a minute into the ride. The slight breeze from the Ferris wheel beginning to circle around ruffled his hair, and where he clutched his hat in one hand, his knuckles had turned white.

"Are you okay?"

That same weird, tight grimace he'd been sporting widened. As though I could be convinced that meant he was. Where had my cheery, hilarious Nate gone? The day had been hot, but it was finally cooling off. It was just the two of us in the little metal cage that looked like a blue umbrella dangling from the rim of a giant, white-painted wheel.

"But really, what's wrong?"

He swallowed, glanced to the side, then whipped his

head back to me. "I, uh... may or may not be mildly uncomfortable with heights."

"Seriously?"

A small nod and nothing else. Everything about him looked wound tight, and he held onto the metal bench for dear life.

"Why would you come on this ride if you're scared of heights?"

"You wanted to."

The words came out soft, gentle. Not accusatory. Not blaming me for putting him in the situation. He flashed a smile, something closer to his real one.

My heart utterly melted. "You could have just told me, crazy."

"I know."

His gaze found mine, and the look there sent a rush of affection and desire through me.

"I'm going to slide over and sit by you, okay?"

I needed to be closer to him. I needed to hold his hand and put an arm around his shoulders, do whatever I could to bring him comfort now that he'd stubbornly, stupidly, and yet adorably put himself in this situation.

"Are you sure? I'm not—"

I slid on the blue skirts of my dirndl in two quick slips, and once my body lined right up with his, reached down and eased the hand holding his hat open. I set the item to the side and laced our fingers together. "These things are really safe. And if something happens, I'll save you."

He smiled, and his eyes took me in, quickly dipped to my neck and slid down, then jumped back to staring at the floor of the little pod. The trail of his attention gave me an idea. Normally, I might not be brave enough to even suggest such a thing, but his genuine fear, and his willingness to face it just so I could ride this thing, had me braving up.

"Listen, if you—"

"Oh, crap, crap."

I stifled a giggle, which turned into a laugh as the ride clanked to a halt. They'd started offloading people far below us. "We're fine. They did that on purpose. For now, we can enjoy the view."

From high up on this structure, we could see much of this end of the military post. Since the terrain was so heavily wooded and hilly, we couldn't see as far as I might have expected for an area surrounded by farmland. But I could see the giant red and white striped tent with people milling in and out, the lines of vendor booths set up in an oval just outside it. The kids had loved this fest last year because they had all kinds of rides, and of course the mini donuts were delicious. I'd buy Nate some when we got off—some fried, sugary dough should help him.

The ride advanced a few feet, then stopped again, leaving our car, or pod, or whatever you'd call it, swinging a bit. Nate audibly gulped.

"I'm amazed I didn't know this about you." I squeezed his hand where I held it.

"I don't exactly advertise it. And weirdly, it doesn't come up that often."

I chuckled, then realized how unlikely that was. "Aren't you both Air Assault and Airborne qualified? Doesn't that mean you jump out of helicopters and airplanes?"

He exhaled through his nose. "I am. I have. I do what I can to avoid it, but the routines of those things do help. And there's some sense of security in the equipment. But I fully admit that jumping out of a perfectly good airplane makes me feel like I'm dying every damn time. Any idiot who pays for that experience needs their head examined."

His vehemence had me laughing full out, but I quickly reeled it in. I loved that humor in him, even when he was more scared than I'd ever seen him. It seemed so strange to see him like this—vulnerable in some way. I'd never sensed any kind of weakness or vulnerability in him until lately, when he showed me little pieces of his feelings for me. Those left him exposed, but this was another level. Eric had to know, but I wondered if maybe Nate kept it locked down super well so maybe even Eric didn't.

"I'll make you a deal, Reynolds," I said after a minute or so of quiet.

His eyes flicked to me, and despite the genuine discomfort, I sensed interest there.

"If you think it would help, and only if you think it would help, you could kiss me to pass the time up here. It's only a few minutes left, but—"

He moved, and even though it happened quickly, it felt like time slowed down for me. The hand formerly gripping the bench settled on my shoulder, and he even leaned forward from where he'd plastered himself against the seat. The hand laced with mine released me and came to the side of my head, fingers threading through my hair and thumb resting just in front of my ear.

Then he tilted his head just as I raised my chin, and our lips touched.

I hadn't thought this through all the way to this moment. I wanted to kiss Nate. I wanted to be kissed by Nate. I'd come up with the idea as a fun distraction, a little act of bravery that would lighten the load of his discomfort and fear.

When his lips touched mine, gently at first, my heart

started racing. But he didn't pull back. After that first sweet press, he returned more insistently. Still closed lips, but the contact sent little rivers of burning sensation through me.

Somehow, I'd been calm before, more focused on helping him loosen up than anything else. But now, calm was a thing I thought I'd probably never been in my entire life.

He broke away just as I grabbed the leather straps of his lederhosen, needing something to hold onto, something to steady me, even though the ride, and the kiss, had stopped.

His gaze flickered between my eyes as we both breathed for a moment, just watching one another. He was so close—I wanted him closer. I must've leaned in, my body driving the action more than my useless brain, because then he closed the small gap with a groan I felt down to my toes. Even the first time, there had been no hesitation, but with this meeting, his mouth felt demanding in a way that thrilled me. He seemed hungry... for me.

The machine ground to a halt, and something next to us rattled open. We jumped as we both registered the stop and released each other. The next minute was a jumble of activity, both of us piling out, then him leaning back in to grab the hat he'd left on the seat. Luckily, I'd worn a purse that had a cross-body strap, or I would've forgotten about it.

"Good distraction?" I asked, voice shaky with adrenaline.

He tugged me to the side, out of the flow of traffic once we were far enough from the ride. His arms didn't stop until he'd brought me flush against him. "Any time you feel the need to distract me like that, be my guest."

His eyes had turned molten and flickered from mine down to my lips.

Right when I could've sworn he'd close the distance and kiss me again, we heard, "Right on, sir!"

Nate froze, then straightened.

"Seriously, sir! Go for it!

He waved them off as I dipped my head, cheeks heating to a blaze in seconds after the first comment. I didn't know them, and they probably didn't know me, but if they did... *humiliating.* Not to be seen kissing Nate—though it felt a little weird that we hadn't told Eric and Livie at least—but generally, to be kissing *anyone* publicly. Just not my thing. I wasn't *out there* like that. Maybe Nate was. Maybe this would be awkward between us once I explained.

My stomach twisted at that thought—this was all my fault. I'd been the one to kiss him in the first place. I'd probably sent the wrong message. I didn't remember how to be with someone in public anymore. Jim hadn't liked me to talk with him, or anyone, if he took me somewhere. We rarely went out, rarely did anything together, especially after we were married. When we dated, he took me to quiet, private places with low lighting. I never felt like he was ashamed of me, but I sensed his possessiveness even then. Foolishly, it'd given me a little thrill. I'd liked that he'd wanted to keep me to himself.

"Sorry. Ignore them," he murmured.

I kept my head low to avoid eye contact, suddenly incredibly embarrassed by my forwardness, and being seen, and just... everything. So far out of bounds from the safe, quiet way of life I'd been clinging to, I could hardly breathe past the lump of self-recrimination balling up in my mouth.

I didn't know how to be with someone like this. Somehow, I'd forgotten all that in the face of his fear, so focused on alleviating his discomfort, I'd done something I never would've otherwise.

Blame the odd circumstances—that was all. And he'd said I could do it any time. I could take Nate at his word. He made me forget some of those habits I'd fallen into—that self-consciousness and sharp awareness of what others were thinking.

But as we walked down the lane of booths, I couldn't shake the oily feeling that came whenever I remembered who I'd been before. I didn't want those feelings now, not ever with Nate, and yet here they were, clogging my throat and keeping me from reaching out and taking his warm, rough hand.

"Stop here a sec," he said and then ordered something in German.

I'd heard him speak the language a dozen times—triple that—and yet it still made my fingers tingle and my heart trip. Maybe because I also knew it was one of a few languages he spoke very well.

"Here," he said and put a hand on my lower back.

I finally lifted my head, and warmth burst in my chest, edging out some of the swirling mess. He held out a little paper cone filled with two-inch wide mini donuts dusted with powdered sugar. He presented a long wooden skewer with a flourish.

"Thank you."

His half-smile made my stomach flip for the nth time today.

"They're your favorite, aren't they?"

I nodded.

"Good."

After that, we strolled, people-watching and plucking the little donuts out of the cone with our sticks, not talking. Kids screamed on the bumper cars and at carnival game booths, and the thumping rhythm of country music from the fest tent floated across the fest platz. We made it to the exit, and with a raised brow, he asked if I was ready to go. I nodded, unprepared to break the silence between us. He was unusually quiet—Nate was a talker, so this quiet between us said one of two things. One, he realized I needed the space and wouldn't want to talk about anything too personal while we wandered around, or two, he felt weird now too. *Ughghghgh.*

Before long, he'd opened the car door for me, then shut it gently behind me. As he jogged around to his side, I scrambled for what to say. What to talk about.

"Thank you for the donuts. And... everything. It's been fun." No doubt he could hear the way I'd forced the words out in stilted, weird phrases.

He glanced at me, but the road was winding in this section of the drive, so he couldn't actually look. "You're welcome, of course. Thanks for being my date."

"Sure," I said weakly and internally cringed.

How had I managed to take things from kissing him, and *being kissed* by him—which was a delight, by the way— to this?

He'd turned on the radio, and that filled the silence for the next few minutes. Though I knew it wasn't like Nate to not confront how things had just gone from kissing to silent, he must've sensed I needed the space. Grateful, I focused on the darkening scenery out the window and tried not to wonder if the guys who'd seen us knew Eric. If they'd tell him. Why I even cared.

Nate's voice shook me from my thoughts just as he parked in his driveway. *Our* driveway.

"You going to tell me what's wrong, or do you need more time?"

CHAPTER TWENTY-THREE

Nate

Ariel's bright blue eyes widened.

That look set off an alarm in me. I already had a few bells ringing, little alerts telling me what had happened for me wasn't the same as what'd happened for her. Seemed obvious, but I feared our experiences of the last forty minutes were miles apart.

For me? The woman I'd wanted for over a decade had just kissed me. Out of nowhere, she'd kissed me, and then I'd kissed her, and though they'd been basic, closed-mouth kisses... *damn.* I'd lit on fire. She'd erased the terror of being up high in a flimsy little aluminum pinwheel, certain death just waiting for the right moment. She'd done it to distract me.

We'd stumbled off the ride, blushing and embarrassed to have been interrupted at the bottom, and then I'd been about to kiss her again, for real this time, when the soldiers had piped up. Moments like that made me wish I tended to be more reclusive, not so outgoing. If I'd been Nick Masters, no one would've dared comment on me kissing a woman.

Alas, they did, and I'd seen the deep red blush creep over Ariel's neck, chest, and all the way up her face. She didn't look back at me. She didn't look up and laugh like I'd expected. Even the donuts had only given me a brief glance at her. She had way too much going on in her head, and if I had to guess, it only was partly to do with me and our kiss.

Or, as I'd worried over the entire ride home as we sat side by side without speaking, it did have to do with me, and she was having serious, life-changing second thoughts.

I'd booted that idea to the side, knowing I needed to focus on her and not my fears. She slipped out of the car and walked to the door without a word. Fifteen different questions jumped to mind, but I waited until we were inside.

"Hey," I said, using my gentlest voice.

She turned to me, reluctantly glancing at my face.

"Where'd you go?"

Her mouth opened, but she pressed her lips closed without speaking. Frustration flared—not with her, but with myself. I didn't want to press her, but I needed to understand what was going on.

"I don't want to sound pushy, Wolfe. But I don't understand what's happening. And I want to. I get that something's up and you might need... time. Or space. Whatever."

Her brows dipped low, and she licked her full bottom lip. "I don't know. I'm not trying to be... whatever this is. I'm not really a PDA person, and I got a little freaked when those guys were talking. I'm sorry."

I'd figured. She hadn't seemed upset when we got off

the ride, though it'd been seconds between exiting and the soldiers hollering.

"*I'm* sorry. They're idiots. And I highly doubt they recognized you."

They probably just saw me with a gorgeous woman. And she did look glaringly beautiful today. The deep blue, white, and black dirndl hugged her arms, shoulders, and waist while doing ridiculously appealing things to her chest. The bow of the apron tied to the side that signified single, I'd noted at first glance. That didn't matter, but strangely, it pleased me since I knew our status as dating meant she wasn't actually available to anyone but me. The skirts flared out over her hips and ended just below her knee, leaving the smooth lines of her calves and ankles exposed before her feet disappeared into dark brown low-heeled shoes. I'd had to make a concerted effort not to look at her for fear the very sight would make me forget this whole *slow* thing.

"I hope not," she said, then dropped her purse and wandered into the kitchen.

"I'm sure of it. You don't have to fear having been seen with me," I tried, hoping the joke would make her smile.

Instead, she pinned me with a look and rolled her eyes. The tension in my chest loosened just a little.

"I'm not scared to be seen with you. But I'm not someone who normally kisses people in public, nor do I want Eric and Livie finding out we're together via soldiers telling him we were making out on the Ferris wheel."

My heart kicked. Then again. *Together.* We'd said we were dating. Was that together? Some people might define it that way, but others wouldn't. And going slow, to me, meant we were dating, but not necessarily together. But out of her lips came the words, and my mind latched onto them.

"We were hardly making out," I offered, amazed at

myself for not saying something about the other part of her words.

She scoffed. "We were clearly kissing. Anyone waiting to load onto the ride saw us. And then you almost kissed me again before they started cheering you on."

I chuckled. "Fair enough. People definitely saw."

She tucked her lips between her teeth and exhaled out her nose. That action sobered me immediately, and I rounded the counter to stand in front of her.

"I feel like I should apologize, but I don't know what for."

She shook her head, looking weary and sad. "No, you don't need to apologize. I'm... I'm a mess. This is nothing new. And I just had this jumble of thoughts about... everything. I don't know if I can explain it."

I chanced touching her, setting a hand on her arm. "It's okay. You don't have to explain. You can tell me if you want, but you don't have to. I just want to know you're okay."

She studied me, those intense blue eyes flickering all around my face before speaking. "I'm okay, Nate. And I had fun with you."

"Good. Me too." And as much as I wanted to push on the together thing, on what was really going on, I didn't. I didn't kiss her again either, but I did one last thing before I'd escape upstairs and give her the space she clearly needed. "Can I hug you?"

She nodded and reached for me just when I did her. I smiled to myself as she pressed her hands into my back and hugged me back, fully and without reservation. Relief hit me, a bit of longing too, and I breathed in the moment. I could be patient—hell, I'd already waited this long. I never expected everything to be perfect or without ups and downs. This wasn't even a down; it was just a bump in the road. It didn't signal the beginning of the end—it only meant we were working through things. And that was good.

If those fears that she wouldn't want this with me—even these small ups and downs—flared vivid in my mind again? Nothing I could do about it. We'd ride it out and see. And I'd be better—I wouldn't push her in any way, wouldn't let myself get caught up in her, even if she kissed me again. The slower pace for us was right, and we'd continue that way toward something great while we were here in Germany together.

Plus, she held onto me just as tightly as I did her. She hugged me back. That had to be a good thing.

It had to be.

CHAPTER TWENTY-FOUR

Ariel

Robby squeezed me as hard as he could around the waist. "I could just stay with you."

I chuckled and hugged him back. Eric shook his head from where he looked on a few feet away. "We'd have fun, buddy, but you've got school tomorrow."

"*Ugggh.*"

Livie laughed, Delia rolled her eyes, and Eric reached for the little boy plastered to me.

"Come on, bud, let's get you home." He peeled Robby from me, then gave me his apologetic grown-up smile. "Sorry. You know he loves you."

"Don't say sorry. I love him. He's my favorite boy in the world." I leaned down to kiss his cheek, eliciting a squinty pout from Robby that always made me laugh. He beamed at the sound. "I'll see you guys Tuesday, right?"

Everyone nodded. I'd be doing kid pick up, homework,

and making dinner. It'd been a while since I'd needed to bridge the gap. Mom had stepped back into her role, and I became the dreaded fifth wheel again. I still joined them for dinner often, especially when Nate wasn't going to be home. It was partly why I'd come with them back to the fest this afternoon—I didn't like just sitting around, because then I ended up thinking about him and missing him, which was just stupid.

But Summer, Bec, Katie, Emily, and I were all having dinner and hanging out at the fest to enjoy the last night, and sadly, what would be my last fest. The thought made me so sad, but it'd be Bec and Katie's last one too, so in some odd way, it helped that I'd get to spend it with other people making a last memory too.

I waved off my family, snagging a quick hug from Delia and a wave from Livie. While she wasn't as sick as she had been, she still had low energy and generally felt bad, so a night out, though she desperately wanted the girls' night, wasn't going to happen tonight. If I didn't know how much she wanted this baby, I'd feel bad for her. But we'd do one last hurrah of a girls' night in a few weeks before we all left... well, everyone but Emily and Summer.

I didn't want to spend more time thinking about *lasts* and leaving, so I wandered to the giant tent where we'd planned to meet. Inside, Summer, Emily, and Katie sat at a table in the far corner. Before long, we'd all gotten our food, and Bec had found us. The music wasn't blaring just yet, so we were able to chat.

"How's the moving prep going?" Emily asked Bec and Katie.

"Good for me. My stuff's actually already mostly gone—they're coming in a little over a week for my main shipment." Bec shook her head like she couldn't believe it.

"Our household goods went last week. We're living with loaner furniture and just our unaccompanied baggage."

My brow furrowed. "What's that?"

As much as I knew about Army life, I hadn't done an OCONUS move as a spouse or even with Eric. I'd just shown up well after the dust had settled. He'd made all the arrangements for their move this summer, but we still had almost a full month before any real packing needed to start, from what I understood.

"Unaccompanied baggage is stuff you get to keep until really close to your actual move, and then in theory, you ship it, and it flies rather than taking a boat across the ocean and months to arrive, so you have the stuff sooner on the other end. Usually, you get about a thousand pounds. People have different methods for what to keep, but it's mostly smaller things, no real furniture—usually kitchen stuff, bathroom stuff, and then toys or bikes, sometimes a smaller TV. You'll hear people call it 'UB' and sometimes 'UAB,' though the official acronym is 'UB.'" She lifted her stein of beer in an air-toast, then took a swig.

Emily's thorough response didn't surprise me. She'd grown up a military brat, I'd learned, and she'd worked in military communities for years.

"What she said," Katie added, and we all laughed. "I can't believe this is the end. I feel like I just got here." She pulled at one of the giant soft pretzels we'd ordered to share, then chomped down on the bite.

I feel like I just got here. That said it exactly. I'd been here over a year and a half now, but I felt like I'd just arrived. I had my feet under me but still had no real idea what I wanted in terms of work or even life at large. I didn't want to wade through that during another move.

And now, starting things with Nate made that feeling even more vivid. We'd just started dating, and I'd even managed to make our first kiss weird in the aftermath because of all my junk. He'd given me so much space to think and feel without pressuring me to talk to him, which only made me like him more. But he'd left early the next morning, before I woke, and I hadn't known what to say anyway.

He'd texted a few times, and I'd been too chicken to respond. I just didn't know how to explain myself, and I did owe him an explanation. I wanted to get my thoughts sorted out before we talked again, which I hoped we'd do tonight when I got home, or tomorrow, if he arrived super late.

I tuned back into the conversation, listening to Summer explain Nick's retirement plans and how they were going to play it by ear. She might say that, but I could tell Summer was sold out for Nick. I was so glad for them.

I looked around the table—only Emily and I were single. Or, I supposed technically, I wasn't single—was I? I was dating Nate, and I had no intention of dating anyone else. I couldn't even imagine wanting to see anyone else, and the thought of him seeing other people made a spike of rage rear up in me.

I needed to talk to him. Desperately. He should know where I stood—or at least I should try to explain why I crawled inside my head and couldn't get out of it.

"So, I have some news," Emily said, a sly smile on her face.

We all quieted so she could speak.

"I may be accepting a move out of education services. If I do that, I'll end up working a few consecutive assignments —the first is looking like Romania, though it may end up being Lithuania."

My mouth dropped open, but I didn't speak. I wasn't the chattiest in these circumstances, even though I felt comfortable with these women. Plus, there was no need, as of course Summer and Bec dove right in.

"Romania?"

"Lithuania?" Bec grabbed Emily's arm and shook her, a huge smile on her face.

Emily laughed.

"I know. I know! It's a huge change, but honestly, you inspired me." She said this to Bec.

"Me?"

Emily nodded. "You realizing you felt stuck pushed me to see the same for myself. I loved getting over here to Europe, but I think I may be interested in looking beyond education. I don't know. This job is kind of a temporary thing, so I technically will keep my position here, but I'll work elsewhere and broaden my view. If I'm understanding correctly, then I can maneuver out more permanently if I like it and they like me."

"That sounds ideal," I said.

"It really does, doesn't it?" She flipped her hair in a usual show of humor, though we'd all heard the tremor of excitement and nerves in her voice as she'd explained. "It may be a massive failure, but we'll see."

"Yeah. You'll fail at this when pigs fly." Bec squeezed Emily's hand, and they beamed at each other.

"To Emily!" Summer said, her mug raised high.

The rest of us joined her, our giant glass beer steins surprisingly heavy where we held them together in the middle of our little circle.

"To all of us! Prost!" Emily said, and we all clanked our drinks together, sloshes of foamy beer spilling over onto the fest table.

We all giggled at the clumsy toast and smiled at each other, enjoying the moment for what it was.

My heart swelled. There was nothing better than seeing these friends rejoice and support each other. This was part of what I'd been missing for years, and I hated that a clock ticked away at the time I could still enjoy it. That feeling—love, dread, disappointment, sadness—it welled up and clogged my throat. I cleared it roughly.

"I'm going to run to the bathroom. I've been chugging water all afternoon and it just caught up with me." I stood and climbed over the bench.

"I'll join you," Summer said.

We made our way through the crowded aisles outside, then across the grass to where the restrooms were. Since this fest happened yearly, they had a permanent building with toilets and sinks, and it was surprisingly nice. German fests usually had temporary toilets, but in typical German fashion, they were extremely clean and nice. I suspected that if the fest weren't a cooperative event inviting Germans to come, they would've supplied porta potties. But that wasn't very hospitable.

The line moved quickly, and I made my way out just seconds before Summer. She told me how Nick would be submitting his retirement information that next day. Such a momentous thing, and she seemed so thrilled for him.

"That's so exciting! I—"

"Ariel."

I looked around but didn't see who'd said my name, so I continued the thought. "I'm so—"

"*Ariel.*"

My stomach lurched.

No.

I knew that voice.

This didn't make sense.

"I'm talking to you."

Then his hand was on my arm, a little too tight, and he whipped me around.

My throat constricted, and my breath came up short. "Jim."

His hand squeezed my arm, and the feeling of that too-hard hold sent me back to so many similar moments. His cold eyes roved over me, hair to shoes and back again. I couldn't seem to find any air.

"Damn, don't you look a sight."

My heart clutched. Any comments about my appearance went bad places. To physical contact I didn't want, or to more words that would linger in my mind for way too long. I didn't want that—him—in my mind. And he couldn't touch me anymore—I wasn't his. He wasn't mine. We were done.

Remembering this shook me from the freeze. I tore my arm from his grasp and stepped away. "What are you doing here?"

He smirked. "Arrived a few days early for the rotation coming up next week. And isn't this perfect? Have dinner with me."

"Are you insane?"

His face shut down. The humor and good nature draining from his expression sent alarm pinging through me, and my heart stuttered again.

"Do you have to be such an ungrateful witch? I haven't seen you in almost two years. I've missed you, darlin', and I just want to know how you've been."

He stepped toward me, and I shuffled out of his reach, clumsy and wooden with each movement.

Light pressure on my back startled me. Summer spoke before I got myself together.

"Summer Applegate. You are?" She tilted her head to the side, waiting for a response, but she didn't extend her hand for a shake.

I'm not alone. I'm safe.

I'm not alone. I'm safe.

Those two thoughts cycled through my mind, Summer's hand on my back grounding me into the now. I owed him nothing. He had no control over me. We were done.

"Lieutenant Colonel Jim Crane, Ariel's husband."

"Ex-husband." Despite the thick fog that had descended on my mind at the sight of him, at his touch, this barked out of me from my very gut.

His eyes cut to me. "Sure. Ex-husband. But you'll always belong to me."

That sent a bolt of lightning-hot rage through me. "I never belonged to you—not in the way you thought. And I definitely don't anymore. That's the whole concept of divorce, Jim. That's why you haven't seen or heard from me since the last meeting with the lawyers. And that's why you won't see me again."

That was exactly how he treated me though, wasn't it? Like something he owned, controlled, and kept for his convenience. Cleaning, cooking, satisfying him physically without the hassle of dating—wives are handy like that. Better if they have no money, no independence, and you wear them down so they don't know whether they're really hurting, really lonely, or if they've imagined all their discontentment thanks to their husband's expert gaslighting and abuse.

Jim's top lip curled in a way that used to send me cowering. I resisted the reflex to duck my head, mentally chanting through the reminder that he couldn't touch me or do anything to me anymore. Summer was with me. We were surrounded by people milling around. He couldn't do anything to me.

"You'll see me again. I'm here for *weeks*, and that's more than enough time to track you down again. We're overdue for a reunion," he said, eyes slipping over me. "A private one."

My stomach soured, and I shook my head. "Goodbye."

Summer hugged me to her as we turned and walked quickly away from him. Once inside the tent, she seemed to know I couldn't stay. She said something about me not feeling well and made our excuses. She walked me out, all the way to my car. She made me promise I could drive, and I said of course I could, though I probably shouldn't have. But I wanted to leave. I couldn't risk seeing him again and certainly couldn't wait another minute before I went.

Somehow, I made it home without crashing despite shaking hands and the muted quality of everything around me, like I'd stood next to a too-loud speaker and just stepped away. Shutting the front door unlocked the tide of emotion, and I stumbled to my room, closed myself in, and cried my guts out.

Nate

I'd been gone three days, hadn't seen Ariel, but also hadn't heard from her. I'd texted a few times, and other than the first day, I hadn't heard back.

Then my one and only workday for the week involved a farewell to Nick Masters. He wasn't quite done, but anyone who submits his retirement packet deserves a good handshake. And then I had a terrible discussion with Eric about me and Ariel. He wanted to know what was up, and though I remained hopeful, I honestly had no idea. The kiss was great, but she'd locked up after that. And I didn't feel like it was my right to tell him anything after the way she'd been so concerned he might find out from the people who'd seen us together.

I'd expected we'd at least chat, joke back and forth, *something* while I traveled over the weekend. After our hug,

I'd said good night, and when I'd left the next morning, she'd still been in her room. The weekend in the Alps should've restored me, but I spent much of the time not sleeping and worrying about every possible negative thing my stupid anxious brain could conjure up.

Eric had finally broached the subject of Ariel's move, of how things were going, and instead of excitedly reporting on the state of our dating, I had no freaking idea what was happening.

Eric's anger, his suspicions that I'd asked Ariel to move in so I could bust a move on her... it fired me up. I could've said we'd agreed to date, or that we'd at least been out, but with the way things were between us, I had no idea. I did know I wasn't going to tell him we were like brother and sister as he'd requested... as if I'd *ever* say such a thing. And he knew it.

So I left there, mildly pissed off, more than ready to see Ariel, and uneasy out my ears to figure out what was happening between us. I'd arrived late last night, and when I left for work early today, she'd still been in her room. Not a peep and hardly a trace of her around the house, frankly. If it weren't for her jacket hanging in the hallway or her coffee mug in the dishwasher, I might've convinced myself her living there was all in my head.

It was ten after six. I wanted to find Ariel and talk to her, have some dinner, and finish packing for my trip, then go to bed.

Actually, that was a total lie. I wanted to find Ariel, kiss her. Kiss her some more. Then talk to her. Or fine, talk to her, then kiss her, sure. But yeah, tied up in all of this was the fact that now I *had* kissed her, and I wasn't likely to forget it anytime soon. Didn't want to, wasn't going to, so there.

I scrubbed my hands over my hair, then splashed water on my face. I'd been home for about fifteen minutes, puttering around downstairs, then venturing up the spiral staircase to my room to freshen up and ditch my uniform. Still no word from her, which did nothing good for my anxiety.

Bypassing her door on the way back down to the kitchen required insane amounts of self-control. But I reminded myself that she lived here as a roommate, and if we were really dating, in any other circumstance, I wouldn't be able to just knock on her door and invade her privacy. She'd likely feel compelled to answer, and that would put pressure on her. Even though I wanted to pressure her, just enough to get a response, I also recognized that was just crappy.

So, I kept walking, down the last set of stairs to the main floor and busied myself with making a simple dinner. My back-up plan was that I could make her dinner and text her to say it was ready. That might draw her out, or at least force a response.

Thirty minutes later, I sent the message. Tension coiled in my gut and hooked into my shoulders and neck. The sound of her footsteps descending the stairs only wound me tighter, anticipation, concern, anxiety all whipping through me at a dizzying rate.

"Hey. Sorry I've been a hermit. I'm glad you're back."

My stomach bottomed out at the sight of her. Lovely, as always, but her bright blue eyes were red, tired-looking, and the dark circles under them suggested she hadn't slept much. "What happened?"

She shook her head and padded into the kitchen past me but didn't speak or meet my eye.

"Ariel. What's going on?"

She filled a glass with water, then set the pitcher back in the fridge. She took a drink, set it back down. Each second that ticked by without her answering tolled a dreadful sound in my head. I pressed my lips together, forbidding myself to prompt her again.

After a second drink from the glass, she turned to me. The expression on her face would've made me stagger and fall if I hadn't been standing still.

"I saw Jim."

"What? Where?"

That was so far from what I'd expected her to say. I'd heard the words in my head too many times over the last seventy-two hours. *It's not working. We're not right together. Let's just call it.* And maybe they would come eventually, but right now? This was a curve ball I hated to hear but could accept far more graciously than what I'd been bracing against.

"At the fest last night."

I rushed to her but stopped short of pulling her into me and hugging her. "Damn."

She nodded. "Wasn't great."

"Did you talk to him?"

She nodded again, smaller this time, and pressed her lips together.

"Are you okay?"

Her sharp inhale sounded loud in the quiet kitchen. I couldn't do it—couldn't keep my distance anymore. I took her by the shoulders and pulled her to me. I would've done this before—this had nothing to do with whatever mess we'd run into over the weekend. Her arms wrapped around my waist, and we were quiet for a few moments before she answered.

"I'm scared. I don't want to be, and so I think I'm also mad that I feel scared."

"You can feel however you want. But I don't want you to be scared. What did he say?"

She looked up but didn't release me. "He said he'd be here for a few weeks, and he was certain we'd see each other again. I don't know why, but it felt like a threat."

Alarm and fury zipped up my spine, and I straightened. "You think he meant it that way? As a threat?"

"I don't know. It's hard to separate all the old feelings of fearing him with the reality that he's *not* my husband, I owe him nothing, and he has no power over me. But the way he said it made it feel like it was."

I exhaled slowly through my nose. "I won't let him hurt you. Not anymore."

The self-loathing I felt at knowing I *had* let him hurt her before had just about offed me once Eric told me how it'd been for her, and every time she let some little piece of their relationship slip. Not again. Not ever again.

One of her hands pressed into my chest, grabbing my attention. "You going to be my bodyguard for the next month?"

I let a little heat enter my gaze, and a smile pulled at my lips. "I will do just about anything for your body, anytime."

She huffed a reluctant laugh and pushed away. "You're ridiculous."

"I'm truthful. But seriously, what can I do?"

"I don't know. I can't very well not go on post while he's here. I'm guessing you or Eric could figure out when he's supposed to leave. And when the busiest part of the rotation is going, I'm probably in the clear. But until it starts next week..."

Then it hit me. The perfect solution to this problem, and potentially an aid for our entire situation. Plus, something I'd literally dreamed of.

"That settles it. You're coming to Italy with me."

CHAPTER TWENTY-SIX

Ariel

The flight attendant smiled broadly as she set down my drink, then Nate's.

I thanked her, still feeling more than a little disbelief at the series of events that had led me here.

Where was here? In a Rome-bound first-class Alitalia seat next to Nate, not even twenty-four hours after I'd told him about seeing Jim.

For the hundredth time since, I shut my eyes and inhaled, searching for calm. I couldn't ignore the niggling feeling that this was running away. Well, obviously it was running away, but it felt like a failure. And I hated that. Jim had prompted that feeling in me too many times, and my jaw ached from all the teeth-gritting I'd been doing at the return of it.

Yet again, I couldn't tell. Was this right? Had I done the wrong thing?

Then immediately, a wave of self-loathing for doubting myself washed through me. Would I ever get to the point where I could do something and feel sure?

"You okay?" Nate asked next to me, solicitous and charming.

As though he and Eric hadn't basically forced me into this trip.

"Mm-hmm."

I hadn't said much to him. I wouldn't call it punishment, my minimal talking, as much as self-preservation. If he felt less than pleased, I couldn't help that.

How did it all happen? First, I told Nate about Jim and all his awfulness. Then Nate got this look and said I should come to Italy with him. At my incredulity, he explained it'd give me the rest of the week away from Jim's general vicinity. The highest likelihood of me running into him again would be in the next few days, since after that, the intensity of the rotation would keep everyone out in the training area and well away from main post. The only other obstacle would be when everyone was loading up and leaving, and after Eric got pulled into the conversation via a phone call on speaker, he promised he could find out when Jim was scheduled to leave and help me avoid him.

Then he heartily supported my going to Italy.

Then Nate hung up, called his travel agent, and here I sat. He was jotting down the confirmation number for my ticket before I ever found the words to fully protest. Then, when I did, I saw a side of Nate I never imagined I'd see.

"You have to be kidding me, Nate. I can't go to Italy."

"Of course you can."

"No, I can't."

"Yes, you can. And you are. Tomorrow at eleven, you'll be on a plane out of Munich. Done."

I stiffened my spine and gritted my teeth—yep, it'd started last night. "I appreciate the offer. I don't want to run away from him. I just want to live my life."

"Perfect. Live it with me in Italy for the next five days." He swiped through his phone, not looking at me, then when he found what he'd been searching for, he slipped it into his pocket. "I've got to pack, and so should you."

That tipped the scales. He and Eric had decided this for me. And yes, I wanted to go—a big part of me wanted to go. I would've loved an invitation before tonight. Granted, we were walking on such baby giraffe legs in this relationship, it would've seemed like far too much, too soon for my request to go slowly, but still. Being backed into the corner and being *made* to go wasn't a thing I wanted for my life anymore, even if it was Italy with a man I had more than a few positive feelings for.

"Nate." My words stopped him before he reached the stairs. "I don't like this."

The muscle in his jaw flexed before he stalked back to me. "I don't either. I don't like your abusive, insane ex-husband threatening you. I don't like you being scared. I don't like you feeling anything but good. I'm solving one small part of this problem because, for once—just this once—I can actually do something to help protect you."

A whole bucketful of emotion crashed through me then, but I couldn't find words. My eyes teared, so then I definitely couldn't speak. I pressed my lips together to stay more crying—I'd cried way too much today, way too much for a lifetime over my ex.

Nate's gaze softened immediately. "I'm sorry this is happening. This isn't about me or my need to help—I get that. But I *can* help. Please let me take you away for a little while. No pressure. Just quiet. And pasta."

I swallowed but knew if I tried to say anything, I'd end up crying. All the fight, any indignation or frustration driving me to that point, deflated completely. He meant well, but more than that, if I refused, he wouldn't force me. I knew that in my heart and in my gut, and that allowed me to agree. So, I just nodded, and we left to pack.

Now, here we sat. Even though I'd agreed, and I appreciated this on some levels, I felt weak. It wasn't Nate's fault—it wasn't really anyone's fault, except maybe Jim's. But knowing that didn't change the way words stuck on my tongue and my nerves were frayed ends of ever-shortening strings. Not shockingly, I'd barely slept the night before, and I looked like death warmed over at just after noon.

"Will you talk to me?" Nate asked quietly.

He had this way of asking that sounded so gentle. I wondered if he had to use that tone with anyone else or if I was a special brand of damaged and required that injured baby animal approach uniquely.

"I'm not trying to freeze you out. I'm just... overwhelmed."

I glanced over at him, and his whole body was canted toward me. His eyes studied me, a little frantic still, but calmed from what they'd been last night when he'd declared he was going to solve this problem for me.

Honestly, when I'd reflected on it, it'd been kind of hot. Nate wasn't an Alpha-type. At least he hadn't been for me. And that worked well for me generally—obviously enough, I'd been controlled plenty. But the memory of his refusing to use those kid gloves in conjunction with still wanting to do right by me sent a thrill through me. I could enjoy that because I knew without a doubt if I insisted on staying in Germany, he would've relented. He would've listened, like he was listening now.

"That's understandable."

I offered a small smile, glad he couldn't read my mind to see the confusing jumble of disappointment in myself, rage at Jim for busting in on my life, and attraction to Nate.

"We'll land in about an hour and take a car to the house. After that, you can spend time settling in, and we'll eat at home, if that's okay. I figured we'll go sightsee a little tomorrow, if you're up for it, but we're in no rush. I have a few things I have to take care of later this week, so I won't be pestering you the whole time."

All this, he said to an in-flight magazine he'd opened and started flipping through.

"Sounds great."

And it did. If I could just let go of some of the negative thoughts, maybe I could enjoy this. I hadn't had a true vacation in a while. Of course, I'd traveled with Eric and the kids, and we'd had some wonderful trips, not least of all the most recent spring break adventure. But a trip without kids, to a city I'd always wanted to visit, with a man I—

Best not to finish that thought in this muddled moment.

Instead, I shut my eyes, hoping to sleep a little. Hoping maybe I'd wake without shame and rage and disappointment weighing in my gut.

Nerves. So. Many. Nerves.

I'd thought about the trip with Nate as a trip with Nate —complex enough considering our current situation. I had not fully registered that Nate's trip to Italy was him going to his family's Rome house to see his sister and mother. So, I was effectively meeting his sister and mother on zero sleep after repeated self-loathing, ex-hating, why-can't-I-just-be-done-with-these-feelings crying jags over the last eighteen hours.

Ideal.

I don't know how I'd blocked that whole part of this deal out, but once I remembered it—once he said, "I'm glad you'll finally meet Maddie"—I had a small internal meltdown.

I couldn't even enjoy the ride from the airport into the city thanks to my roiling thoughts. The Reynolds family wealth had been obvious in some ways over the years, but I didn't have a true sense of its scope until Nate mentioned *the Rome house* a few weeks ago and then admitted to their owning multiple international properties. That was not a thing normal people had.

On top of that, I already knew his younger sister, Madeleine Reynolds, was some kind of tech genius and ran a Fortune 500 company as one of the youngest women ever to be a millionaire or something insane. I'd come across the article while we weren't talking, so come to think of it, I'd never asked him about it.

From Nate, I knew Maddie only as Maddie, his irritating and beloved little sister. I knew they were close, maybe even closer than me and Eric, or had been when we met. And I remembered that Nate was meeting his sister in Rome, so I was about to walk myself into a family reunion with people I'd never met as a semi-non-sort-of-dating-friend. Yes, we'd determined we were dating, but that was before my awkwardness after kissing him, and then all this mess... I didn't know where we stood. Yet again.

Just so completely ideal.

"What's going on in that head?" he asked.

"Nothing." I cleared my throat, then to avoid sounding sullen, added, "Just excited to see your family's house."

When he didn't respond, I glanced at him. He'd worn a lightweight, light blue button-down shirt and khaki pants and he looked good. Ridiculously cool and comfortable while also being stylish and worldly. My jeans and T-shirt with sneakers felt dumpy in comparison. Thank goodness I'd showered and washed my hair, at least—when my alarm went off and I saw I'd only slept for about two hours, I'd considered sleeping that last forty minutes.

"You know there's no pressure about anything while we're here, right?"

My stomach flipped. That could mean so many things, and knowing Nate, he meant all of them. No pressure about performing for his family. No pressure on our relationship. He was so thoughtful to say that, though it didn't relieve much of the anxious knot in my chest.

"*Abbiamo arrivato, Signoré.*" The driver spoke just as the car stopped in front of a nondescript building.

"*Grazie, Paolo.*"

I'd heard Nate speak Italian how many times already today? It hadn't penetrated the fog on the flight, but after we landed and he greeted the driver, Paolo, and then chatted about... whatever they chatted about, I got an earful.

I hadn't been able to look at him speaking it. It would be too much for this fragile little shell of composure I'd cobbled together today. Maybe after a decent night's sleep, I could enjoy it—appreciate it more completely. Because honestly, I'd thought about the fact that Nate knew Italian more than once over the years. It appealed to me on a level I didn't fully understand, and yet hearing his smooth, low voice speak even the simplest of phrases made me feel like something at the heart of me was thawing.

"Ready?" The doors swung open, and Nate flashed me a smile before stepping out his side.

I clutched my purse and exited where Paolo stood waiting patiently for me to get out of his way so he could close the door. Did he work exclusively for the Reynolds family? That seemed far-fetched, though the way he and Nate had shaken hands seemed too familiar for him to be just some random driver.

I rounded the car to Nate who had an odd expression on his face. To be fair, he wore mirrored sunglasses, so I couldn't see his eyes. Before I could ask him what it was, he tossed his head to the side.

"This way."

We passed through a nondescript door, and as soon as I saw the other side, I sucked in a breath. A three- or maybe four-story building sat in front of winding, shaped boxwood shrubbery cut to low, neat lines. Closest to where we stood, at the edge of what I now realized was a small courtyard, there were mature trees and even some small beds with flowers. Close-cut grass created a bright green carpet leading up to an edge of topiaries. The choice to use light gray stone on the walkway, or maybe it was even somehow a driveway, made the shaped shrubbery look even more vibrant, especially paired with the gray stucco façade of the building itself.

"Wow. I wasn't expecting that," I said.

"Kind of fun, huh?" Nate smiled, then led the way to the entrance.

Before he could open it, someone opened the door and stepped through. Nate thanked the man wearing a uniform of navy coat with red buttons. I was about to do the same, when a woman's voice stopped me.

"My baby is here!"

The *clack-clack* of high heels sounded in the large

space. I blinked rapidly as though that might help my eyes adjust faster to the darker inside of the house.

"It's been too long, Nathan. Too long."

A woman I could only describe as glamorous reached up a hand and turned her face away even as she stepped close to Nate, who kissed her waiting cheek.

"I'm sorry. I'm glad I could come. I brought a friend." He gestured to me. "Mom, this is Ariel Wolfe. Ariel, this is my mom, Annette."

Nate's mom was petite—probably four or five inches shorter than my five-foot-seven, and easily twenty or more pounds lighter. Her lightly tanned skin had a healthy glow, though her face was practically wrinkle-free. She wore light makeup highlighting delicate features framed by a lustrous golden shoulder-length blunt haircut, simple-looking jewelry, and an outfit of black cigarette slacks and a nude silk blouse. On her feet were heels, though I didn't get a good look at them.

Her dark lashes blinked twice, then a manicured hand extended to me.

I took it. "So nice to meet you, Mrs. Reynolds."

Her brown eyes slipped over me. "Likewise. Welcome."

She turned abruptly, flicked her wrist, and rattled off something in Italian. Nate responded, then did the nod, head dip thing to indicate we should follow her. They went back and forth, completely in Italian, as we walked. I tried not to feel frustrated, but it seemed a little rude. That said, we were in Italy, so maybe I was the rude one for showing up without knowing the language. And from the way Nate had said, "I brought a friend," he may not have given her a heads up.

We walked along a white marbled floor under a double grand staircase with wrought-iron railings that led to the second story and highlighted the high cathedral-style ceiling of the entrance.

"Madeleine is working, but she'll join us for dinner. I assume you'll be eating here tonight?" Annette didn't turn to ask.

Nate glanced at me and winked before responding. "Yes, we will. Thanks."

The wink and the manners made me smile, even with the sinking sensation that I did not belong here settling in with every step we took.

After walking past several doors and entryways, Annette paused at another marbled staircase.

"I imagine you'll want to freshen up." She surveyed me in a glance, then turned and began walking away. "You're both in eight. Everything else is taken."

Nate stiffened next to me. "What do you mean?"

She turned. "Exactly what I said, Nathan. Everything else is taken. If you'd made me aware of your guest, I would've been prepared, but since you did not, I only have eight available."

Well, there we had it. Clearly, he hadn't let her know, and she wasn't happy about it. And I got the sense that there was some amount of bad news there that I didn't understand since Nate ran a hand through his hair and grumbled something I didn't catch.

"Follow me. They'll bring our other bags in just a minute." He sounded a little off, further alerting me to something wrong.

"Is everything okay?" I asked, nearly at a jog to keep up with him.

He made an irritable sound. "It'll be fine. Basically, there's only one room, but we'll figure it out. It'll be fine."

CHAPTER TWENTY-SEVEN

Nate

The small "Oh!" came low and quiet behind me.

Dammit. I didn't want her to feel cornered. Hadn't I brought her here precisely to get her out of a bad situation? Now this nonsense.

And it was all because I hadn't given my mother the heads-up. She could be so lovely and warm sometimes, but if you crossed her... beware. She had claws she sharpened nightly. Or, more accurately, she had claws she paid someone to sharpen—wouldn't want to expend any extra effort DIY-ing it.

I exhaled a long gusty sigh and rolled my shoulders. I'd sleep in the living room or something—it'd be fine. Or, more likely, I'd talk my mother into letting me have one of the five bedrooms that had to be free. With us, Maddie, and her here, that meant only three of the eight bedrooms were occupied. I'd call BS on the lies later, but for now, I needed to get Ariel settled and help her relax.

The temptation to think of all the ways I'd like to help her do just that flitted through my mind, but I batted it away with a steel beam. Couldn't be having any of those thoughts just now. Or anytime soon.

"Here we are," I said and pushed the ten-foot door open.

She didn't meet my eye but did proceed through the door, so I followed and strained around to look toward the bathroom so I wouldn't end up admiring the way her jeans fit.

Well. They fit very nicely. I could attest from past acquaintance—and yet again, *stop thinking about how her jeans fit, you idiot!* Why my brain had decided to start fantasizing about Ariel's body *right now*, I didn't understand. Maybe it was the whole room-sharing situation, but we'd get that worked out. Or I'd banish myself to the floor.

Or not...

I crushed my eyes shut and exhaled slowly.

"This is beautiful."

She stood in the middle of the room, slowly turning and taking everything in. Modern art decorated the walls with bright colors on stark white canvases. The wood floors weaved together in an intricate pattern partially hidden by a giant, thick rug that extended well beyond the large bed centering the room. The headboard was made of ridiculously soft leather and took up much of the far wall, creating a giant light brown focal point. The bed itself was something like a king-sized—maybe not quite, as European sizes differed. It was made up in light gray and white linens, as usual. I often thought of this house as just that—white and gray. Except for the rooftop garden and lounge area, it never struck me as particularly homey.

"This is the room I usually stay in," I said, setting my bag on a light brown overstuffed leather chair.

"It's really beautiful. Everything is."

"Yeah, it's a nice place."

Her eyes found me. "To say the least."

It made sense. Not everyone was used to this kind of living. I knew that. I didn't want to seem like a jerk. But the niceness of this house had nothing to do with me, so saying thank you for a compliment about it felt weird.

"Let's get you settled. I think maybe you should nap, and I'll go hunt down my mom and figure out the room thing."

Ariel set her purse gently on the bench at the end of the bed. "She didn't seem very happy about my being here."

I stepped toward her and almost grabbed her arm but stopped myself. Something about this whole situation had made me hesitate to touch her. I missed the feel of her to a ridiculous degree considering we'd had all of two kisses and a few minutes of handholding. Still, I wanted to reassure her, so I'd do it with words.

"I'm sorry. She's not upset with you. It's completely my fault I didn't give her the heads-up. But she'll get over it, and she's going to love you."

And if she doesn't, I don't give a damn, because I do.

"I feel like I'm intruding," she said, arms wrapping around her waist.

"I invited you. I practically dragged you here." I moved a little closer. "Let me go talk with her while you get some rest. I'll come get you in a few hours, and we'll grab some food and break the ice, okay?"

Those killer blue eyes gazed back at me. The storm behind them clearly hadn't been placated by my feeble attempt to reassure her, but maybe now she'd rest. She looked exhausted. In another version of this story, I'd kiss her slowly and curl up next to her to sleep, our bodies nested close.

Another version.

"Okay."

Before I did or said anything stupid, since I was evidently mildly overcome by standing in a bedroom I'd slept in a hundred times before with Ariel here next to me, I gave her a poor excuse for a smile and left to find the woman of the house.

~

"It's rude."

"It is *not* rude. I invited her. I'm sorry if *I* was rude by not telling you—I should've. But it was a last-minute thing, and she had nothing to do with my failure to tell you. I cannot believe you're being like this."

My mother glanced at me from the desk where she sat, dipping her head to look out above the reading glasses she'd donned to do whatever task she had on her computer. It'd taken quite a while to track her down, but I'd admittedly taken my time to start the hunt. I'd needed a minute to clear my head of all the crap flying around in there, and a few more to brace for this conversation.

"I'm *being like this* because this was supposed to be a family trip." She raised her chin to look at me with an all too familiar air of hurt.

"I'm sorry about that. I know it's been too long. Ariel needed to get away, and plus, we've just gotten started dating. I care about her. I want her here with me." *Under-statement.*

Her brown eyes skewered me. "Well, I should probably tell you we have guests coming in tomorrow night, so that's one reason the rooms are all occupied. But if you're just starting out, maybe you and Maddie can share—"

"It's fine. If the other rooms are actually taken, then it's fine."

She narrowed her gaze and pursed her lips. "They are. But we could get her a hotel room, no problem. My treat! I'm happy to."

There it is. It made no sense that she would be unhappy about me bringing Ariel and yet shove me in a room with her—she wanted an excuse to kick her to a hotel. *Seriously?* I wondered if this had anything to do with the upcoming meetings we'd have with my father. She got particularly weird about everything when she knew she'd interact with him. If I hadn't hated their dynamic already, the way my mother morphed into this competitive, mean-spirited person any time contact with my father loomed never failed to clinch the dread I felt when thinking about marriage to the wrong person.

I exhaled a controlled breath, fighting the urge to scoff or roll my eyes. I was too old for those reactions to her, but the woman could drive me insane. "Absolutely not. I invited her here. I'm not about to shove her into a hotel. If she goes to a hotel, so do I."

"Oh, nonsense, Nathan. You'll both stay."

"What's all this?" Maddie's voice cut in as she stepped into the room.

The tone told me she could tell I needed rescuing. I didn't. Not really. But I'd take the assist.

"Ariel's with me. There's only one room available,

apparently, since I so rudely neglected to mention her coming in the last-minute change of plans."

Maddie's brows rose. "She's here?"

I nodded.

A look flashed across her face, but she smoothed her expression so quickly, I couldn't tell what it meant. She'd made clear her skepticism of our dating, but that came from her being a protective sister. I loved that about her—that she wanted the best for me. She just didn't realize that the reason I'd been hung up on Ariel so long was because she was, without a doubt, the best.

"Can you both just... be nice to her? She's important." *And I only have so much time left with her.*

"We'll be fine. Go clean up and get ready for dinner. Settle into your room and figure out how you're going to manage your *there's only one bed* situation." Maddie shuttled me out the door of my mom's office but stopped me with a hand on my arm before I stalked away. "I'm excited to meet her, really."

My heart warmed, and I pulled her into a hug. "I'm excited for you to meet her too."

I released her, but not after messing up her hair because that would be my job until she found someone else to do it for her.

She glared and smoothed it away from her face. "You should've given her some notice, though."

She meant our mother.

"I should have. I didn't mean to keep it from her, but honestly, it all happened in the last eighteen hours. It's been a whirlwind." The tension in my shoulders cinched tighter. "Ariel's ex showed up at Kugelfels and threatened her. I insisted she come down here, get away for a bit. It's not like

I invited her here on some romantic getaway to meet my family."

Just the thought of something like that made longing flood in. But frankly, I was so familiar with that feeling—that gut-deep wanting and only a thread of stubborn hope to pin it on—I hardly noticed.

"Is she okay?" Maddie's tone held genuine concern.

That brought a smile out of me. I loved this woman's tender heart, even in the midst of her skepticism about my being with Ariel. "I think so. But it threw her. I'm hoping she's getting some rest now because I'm positive she didn't sleep much last night."

Her brow arched. "Positive, huh?"

I shoved her. "Not *that* positive. Just… she's exhausted."

Something about saying that made the sight of Maddie click with her words from last week when we spoke. *She* looked exhausted. Her brown eyes had no bags, nor would they, since my sister had perfected subtle, expert-level makeup in her early teens and rarely went without it. But they were reddened and tired, right along with her general demeanor. Maddie normally had this grit and energy to her, like at any moment she was planning some brilliant new business venture and simultaneously developing an influential charitable foundation. She was just one of those people who got more done in an hour than everyone else.

But right now, that buzz of energy was missing, like someone muting a TV during the best scene of a movie. How had I not noticed the second she walked in?

"You seem like you need some rest too, Maddie."

She laughed softly. "Yeah. That's why I'm here. I refused to miss this like I missed our trip in March."

"Good. Then we'll all rest and relax and you'll finally

meet Ariel. It'll be simple and low stress, and it'll be great." I smiled and patted her shoulder. "I'll see you at dinner."

~

A short run helped work out some of the anxious energy, but Ariel was still sleeping by the time I showered, dressed, and saw we only had an hour until dinner. I hated to wake her, but she wouldn't be happy if I let her sleep. She wouldn't sleep tonight, and it'd just start a cycle of bad rest, so at just less than an hour until we were supposed to head down to eat, I sat next to her on the bed.

My heart clutched as I looked down at her. She lay on her side, one arm under her pillow, the other tucked into her chest. Her face slackened with sleep, she looked peaceful and beautiful. How stupid, my reaction to this, but I'd very rarely gotten to see her asleep. It was an intimate thing, to see someone sleeping in a bed. And here she was.

"Ariel." I used my softest voice, but no luck. After another try, only slightly louder, I pressed my hand to her shoulder and gently squeezed there. "Wolfe, it's time to get up."

The hand that had been tucked into her chest slipped over mine. The warmth and unexpected touch sent my heart skittering. Then she rolled over, and our hands moved with her, sliding from her shoulder to the center of her chest. Her palm still pressed into mine, and the other arm that'd been cradling her head under the pillow joined to hold me against her.

Had I ever been able to breathe properly? I couldn't recall a time when it'd been easy. But to be fair, I couldn't think of anything in this moment except her warm hands on mine and my skin against her chest. My fingers were splayed over her sternum, the first two at her collarbone and the others spread out toward her shoulders.

She inhaled long and slow, then exhaled. And finally, her eyes opened.

My hand spasmed, just barely, at the sight of that blue gaze, and she blinked in response. Maybe she hadn't realized she'd held my hands to her? I honestly had no idea what the hell was going on, but I wasn't going to do anything until she did.

"Everything okay with your mom?"

I swallowed and made a weird sound I could only describe as *"guh"* because I had not expected a chat about my mother. Most of my concentration now centered on not leaning down and kissing her. I couldn't remember why I shouldn't do that.

In fact, why shouldn't I?

"Nate?"

I cleared my throat and shook off that inane mental conversation. "Uh, yeah. It's all good. Dinner's in about forty-five minutes. You can stay here if you want, but if you want to come down—"

"I do."

I swallowed again, though my throat had long since dried out. "Okay."

And then she just looked at me. I would've given anything to know what she was thinking, what she wanted in that moment. I would've sworn in front of a judge that her expression spoke of ideas like the ones I'd been fighting off all afternoon.

Neither of us spoke, but after a moment, she lifted my hand and brought my palm to her lips. She kissed the center of it, then released me.

"I should get up," she said, then sat up.

I stood quickly, moving out of her way. She grabbed a bag and disappeared into the bathroom, and I slumped into the leather chair and cradled my hand, inspecting it. It felt different. That small touch of her lips had done something to it—to me. I didn't understand what it meant, and maybe it meant nothing.

Or maybe it meant everything.

CHAPTER TWENTY-EIGHT

Ariel

Not for the first time tonight, nerves and more than a little dread dripped into my belly. The first had been simply stepping out of the room, knowing I'd see his mom again and meet Maddie for the first time. I didn't know what to expect from his sister, but I wanted her to like me. She mattered to Nate, and they were close. I wanted her approval, and I also knew we were basically polar opposites.

Then we'd walked the halls to the dining room, and I'd more fully absorbed the opulence of the place. Marble, tapestries, art—everything oozing wealth and privilege without being overbearing. It was absolutely gorgeous, and though I'd showered and changed out of my jeans and tee, I still felt raggedy.

And now, Mrs. Reynolds—*Annette*— had just asked me

a question I knew would help her evaluate me on any number of scales she kept.

"So, Ariel, what is it that you do?"

"I've been nannying for my brother since I moved to Germany, and I volunteer at the kids' school a few times a week. I also recently started working with the Red Cross on post."

It wasn't shame or even embarrassment I felt. I had loved being a nanny for Robby and Delia. Getting to see them grow up after missing out on years of their childhoods while I was with Jim meant the world to me.

It was more that all of that was coming to an end, and I had no idea what would come next. I'd decided I wouldn't nanny for them anymore because my mom would be moving with them and she loved it. But... what *would* I do? I'd never been someone with huge ambition. And I had grappled with some shame about that, but I couldn't summon those feelings in this moment. The post-divorce therapy had helped, but maybe I'd just matured and accepted that about myself. Wouldn't it be magical if it happened so easily?

I'd certainly loathed it harshly enough in the wake of the separation and divorce for a lifetime. Accepting what I wanted, or rather what I didn't want—an impressive career, for example—sat at my fingertips. In the last few weeks as I'd thought through the reality of my situation and what I wanted going forward, the disappointment in myself for not even *having* a clear career track had waned.

And just now? Mercifully, I didn't get dragged under by Annette's clear lack of regard for my meager resume. *Not* feeling humiliated by someone else's disapproval was something I happily claimed as a benchmark win.

I knew with certainty my current position in life did not

meet with Annette's approval, whether she was aware that me and Nate were dating—assuming we still were. I mean, he seemed definitive, but I'd kind of flipped after the date and kiss, and then Jim happened, and here we were.

"Ah. How... varied." Annette's voice and miniscule smile were tight.

"Ariel has been indispensable for Eric. She's been a godsend for the kids, and I know he and Livie have been so thankful to have her." Nate spoke to his mom and sister who sat across from us at a long table in a dining room that reportedly wasn't even the formal one.

At his words, Maddie's face brightened. "How is sweet Eric?"

Sweet Eric? I was about as big an Eric Wolfe fan as a girl could get without being married to him, but *sweet* wasn't usually the first way someone would describe him. He could come off a bit stern, even.

"Oh, don't start, Maddie. He's happily remarried, as you know." Nate gave his sister a glare.

"You can't blame me. He's your best friend, he is insanely attractive, and he's incredibly successful in his field. That's catnip for me."

I chuckled, relieved the discussion had shifted from me. Nate took the reins then and ran with it, bless him.

"Sure, sure, I don't blame you. Especially when you've been dating smarmy little computer-loving vampires for the last decade, I'm sure—"

"You did *not* just say that—"

"I'm just saying, you've got a pattern—"

Nate broke off when Maddie raised her hand, spoon ready to throw at him. He looked happily stunned, like the idea that she'd attempt to bean him with a utensil simply delighted him.

"The reality is, neither one of you has found the right person because you're looking beneath you. Once you stop that, you'll find someone worth your time and energy, and who'll receive our blessing."

Her words burned into my ears. *Wow.* What did that even mean? Other than a not-so-subtle suggestion that I certainly wasn't good enough for Nate—and I couldn't argue that—what measurements was she using to identify someone beneath them? If it was money, they'd be hard-pressed to find actual humans able to one-up them, based on the second dining room we were currently slumming in, here in an actual Roman villa.

More than that, her disapproval of Nate *and* Maddie rang clear. She'd made a handful of other jabs at Nate in particular, and at this point, I was just done with her. She seemed to both dote on and criticize him, and she had equal parts admiration and disdain for Maddie—the oddest dynamic I'd ever seen.

Maddie sighed audibly and set down her utensils. "Yeah. Well. I'm not sure."

Nate had ducked his head and shifted food around on his plate. I couldn't have said what I wanted him to say in response, but I expected something—some retort to refute her idea. Some defense of his life and all he'd accomplished, whether or not he had a partner or spouse his parents approved of.

Annette waved off all the silent revolt. "You'll see."

One of the waiters—butlers? Honestly, I didn't get who these people were because there were entirely too many people doing basic jobs like opening doors and delivering plates to the table. Anyway, one of the at least six people I'd counted thus far at work in the home came and cleared the plates then. We all declined dessert, mercifully, and seconds later, Nate jumped up and pulled my chair out just as I stood.

We said good night to them after another awkward moment when Annette asked if she'd see Nate tomorrow and he said probably not. Just *probably not*, without an explanation. She nodded once, then turned and clacked away in spiked heels that perfectly matched the black retro sheath dress she'd donned for dinner.

I followed Nate back to the room I'd napped in earlier. Maybe the room we'd be sharing? I didn't understand what was going on there but didn't feel like I could press. Tension had reared its head off and on the whole evening, and I'd felt less and less confident in Nate's choice to bring me. More than that, a strong sense of wanting to defend him from his mother's passive-aggressive comments had taken root.

I had no say, no place to speak up, but I'd had to bite my tongue by the end to keep from screaming at her about all his accomplishments, only some of which I even knew about. The point was not about what he'd achieved but about who he was. Maybe she knew how special he was, but after that dinner and enough comments he'd made in the past about their dynamic, I doubted it.

He opened the bedroom door for me, then followed behind. I slipped out of the flats I'd brought. I had one pair of heels, and they were more *night on the town* heels I'd thrown in as a hopeful gesture that maybe we'd go out on a date. This was before I'd remembered the family element, and long before I'd realized his mother would be here too. More than ready to change out of the skirt and blouse I'd worn for dinner and bury my head in a book, I gathered my pajamas and headed for the bathroom.

"I'm sorry. Again. I feel like I'm going to end up saying

that a lot this trip." He'd slumped into the leather chair, looking truly weary.

My heart ached. I knew a little about his relationship with his family over the years, but seeing his mother's subtle disapproval hurt me. I couldn't imagine how it felt to him or Maddie. I had the sudden need to tell him just how great he was—how much I thought of him, even if his mother and father—wherever he was—didn't.

I tossed my things on the bed, crossed to stand in front of him, and stood so my legs were inside his splayed knees. His eyes perked with interest, though he stayed reclining in the chair, head resting in one hand.

"You know you're amazing, right?"

His brows furrowed, then one arched.

"You've mentioned in the past that your parents don't understand you. And I don't know your mom at all, of course, but seeing her tonight, I got a hint of that, I guess." I reached out a hand, not entirely sure what I wanted but certain I needed him to understand.

He sat forward, and his warm palm slipped against mine. A thrill chased the contact. His fingers wrapped around the back of my hand, and his thumb skated across my wrist. My pulse ticked up, and my cheeks heated.

When I spoke, it came out softer now that he'd come closer. "You seem down. And I don't like seeing you like that."

His somber expression made my heart skip. The line of his brows and his cheekbones stood out in sharp relief in the dim light. He was ridiculously handsome.

"Thank you."

"Do you ever challenge her? Try to help her see how amazingly accomplished you are? That she shouldn't..." I trailed off, frustration with his situation, and a little with him for not pushing back, clogging my throat.

"I used to. Maddie and I both learned a long time ago it didn't change how she talked to us. It's how our family functions, as messed up as it is. But I don't need to scream and yell at her to get her to see me the way I wish she would. She'll only do that if she decides to."

My brows raised.

"Don't be impressed. It took me years of therapy to get to that point." He huffed a reluctant laugh. "Thank you for caring."

The graveled quality to his voice made my stomach clench, but I shook my head and spoke past the shimmering in my chest. "Thank *you*. I was so selfish, I didn't think about how my coming would affect you and your time with your family. I was so focused on myself and Jim, I didn't realize this was going to cause friction with your family. You don't have to worry about entertaining me or anything. Do whatever you want, and I'll be fine."

Something flickered in his expression, and I could've sworn it turned heated as his gaze searched my face.

"All right. I'll only do what I want."

I noticed his eyes drop to my lips, and my heart sprinted. Why did those words sound suggestive? Why did I feel like my insides had turned liquid just from his fingers on my wrist?

"Promise?" I managed in a voice just shy of a whisper.

"Absolutely."

"Good."

His thumb arced along my skin again. Neither one of us looked away, but the room shrunk to just the two of us.

"Question is, will you do what *you* want?"

Heat bloomed in my belly. Would I?

For all the lack of clarity about what I wanted in my professional life, or where I was going in life more generally, I had none of that here. The last forty-eight hours had distilled my feelings for Nate. A bit unexpectedly, since at first, I'd been so wrapped around the upset over seeing Jim and all the feelings that encounter had stirred, but something had clicked into place between departing from Kugelfels and leaving that dinner table.

I stepped closer just as his other hand settled on my waist. And I did something I'd wanted to do for a long time—much longer than I'd ever admitted to myself. I traced the left side of his jaw with the fingers of my free hand, then let them slip back into his hair.

His eyes got a heavy, lazy look in them. "What do you want, Ariel?"

Every nerve I had announced itself, a little cacophonous symphony of doubt and memory. I ignored them all and answered him by inching closer, leaning down, and touching my lips to his.

It'd been five days since our first kiss. Five days since I'd gotten locked in my own head over my past. Then Jim literally materialized out of seemingly nowhere to confirm everything I remembered about him. And a day after that, Nate came home and proved to be even better than what I already knew to be true about him.

The confusing amount of desperation and desire I felt for him now made me physically shake. Or maybe that was the adrenaline rushing through me right along with my pulse.

Nate kissed me back, but gently. He released our hands and brought his now free one to the other side of me with a thumb at my hip bone and fingers spread out on my waist. He held me close, but he didn't take over.

I held his face and pulled back after a few soft, singeing kisses. I wanted more of the heat, to take more from him. But as they so often did, emotions clogged my throat and tears gathered. Tenderness and love for him shot through me, crystal clear. Not the love of our friendship and our past, but a clarified, new dimension. A watery chuckle escaped at the realization.

"What are you thinking?" he asked, hands still gripping me, eyes glued to mine.

"I just..." I crawled onto his lap, straddling him, and wrapped my arms around his shoulders. I hugged him to me with all my limbs, my heart glowing so brightly, it felt like sunbeams might burst through my chest.

It was a full body hug, warm and sweet. His arms held me across my shoulders and at my back. His face tucked into my neck, and I pressed my cheek against his head.

Recognizing that moving from a kiss to this odd, clutching hug might need explanation, I started. "Sorry to go from a kiss to this, but—"

He pulled back enough to see my face. "You never need to apologize for hugging me. I'm going on record right now."

The smile in his eyes and on his gorgeous lips confirmed it, and I fell a little farther for him. "Good to know."

CHAPTER TWENTY-NINE

Nate

Morning dawned, and I sat up feeling every minute of my thirty-seven years. More and more often lately, I reminisced about how I could sleep on a couch at twenty-five and spring out of bed, ready for anything. Now, I moved gingerly, waiting for whatever pinched nerve or aching joint might announce itself thanks to sleeping balled up on a sofa.

I scrubbed my face and took a moment to remember last night. She'd kissed me, then that hug. The best hug of my life. If I could order a full-body—Ariel in my lap with arms and legs wrapped around me and head resting on mine—hug every day for the rest of my life, I would. Take anything from me—I'd pay it.

If only *the rest of my life* was an option for either of us. Her leaving was the natural breaking point, and it'd save us from an inevitable and messy breakup down the road. I'd lived my life knowing that's how things ended—or worse, like my parents—and I wouldn't send me and Ariel hurtling in that direction by hoping for more.

If that determination sounded weaker by the minute, I couldn't do anything about it. I certainly couldn't pretend she affected me any less than she did, which was completely. My mind thankfully flipped back to memories of last night.

Though desire hung heavy around us in the wake of the kiss, the mood shifted as we held each other and breathed. The exhaustion of the day had dragged at both of us, and after a few more minutes, she'd moved. Before she shut herself in the bathroom to ready for bed, I had kissed her cheek and told her I'd see her this morning.

Because however tired I might've been, her words, her touch... *yeah*. I was not about to stick around. Self-preservation demanded I exit the room and get a grip, get some sleep, and start fresh today. If I'd been there when she came out of the bathroom in that little blue robe, if she'd given me another heated look or touched me *at all*, I would've wanted to move from *slow* to autobahn on a clear low-traffic day fast.

Good. Grief. How I wanted her.

And terrifyingly enough, she appeared to be feeling the same about me, which seemed impossible after those feelings going unrequited for so long. Even after the disaster of a dinner last night. Maddie hadn't been warm, exactly, but she'd asked Ariel a few questions and been polite enough to change the subject after my mom grilled Ariel about her jobs.

I did want to talk to Ariel about all of that, though—it'd been a while since we had discussed jobs and where she was heading. Most specifically, when, exactly, she was leaving Germany. I knew Eric's schedule, and I figured she was going with him, but I hadn't confirmed with her. I didn't want that ticking clock to be even more vivid, but that small part of my mind that shouted at me in self-preservation demanded I know when all of this would come to a screeching halt when she left. Because it would.

It had to.

I pushed off the couch. Time to get on with it. And I'd need to press my mother on a room again because I couldn't do another night on the couch in a villa with eight bedrooms and four people living here.

A half hour later, I'd showered and changed in one of the extra bathrooms. Strangely enough, the villa had eight bedrooms but upward of ten full bathrooms and a handful of half baths. I'd never understood that, but today, it came in handy.

My knock on Ariel's door yielded an immediate "One sec!" from the other side. I was enamored enough to find even that adorable.

She peeked out of the room, then waved me in. "Sorry I'm running late. Just need to slip on my shoes and grab my purse."

"You don't have to apologize. You're not late. I'm five minutes early."

I took in the room while she sat on the bench at the end of the bed and worked on her shoes. She'd tidied the bed, and there was nothing out of place—almost like she hadn't slept here. Other than her purse on the dresser and an e-reader on the left bedside table, I wouldn't have known she'd been there.

"Ugh, you're right." She straightened and put her hands on her hips just above the waist of her jeans. "I'm not sorry for not being late."

I closed in on her, hoping the night hadn't scared away that bit of closeness we'd shared—the ground we'd gained. She didn't shift or move away as I took her shoulders in my hands, enjoying the smooth skin under my palms thanks to the cap sleeves of her shirt.

"Good. Now, you *finally* ready, Wolfe?"

She shook her head. "Yes, *Reynolds*. I'm ready."

We left with only a few of the staff noticing and no run-ins with my mother, so my faith in the Almighty held strong. I wanted this day with Ariel, and I needed distance from Annette Reynolds.

We grabbed pastries and coffee at a small café, then kept walking. We hit the typical Roman must-sees early since the villa was only a fifteen-minute walk from the colosseum, Trajan's market, the ever-impressive Altare di Patria, and then strolled to the Pantheon.

We took our time, talking and laughing together like we used to. She'd never been to Rome, so seeing the history come alive for her made me fall in love with it all over again. Nothing in the US could compare with the feeling of encountering ancient history. Granted, the national parks had some amazing natural sights that held another layer of significance, even, but revisiting these classic tourist destinations felt oddly refreshing. I hadn't toured around Rome in years.

We stopped for lunch somewhere between the Trevi fountain and the Spanish steps at a little trattoria that had a nice sidewalk section for al fresco dining. The May day was still blessedly mild, though notably warmer than the

German spring weather we'd left. Had it really only been twenty-four hours?

We'd visited a few shops as we neared the Spanish steps after lunch, then found a small gelateria. I got pistachio, and she chose stracciatella—cream with little flecks of dark chocolate. We slipped back out of the cramped, tiny store, but I caught the moment she took her first bite of the gelato. Her face relaxed into a little smile and her eyes shut as she tasted, then swallowed, her lips soft and pleased.

My mind turned to water and my body went up in smoke.

"Mm, so good. I ate gelato every day we were in Venice last year. I hope I can do the same here."

"Mm."

She tilted her head and eyed me as we walked—somehow, my feet had remained corporeal, and I'd managed to keep pace with her instead of disappearing into a shadowy singed place on the cobblestones at the sight of her licking the cream and chocolate sweetness off a mini plastic spoon.

At some point, once my Ariel-addled mind returned to itself, I'd censure myself for acting a fool. For being so affected by any new experience with her, any moment remotely sensual or special or mundane. I couldn't escape the compulsion to hoard every second of time with her, to stuff it into the box long ago marked *Ariel Wolfe, Unattainable Dream Girl* and pray I'd be able to tape it shut and shove it into the darkened parts of my heart when this was all over.

"Nate?"

"Hmm?"

"Did you hear me?"

That head tilted again, but then I realized we'd stopped

at the side of the walkway and the heat of her free hand seeped into the skin of my forearm.

"Uh, no. Sorry. I was just too lost in the pure bliss that is pistachio gelato."

She laughed. "Well, that's what I asked you—how come pistachio? You're not really a nut person normally, are you?"

We returned to our strolling pace.

"No. I don't mind them, but they're not a particular love. Pistachio gelato is just... delicious. I suppose it does technically taste like an actual pistachio in some way, but mostly it's just good. Here. Try."

I stepped close to a building, out of the flow of walking traffic, and held out the small cup.

She raised a skeptical brow but dipped her spoon in and took the tiniest bit. She met my gaze just as she brought it to her lips and closed her mouth around the bright green scoop. Her lashes fluttered and then she licked her lips and smiled. "Okay, that's really good."

Pressure had built. Maybe my core temperature had spiked and caused system failure. Whatever the case, I moved without thought. I turned my body toward her, and with my free hand at the side of her face, I kissed her.

The stunned stillness of her immediate response melted in seconds. I stepped closer and she pressed into me, her arm wrapping around me and clutching at the back of my shirt. She tasted sweet, like cream and chocolate. Her tongue was cool, but her lips and her mouth were warm.

A low, quiet moan of satisfaction sounded between us and it hit me straight in the gut. Before I did anything stupid, I pulled back, desire a pounding pulse through my body.

Her blue eyes were bright as they blinked, and she released me. "You're really good at that."

I chuckled, relieved she wasn't upset, though the way she'd kissed me back should've told me that already. Maybe I'd always be a little needy, a little hungry for reassurance where she came in. "You are too."

She ducked her head and hid a smile. We walked quietly for a while, but the closer we got to the villa, the more the anxiety of our situation clawed at me.

"So, can I take you to dinner tonight?"

Her answering smile seemed perplexed. "Of course. I came here with you. I don't want to be in your way or keep you from spending time with Maddie or your mom, but I want as much of you as you'll give me."

The words struck right between the ribs. Oh, she had no idea how much of me she already had. How much I wanted to give her. I feared she wasn't ready, especially after last weekend, but maybe this week would change all that.

"Well, I definitely want to give you dinner. Let's start there."

CHAPTER THIRTY

Ariel

We had a perfect day. After we arrived back at the villa, he dug through the bag still sitting just inside the door of my room and said he'd make a dinner reservation for eight. That meant I had four hours to fill by myself.

I mostly wanted him to stay. To lay down next to me and rest or kiss me some more. But I also needed time to recharge, especially if I had to interact with anyone else or if his mom decided she wanted to join us. I couldn't really see her doing that, but since I didn't know her, and I did know she wasn't all that happy about Nate having his own plans, I couldn't rule it out.

After a nap, shower, and my best efforts at looking good for our date, I left the room in black jeans, bright red flats, an off-the-shoulder top that matched my eyes, and a light jacket in case it got chilly. I'd agonized over only having one more dress. I had done a terrible job packing, but I couldn't blame myself considering the circumstances. If he'd planned a formal dinner, he would've told me.

Right?

Yes. Completely. Nate was thoughtful like that, and he was already worried about my feeling uncomfortable. Not much we could do about that because I definitely did, but the day together had calmed some of that riot in me.

I shut the door behind me and padded down the hallway. The wooden floors and open air gave a hollow feeling to the space. Once I reached the top of the stairs, I admit it... I hesitated. Annette's voice immediately pinned me in place, and my stomach twisted.

"You brought her here, Nathan. I don't know what you expect *me* to do about it."

Nate responded too quietly for me to hear.

"My guest will be arriving soon. Someone canceled so there is now one other room available. *You're welcome.* But at some point, you'll begin to take responsibility for your actions... someday."

That "someday" came on a weird sing-songy note, and then her heels clacked a few times, though not enough to have left.

I gritted my teeth and steeled my spine. It would be completely inappropriate for me to say something, but this woman was *not* a nice person. Treating Nate like an irresponsible child for bringing me here, especially when he'd done it to help me out of a nasty situation back at Kugelfels? It made me want to scream at her.

I wouldn't. I hadn't screamed at anyone ever. My fight mode, my opposition press, my defiance, all came with dead and steadfast silence.

Halfway down the stairs, I could see Nate's head. He'd

styled his hair with a part at the side. Over the years, I'd seen him with a few different haircuts—buzzed during his time at certain units, or a little longer like now. The part and length made me want to run my hands through it and mess him up a little. He looked good polished, but after living with him, I knew he looked fantastic a little roughed up. His two days of beard growth added to the rugged effect, and by the time I reached the ground floor, my breath came out shallow and quick.

"Ready?" I asked while approaching.

He turned and smiled, those hazel eyes meeting mine, then slipping down over me. Neck, shoulders, lower—all the way to my bright red flats.

"You look great."

"Thank you. You do too."

Somehow, the four hours apart had created even more tension between us. But this was the good kind. Over the last few years, there'd been a few different kinds of tension between me and Nate, some of them downright wretched. This, however, felt more like a magnetic pull—like if I didn't mess up his hair and taste his lips, and soon, I might crumble.

"Ah, she's here." Annette's voice cut through the moment.

I exhaled the pent-up feeling and turned to her just as Nate asked, "Who's here?"

We followed her through the house to the front entrance as she spoke. "Did I not tell you? It's Juliet! She's joining us for the next few days."

I didn't know the name, but when I glanced at Nate, I saw that of course he did. His jaw clenched and the set of his shoulders stiffened.

"Who's that?" I asked just as we stepped through the

front doors to see a tall, gorgeous blond woman exit a bright red Ferrari from the driver's side.

"My ex," he gritted out.

My stomach sank. *This* was his ex? The way he said it made it sound like there was significance there. Not just a woman he'd dated casually, which had been the majority of his relationships—or so I'd thought. *His ex*, almost like I'd say about Jim. Almost, except without the loathing. The rigid posture and clenched jaw seemed mostly in response to the surprise, not the person.

"My darling, welcome. Welcome!" Annette threw her arms wide as she approached the woman.

Long, long, long blond hair reflecting the sunlight, giving me the sense I was looking at honey and gold melted together. Her giant smile had that toothpaste commercial whiteness and gleam. Her makeup made her light skin look flawless and highlighted her cheekbones, deep brown eyes, and long lashes. Or maybe that was just her natural beauty. She wore white wide-leg slacks and a black top cropped just above her navel, a sliver of porcelain skin peeking out.

She had one of those athletic, slim bodies. Actually, she had one of those model bodies, between the height and the general splendor of her. Heck, I wanted to take a picture of her.

I didn't dare look at Nate. I could feel his frustration, maybe even anger, but that was for his mother and this situation. What I didn't know was how it had ended between them, and whether seeing her here would hurt him, or make him want—

My throat tightened, and a numb, still sensation cloaked me. This woman was physically the opposite of me. If this was his ex... I couldn't even think. She'd turned that bright smile toward Nate, and my heart cracked.

"Nate!" She scuttled up to him and threw her arms around him.

He caught and hugged her, then released her and stepped back. "Juliet, this is Ariel Wolfe."

Her eyes widened and double-blinked, then her attention shifted to me. "Ariel. Wow. So, so happy to meet you."

Though she did seem surprised, her words sounded genuine. Not that I had any idea what false or genuine sounded like for this woman, but she had a warm, lovely, irritatingly attractive glow about her that made me want to like her even though self-pity and misery had taken root in my belly.

"Very nice to meet you, too." *Did anyone else think my voice sounded weird?*

"Maddie and I are having brunch later this week. Will you come with us?" She squeezed a hand I didn't remember her taking, and her eyes sparkled like she might really mean this too.

"Uh, I'd love to." I glanced at Nate.

He'd plastered one of his easygoing smiles on. I knew him well enough at this point to know it was, in fact, plastered, but I didn't have a clue about what made it necessary. A bucket of questions for him filled in my brain.

"Perfect. Okay, then I'm going to run in and find that rotten sister of yours. Have a great evening!" She pressed a hand to my shoulder like we were old friends and took a large leather bag from the man who'd opened her door.

I heard Annette's voice inside say, "So, tell me everything!" like she was giddy to hear news from this woman.

"You ready?" Nate asked.

"You still want to go?"

His brows furrowed. "Of course. I've been looking forward to it."

I summoned a smile for him and followed where he led. We wound through the bustling Roman streets in dimming light. I focused on the stores we passed, the people sipping wine sitting at wicker tables on the sidewalk... anything other than the hundred warring questions I needed to ask Nate. Fifteen minutes later, he held the door to our dinner destination. Good news, because the gnawing in my gut needed something, and I hoped it was food.

Bad news? We'd hardly spoken on the walk, and when we did, it had been observations about the city. Were we really going to ignore this?

We sat. A waiter delivered a menu, and Nate ordered water and bread in Italian, and maybe something else too. I put up blockades against the thump of my heart that inevitably came at the sound of him speaking the beautiful language.

I couldn't see the menu—couldn't think about anything other than what on earth I was doing here. How foolish to think I fit in his life, with him, in any way other than casual friendship. I was nothing like that woman. I had virtually nothing financially. I was far shorter than her, probably outweighed her by a toddler or two. Blue eyes, not brown. Dark hair, not blond. There were so many things right about her, I couldn't help feeling their absence meant something wrong about me.

"What looks good?" Nate said after a few minutes of quiet between us.

"I'm not sure."

"This place is reliable. It's a favorite. You can't go wrong. Or, if you need help..."

"I'm fine."

I didn't look up from the menu. He didn't speak again,

but another minute or two, then he put a finger on the top of my menu and pushed until I let it drop to the table.

"What's up?"

I swallowed, then smiled up at the waiter as he brought our water, bread, and a small plate full of cheeses, meats, and olives.

"Ariel?"

"Juliet was really nice. Did you know she was coming to stay?"

His face fell. "No. I'm sorry about that, and definitely no. She's one of Maddie's best friends, so it's not totally out of place, but I wasn't expecting that. I'm not sure she knew I'd be here, either, though who knows."

I sipped water again. Picked up some bread, then set it down again. "She's beautiful."

Nate looked into my eyes with a set expression—determination, maybe? The muscles at his jaw flexed.

"I've known her for years. We dated for a while a few years ago. We broke up about two years ago. She knew why, and though I felt bad about it, we're friendly. I don't talk to her regularly or anything. It's not an ongoing relationship aside from her being in Maddie's life. She's a good person."

I nodded. "She seemed lovely—genuine and warm. I can see why you liked her."

Loved her? I didn't want to know. The thought of him loving that paragon of all that is lovely made me want to cry. I shouldn't dread knowing he'd loved someone. I didn't want him to have lived without love. And yet, that tightness in my chest wasn't going anywhere.

"She is. She's a good friend to Maddie, too." He reached across the small table and took my hand in his. "But I'm here with you. And though I know it's not like we planned to travel together as a dating couple, I am dating you and only you. I want to date you and only you."

My heart raced and pounded, and I squeezed his hand.

"Tell me you believe that, Wolfe. Please."

"I believe you," I said, voice shaky with relief and thrill.

One thing I would always appreciate about Nate was his straightforward approach to our relationship. He'd been this way in friendship, and I couldn't say enough about how much it meant to me in this new version of us. It helped ease some of the snarling fear that reared up at the thought of what we might be doing to our friendship even now. Even in this moment of going out on another date in this beautiful city, talking like something far more than friends.

His hazel eyes dipped to my lips, then dropped to the table. "Let's get our food ordered, and then I want to hear your thoughts on Rome."

CHAPTER THIRTY-ONE

Nate

Matricide.

That was the fleeting word that crossed my mind when Juliet got out of her car and my mother squealed with glee.

To be clear, I would never harm my mother or anyone else. But I gritted my teeth so hard, I had a headache on the walk to dinner. She could've told me Juliet was coming. She'd had every opportunity to give me the heads-up, and she hadn't taken it. Neither had Maddie, of course, but we hadn't spent much time together so far.

The worst part of all this, aside from it putting that look of confusion and surprise in Ariel's eyes, was that Juliet would recognize the ploy. No doubt my mother wanted me back with her. The fact that this all coincided with Ariel meeting her and Maddie for the first time made me want to scream.

Even if I'd come alone, shoving me and Juliet together wouldn't have changed my mind. Of course my mother had no idea about my long-held feelings for Ariel. But she knew damn well that I'd broken up with Juliet years ago, and I didn't want to go back. No offense to Juliet—she simply wasn't Ariel.

The woman herself held my hand as we wandered back to the villa under a sparkling Roman sky. After clarifying that I didn't want anything from Juliet, she seemed to relax into the evening, and by degrees, things returned to a more comfortable dynamic. But she'd gotten quiet again in these last few minutes while we walked. I'd slipped into my own thoughts, wondering if she was second-guessing this whole trip. Or maybe even the whole us dating thing. But we were nearly back, and I didn't want to end the night without something... more.

"I'll be busy most of the day tomorrow and some of Friday, so you'll have some alone time." I squeezed her hand, hoping the promise of a break from me might help. Though, frankly, also hoping she didn't need it.

She glanced at me. "What are you up to?"

"I have meetings, strangely enough. Just a few video conferences with my father and the board, but while we're all together, they wanted us to meet. Nothing exciting, but I can't miss it. Then we have lunch, which I'm sure you could join us for—"

"Uh, no. I think you should keep this one in the family."

Her answer came so quickly, I laughed. "Are you avoiding my mother, by chance?"

"She's disappointed I'm here. I get that. I don't want to make it any worse."

We halted on the spot, and I turned to her. Ducking my face close, I spoke. "I want you here. I brought you here.

Yes, there was a catalyst for my asking, but honestly, I would've asked without your jerkwad ex's nonsense if I'd thought for a second you'd say yes and it wouldn't seem like too much, too soon."

The darkened street made it so I couldn't see her eyes—at least not that vibrant, gut-punch blue of them. But I could see and feel her focus on me.

"Okay."

"If my mother's plans are upset, then oh well. I'll talk to her tomorrow, but I want you to know that it's okay if she's upset. It's a big enough house we don't have to even see her again—if you don't want to see her again, it's done."

She made a sound like *huh* and her free hand fell to my chest. "No, no. It's her home and I've invaded. You know I'm happy being alone—I'll make myself scarce if you're busy and she's home."

"You don't have to do that."

"This is your family, Nate. They matter to you, just like mine does to me. It's okay if your mom doesn't love me, although I hope one day maybe she'll at least *like* me. But I'm a change of plans she wasn't expecting, and I can't fault her for that. Don't worry about me. You need rest this week too, and stressing over my feelings about your mom? Not restful."

That hand on me, her nearness, her entire being cut into my reason and control—I wanted to pull her to me and devour her. Her sweet words, the quiet jokes and thoughts we'd shared all night. That insistence on helping *me* rest...

I stepped back quickly. "Let's get inside."

Down the last stretch of the street, through the door, into the courtyard, through the front doors swung open by one of the staff. "Grazie, Bruno." Down the hall, up the stairs. My mind moved a step ahead of our bodies, but I nearly dragged her. Her unwillingness to be cowed by my mother, even in the midst of self-doubt and crazy emotions after seeing her ex... it made my mind clamor for her. Like someone walked into a small room and banged cymbals until the walls cracked.

I'd brought her here to help her, but she didn't seem to need help. And here I was thinking I was doing something good for her, then I thrust her into this mess with my mom and Juliet, and even Maddie being a little stand-offish, though I doubted Ariel could tell. And she rolled with it.

"What's happening right now?" she laugh-whispered as I practically dragged her down the hall. She was jogging behind me as I closed in on her room.

"We need privacy."

"We do?"

"Yes." I threw open the door to her room, pulled her in, twirled her around, and paced her back against the door. "We do."

Her chest rose and fell, her gaze searching mine.

I pressed a hand to the right of her head, though I kept my body back from her, just enough so she wouldn't feel trapped. If she didn't like this, anything about this, she could step to the side and be done.

But good grief, I hoped she wouldn't. I needed to be closer to her. Closer than talking at a restaurant or holding hands walking home. Closer than not knowing how she really felt, what she wanted for us. I wouldn't solve that tonight, and I could admit that. Plus, at this range, I caught the faint scent of her perfume and my stomach clenched. My mind muddied with her, her, her.

"Nate?"

She watched me. No fear—just curiosity, urgency, and maybe, if I was lucky, heat.

"Can I kiss you? Please, tell me I can kiss you, because—"

Her lips on mine cut me off, and I'd never been happier for an interruption. Her hands fisted in my shirt at my pecs, and she pulled me in. I obeyed the silent command and stepped closer, slipping my arms around her waist and sliding my hands to her lower back.

A ridiculous growl-moan sound came from my throat as she opened her lips for me, and the soft heat of her tongue met mine. I couldn't find it in myself to be embarrassed because she was right there with me, pressing back against me, meeting each kiss with another.

Kissing Ariel was better than I'd imagined, by the way. And yes, I'd imagined it more than a few times over the years. Was it possible we'd only done this four times? At the fest, last night after dinner, the stolen street kiss today, and now? It felt new and familiar all at once. It was that game *good, better, best*, and it was all three.

My lips coasted along her jaw. Kiss, press, slide to behind her ear. Her shirt left her shoulders bare, and clearly, there was one thing to do. Her smooth skin called to me—I'd fantasized more than once about kissing this place at her jaw, where her neck met her shoulder, the dip in her collarbone.

Her palm pressed into my chest, unmoving, and her other gripped my right bicep. If she hadn't been kissing me back with enthusiasm, then tilting her head to give me room as I explored, I might've worried. Instead, her hold on me seemed more unsure or even shy.

Before that thought fully developed, a knock jarred us both. Ariel gasped and physically jumped enough that I did too and backed away.

"Ariel?"

Maddie. I'd guess she had no idea I was in here, but maybe she did. Perhaps she hated me, and this was her new way of showing it. Maybe she just wanted me to hook up with Juliet so they could be sisters, which had been one of her main selling points back when we dated—and all through high school long before we dated.

"Uh, yes?" Ariel's voice sounded pleasantly rough.

I did that. Forgive me, but I couldn't help reveling in knowing she'd been lost to the moment, right there with me.

"Sorry to interrupt. I saw your light was on." Maddie's muffled voice came through the still-closed door.

Ariel gave me a look I interpreted as a question. Would I hide or stay standing right there? That she had to ask made me smile, and a little starburst ache set off in my heart. There was nothing I wanted to hide from anyone about the way I felt for her. I hadn't shared with my mother because we'd only been dating for a few weeks and I didn't want her pressure. I suspected, even though Ariel had no money and didn't come from an "influential family," if we got to the point I wanted us to—marriage, babies, aching backs as we aged together—my mom would get on board.

Wait. What?

A mental record scratch cut across my mind at that. *Marriage? Babies?* Had I really just gone there so easily? I waited for the alarm bells, the usual wariness and dread of being tied to someone who'd eventually resent me to clang through me. But nothing did.

No need to go there, idiot. You've got less than two months left with her. That cruel thought arrived, an effective slap in the face. The moment had indeed run away with me. The natural end point to all of this, the one barreling toward us far too quickly, was another reason why my mother's feelings about Ariel didn't matter.

I grabbed the door and swung it open, making no attempt to hide my irritation. My pulse still sprinted in my veins, and my breathing was a little ragged, so the glare I gave Maddie came quite naturally.

"Oh. Sorry. Yikes. Uh..." She looked genuinely uncomfortable, so she must not have realized I was in here.

"Need something?"

Ariel tugged on my hand and gave me a stern look before saying, "Everything okay?"

"Yes, totally fine. Juliet and I wanted to invite you to brunch on Friday. I'm pretty sure this one has a tight schedule toward the end of the week, so I figured you could use something to do." She smiled at Ariel, then raised a single brow at me.

That brow had been the voice of a thousand expressions, insults, challenges, and jokes in our lifetime. The sight of it, especially after so long since last seeing her, had me shaking my head even as gratitude washed through me at her offer.

"That's so nice. I'd love to."

We said good night to Maddie, but before Ariel could close the door, I kept a hand on the panel and leaned against it.

"I'm going to go."

"Already?"

Hoo, boy! The look in those eyes hit me straight in the gut. But...

"Yes. Because I'm at another one of those times when I don't want to go slow, but I recognize that's good—the going slow plan. Being here hasn't accelerated us or changed that. So, I'm going to kiss you one more time—" I leaned forward and kissed her forehead, then stepped back, "—and I'm going to see you tomorrow afternoon when I'm back from meetings."

She shook her head but smiled bright and genuine. "Okay then. But please note I'm not asking you to leave."

Longing and desire threatened to crush that little shred of willpower I'd summoned, but I edged it out. When I spoke, though, my voice came out low and gruff and reflected a fraction of those things. "Noted."

I walked back to my room—yes, the one that'd magically materialized as soon as Juliet had, like me not staying with Ariel would somehow make me more willing to reunite with my ex. I breathed deep, working to calm all the ravenous pieces of me. Building a relationship with Ariel had been something I'd wanted for too long to let physical urges drive the train—even if said urges were steel track laid in a very clear direction.

No. We wouldn't rush this. *I* wouldn't rush this or push. I didn't want her to have any regrets because God knew I wouldn't have a single one. I'd already nudged her out of her comfort zone by coming here. We'd go slowly, just like she said. Just like I repeated to myself almost every time I touched her.

Making the most of *now* didn't mean rushing. We still had time. I ignored the impossible voice that whispered a thought I'd had to push away all too often lately. *If I had my way, there'd be a lifetime with her.*

CHAPTER THIRTY-TWO

Ariel

The time here in Rome had been restorative. Since that flaming kiss on Wednesday night, I'd barely seen Nate. Some meeting got rescheduled after the lawyer, or whoever it was, ran late in the morning, and then the whole thing took ten times longer than anticipated. Nate swung by for a kiss after he returned to the villa after ten that Thursday night. It was sweet, passionate, full, and as had been happening lately, made me feel fluttery and weak in the best way.

Since I'd planned on him being gone most of the day anyway, I took to the city. The May weather was perfection. The city bloomed with life and vibrancy. It wasn't full tourist season in Europe, which meant it wasn't crazy crowded either.

I walked through the magnificence of St. Peter's and gave myself plenty of time to view the *Pietà*, a sculpture I'd always wanted to see. Jesus's lifeless body in Mary's arms stirred in me a deep, complex sadness and regret, and yet it was so strikingly beautiful.

After wandering a bit more, then leaving the hallowed space, I celebrated that tunneling, one-with-the-world feeling I sometimes got when I looked at famous art by having a pistachio gelato. It was a small way I could bring Nate with me—eat his favorite flavor, which was actually delicious. I tried to ignore the regret I felt at not having booked tickets to the Sistine Chapel and Vatican Museum—it might not have been high season, but my search this morning showed tickets were sold out the rest of the week.

I'd come back, though. I promised myself these few days in Rome wouldn't be my only chance to be here. How and when, I couldn't say. I'd be moving back to the US, and I'd try to find a job and live a normal life again after all this. The ability to travel overseas again wouldn't come easily.

Yet, the vow to return settled deep in my chest, and I carried it around with me the rest of the day, promising myself it wouldn't be the last time I saw this beautiful city.

Today, Nate had plans to meet a friend he lived with when he studied here during college, and though he'd invited me, I had Maddie and Juliet's invitation and didn't want him to feel suffocated by me.

At the same time, I had to check those kinds of thoughts. Was that a normal thing for a woman to think in a situation like this, or was it something that cropped up thanks to Jim's influence and his ability to make me feel like whatever I did was wrong? If I was affectionate? I was being clingy, needy. If I gave him space? I must've been hiding something, planning something, thinking something I shouldn't.

In this case, I believed Nate wanted to be with me. I

also knew that he hadn't originally planned on me coming, and he'd been looking forward to seeing his friend Michele. Since I had another clear option, even if it made me feel a little ill from nerves just thinking about it, I took it.

That was how I found myself standing at the front entrance to the villa, wondering if it was all a big joke and Maddie and Juliet wouldn't show, remembering the goodbye kiss from this morning.

Nate had knocked on my door, and my breath had caught when I opened it and saw him.

"Hi," I'd said, somehow. That I could utter intelligible words should've won me some kind of prize.

He'd stepped in enough to lean on the doorframe. "'Morning, Wolfe. You looking forward to brunch with—"

"I don't want to talk about that."

He'd chuckled, and his brow had furrowed. "Okay. Then do tell—"

"Are you going to a photo shoot or something?"

I'd lost all manners. I'd lost all thought. The man wore a medium-gray suit that was undoubtedly custom-made. Or maybe not. Frankly, I had no idea if it was or not, but the way it fit him, I had to assume it'd at least been tailored in some way. Gray suit, crisp white shirt open at the collar, no tie. His beard had grown in enough to make him look rugged, but paired with the sophisticated suit, it just worked.

Oh, my, how it worked for him.

I'd felt his eyes on me and finally met his gaze again. He'd looked amused, but there had been that little flame in the back of his expression. I'd wondered if I'd seen it before —not this moment, but in years past—and just hadn't recognized it, or if he'd kept it banked.

"Like what you see then, huh?" He'd given me an obnoxious little smirk and wink.

"I am woman enough to admit that, yes, I do. You look great. This suit looks so good. I knew you looked good in a suit, but now I feel like I need to come up with reasons for you to dress this way when we get back to Germany."

His smile had widened and he'd pushed off the wall to move toward me. "I'll wear whatever you want, whenever you want, Wolfe. Say the word, and it's done."

That rich, low voice had made my stomach twist. He'd stalked closer, took me in his arms, but stopped right before our lips met, those hazel eyes boring into mine.

"Whatever you want," he'd repeated.

Then he'd touched his lips to mine—just the barest, sweetest press—said something in Italian with those flames back in his eyes, and he'd gone.

It had taken me more than a few minutes to recover from that—all of it. Him and his ridiculously good-looking, GQ gorgeousness. The insinuation he'd dress how I wanted, as though I actually cared. That last little kiss. His openness about... wanting me.

It still threw me. He made it clear, but not in a possessive, showy way. It wasn't like Jim's harsh, consuming interest that ended up holding me so tight I couldn't breathe, couldn't think. It was freeing. It helped me know where he stood. And maybe he didn't even mean to do it, but he kept putting the control in my hands in simple ways like telling me he'd wear whatever I wanted. What?

I didn't think of myself as someone who needed control in a relationship, but maybe in the wake of things with Jim, I did. Especially since every time Nate did something like that, it made me all kinds of hot.

"There you are! We were waiting by the stairs. You must've beaten us down."

Juliet's lovely voice burst through the memory. I plastered on a smile and hoped my cheeks weren't red from reliving the encounter and the ensuing appreciation of all things Nate.

"I'm sorry. I thought out here was best."

Juliet waved that away with a perfectly manicured, delicate-looking hand. "No worries. We're taking a car so we can drink champagne to our hearts' content and not have to drive home."

Both women wore jeans and blouses—Juliet's a pale jade and silky thing that draped and gathered in some mysterious, perfect way, and Maddie's cream linen-looking material flattered her without fitting closely. While my own top was simply a light blue button-down with the sleeves rolled, relief hit bright and true at the discovery we were at least in the same general league of attire for the outing.

In the car on the way, Maddie sat in front, and Juliet scooched in next to me in the back. Clearly, she was the more talkative one, though Maddie hadn't struck me as particularly retiring or quiet in our past interactions. Maybe the difference had been Nate—he'd been with me every time we'd spoken.

Juliet had this radiance about her. It was magnetic and charming. I wasn't sure how old she was, but she seemed young, oddly. Sophisticated and worldly, but almost sweet in a way I never imagined a model-level beautiful, wealthy woman in her thirties could ever be. That said, Nate wouldn't date someone horrible, so I also couldn't be surprised that she was lovely.

Minutes later, we pulled up to a chic-looking façade on a quiet street. Maddie led the way inside, and the waiter seated us at a table with giant bamboo chairs that had elaborate arcs at the back and plush bright white and yellow pillows cushioning the back and seat. We all sank into our places, and Juliet sighed.

"You know, I'm just so glad you're here, Ariel. So completely delighted."

Again, she sounded genuine. If Annette had invited her as a ploy to get her alone with Nate, which I'd considered several times since her arrival, then Juliet didn't know about it. Either that or she should get into acting stat because she was laying out the performance of a lifetime.

"I'm really happy to meet you both as well." I couldn't say that I'd heard much about Juliet, honestly, but I'd often heard stories about Maddie.

For her part, Maddie only smiled and focused on her menu. After a bit of small talk, Maddie ordered in perfect Italian while Juliet and I had to go for boring old English. Then we settled in with delicious Italian coffees, and Juliet's attention returned squarely to me.

"So. You and Nate are dating."

I shifted in my seat. "Yes. Very recently started."

She beamed. "Going well?"

"Uh, yes. As far as I'm concerned, everything's great."

Maddie's eyes bore into me, so I returned her gaze. She'd been so nice to invite me and had been cordial to say the least, but I couldn't figure out what was going on with her. Did she know something I didn't about how Nate felt things were going and didn't want to say?

That didn't ring true. But what was it?

Juliet clapped, then raised her demi-tasse as though people often toasted with espresso cups. "To love finding a way."

Her soft smile made my throat tighten, and for some

reason, it felt like she'd just hugged me. It was honestly one of the weirdest and yet most comforting moments of my recent life, and it made no sense. I barely knew this woman, and she'd dated my boyfriend—if he was even considered my boyfriend? But here she was toasting...

"Good Lord, you're a little romantic cheeseball," Maddie said with an eyeroll.

"Hush, you."

I chuckled at their exchange and used it to diffuse my odd emotional response. "To love finding a way."

Our cups clinked, and we all sipped. Even with Maddie's odd dynamic, I felt welcomed and more eager for the day now than I had for the several leading up to it.

"I won't make you tell us all about Nate, because I fully understand how weird that would be. So, let me tell you about my recent failure of a relationship, complete with the man crying on his knees when I broke up with him."

My eyes widened. Maddie snorted.

"Oh wow, he must've really cared for you," I guessed.

She did that elegant hand wave thing she'd done earlier. "Not a bit. He loved my money. We'd been dating for a week. It was completely bananas."

CHAPTER THIRTY-THREE

Nate

I knocked quietly on Ariel's door. I'd been busier than anticipated and had texted her to apologize more than once. She'd reassured me she wasn't upset, and I wanted to believe it. I did. Mostly.

And honestly? A not-small part of me still waited for her to pull away. After all this time, I was waiting for her to call it. After so many years of her *not* choosing me, I couldn't relax into there being an *us*, no matter how much I wanted to.

I'd have to get my head around that. *And if she does pull away, that's it. You have to be done.* Even if it came sooner than the natural end to all of this when she moved from Germany. But for now, this was our shot, and I'd enjoy it while it lasted. That cruel *too little, too late* element at play—the bad timing, the necessary slower pace... I couldn't regret it. It was better than never having a chance with her, even if this one would be automatically short-lived.

It wasn't like that was bad. For me, I at least had a few months being with her. It would never be enough, of course, but... I loosed a breath. The usual line of thinking, that *but at least we wouldn't face the same end all relationships do* was harder to summon tonight. Aside from me, she'd have a rebound under her belt. She'd be free to give someone else a go.

Crap. That thought hit like a knee to the gut. I sure as hell didn't want to think about Ariel with someone else. That was part of the whole *be here now* approach I was doing my best to take. A perspective that had clearly failed me tonight.

I shouldered that thought right out the window to my left and focused up. Despite the lack of interest for years prior, she hadn't been inconsistent or anything but encouraging so far. Maybe nervous, unsure, and most comfortable with slow. But I had no reason to doubt her at this point.

I also knew she didn't feel particularly welcomed here. I hoped the brunch with my sister and Juliet had gone well. Maddie wouldn't be openly hostile or rude, and Juliet was basically bottled sunshine in human form, so even if Maddie showed up with a little edge, Juliet would smooth her out.

I'd seen Juliet downstairs, padding her way to the kitchen in a robe. She had a way of becoming immediately at home in whatever place she inhabited. She'd squeezed my shoulder and raised her eyebrows as she went, saying only, "She's wonderful."

Juliet made my heart ache. Not for me, but for her. She, like Maddie, was a downright excellent human, a great woman, and wanted love. Deserved it. I hoped she'd find her person. As I took the stairs two at a time, I prayed they'd both find it. And I may have said a prayer for myself, that the woman I raced to meet, the person I'd wanted for so long, would find her person *in me*.

God forgive me, I did it. It slipped right in there. I knew this couldn't last beyond the summer, but selfishly, I wanted that. Of course I did.

Something had shifted while being in meeting after meeting, and even while catching up with Michele. It was this low-grade pulsing, like each beat of my heart was stacking up to a clear revelation. One I'd pretty much always known, but now that we'd talked a few miles down this road, I understood and couldn't ignore.

When Ariel answered, she looked sleepy. My spirits sank a touch. She needed to sleep. It was after ten, and she probably hadn't been sleeping all that well. I'd hoped maybe we could watch a movie or have a late dessert, talk a little and maybe I'd work around to hinting at this being some-thing. *Something*. But she wore a set of small white shorts that hugged her body in a way that was hard to look away from, and a tank top that I didn't allow myself to look at in the first place, and they were clearly pajamas.

"Sorry it's so late." I kept my voice low, though the next occupied bedroom wasn't anywhere nearby.

"Come in, and don't apologize. You texted me how many times to do that already today?" She reached out and tugged me inside by the placket on my shirt.

I went more than willingly, of course.

"I just feel bad. I thought we'd at least get one more dinner together."

And I did hate that. Somehow, the trust meetings had gone sideways and thanks to the particularly sharp antagonism between my parents, everything that should've happened in a matter of hours took three times as long. I wished I'd stayed with Michele, but I'd promised my mother yesterday that I'd be there for her again this afternoon.

"Don't. I had a wonderful time. Brunch was great, and I honestly love wandering around by myself." She sat on the end of the bed and watched as I tossed my suit jacket on the leather chair.

"What'd you do for dinner?" I unbuttoned the cuffs of my shirt and rolled them up.

Eyes on my forearms, she said, "I stopped at a trattoria. Ate antipasto and pasta and bread while I read my book. It was perfect."

I chuckled as enjoyment filtered through me at hearing her say that. She'd always been like that before—she liked solitude, loved reading, didn't mind eating alone. Some people couldn't handle doing that. They'd feel conspicuous and embarrassed. Ariel never did because, as she'd told me once, when she opened her book, she'd be dining with friends. *God, I love her.*

Instead of that, I said, "It does sound perfect. I only wish I'd been sitting across from you."

She tilted her head and scrunched her forehead like she was considering it. "Would've been okay, though you probably would've insisted on talking."

"Fair enough. I wouldn't want to miss the opportunity of having you all to myself."

She laughed. "You've had me all to yourself this whole week."

"Hardly." I plunked down on the bed, which made her bounce next to me.

She set a hand on my arm to steady herself.

"Seriously, I'm sorry I ended up working so much. I'd be annoyed by it even if you weren't here, but knowing I missed out on keeping you company..."

I'd bitten back sharp comments, and at one point, outright anger, during the meetings more than once today. Maddie had seemed just as irritated that our family vacation meet up had turned into a full-blown work session two days in a row. My dad was retiring, and his retirement changed board positions and all kinds of things with the foundations and business the family money was tied up in. It wasn't worth detailing out, but needless to say, we'd gone through the fine print and then some this week.

Ariel, who hadn't let go of my arm, shook me. I looked at her. "Don't apologize. Just be with me now."

I blinked back at her. She'd said words I'd been chanting to myself, begging myself to be here now and not get twisted up about the future. But damn if that wasn't becoming harder to do by the second.

She looked earnest and happy. My heart thumped in my chest, and I angled myself toward her. "I would very much like to do that."

"Good. You can start with a kiss."

My pulse skipped, but I did as requested. With one hand in her hair, I moved close and kissed her. The kiss moved from slow and tender to wildfire-spreading passionate, and before I knew it, I lay next to her, my arm supporting her head, her arm around my back and her hand in my hair.

The full crush of desire I held for her pulled at me, driving me closer. She met me kiss for kiss, touch for touch. She was soft and pliant, but insistent in her own way.

Things were escalating quickly, and as much as I wanted her, all of her, with every bit of all of me, I didn't want any regrets. I couldn't shake the real terror of messing things up between us by rushing her.

Because the thought had slipped in that maybe, just maybe, they weren't destined to end. Maybe there was more here, and rushing it, just taking for now and ignoring the future, would be the very thing that did ruin it.

She knew herself and knew her mind, so I'd ask her. When I leaned back to look at her, feeling drugged by the force of this moment between us, she pulled at my neck.

I shook my head. "Wolfe. You've got to let me catch a breath here."

Those bright blue eyes gazed back at me, and her chest rose and fell with a great exhale. "I guess that'd be smart."

I felt a drop of disappointment, because no small part of me had hoped we could continue, but at the same time, I didn't want anything she didn't want to give freely. "Okay. Okay."

I slipped out from under her and sat up, elbows to knees, focusing on breathing slowly and ratcheting down the desire pounding through my bloodstream.

"Sorry. It's not that—"

"Don't apologize. Weren't you just telling me that?" I gave her a smile.

She licked her lips, which did not help my efforts.

"I guess so."

She scooted to the edge of the bed and sat with me. "Would you sleep with me? Go get changed and do whatever, and come back and just spend the night next to me?"

My throat worked, and after a beat, I managed to swallow. "Absolutely. Be right back."

I kissed her temple, then stood to gather my jacket and slipped out of her room. In minutes, I returned in a T-shirt, shorts, and the necessities taken care of. I let myself into her room and found her sitting against the headboard, reading.

I had this thought. One I'd been having way too often considering how new this all was. *I want this.* Not in the physical way—not just her body. Trust that I wanted that too. But *this.* I wanted her reading quietly while I got ready for bed, and then looking up at me like she'd been waiting for me to join her. I wanted her bed to be my bed. *Ours.*

"That was fast." She smiled and set down her e-reader.

"I'm a highly motivated man with the right incentive."

Standing at the opposite side of the bed from hers, I paused a moment. The reality of what I was about to do hit me in a weird way that made my knees quake before I slid in between the cool sheets.

She clicked off the lamp, and darkness shrouded the room but for the moonlight filtering in through the drapes she'd left open a few feet.

"You're staying all the way over there? Are you against cuddling?"

I didn't cuddle—not with anyone else. But did I want to cuddle with Ariel? *Obviously.*

We each inched toward the middle of the bed, not exactly tentative, but in a way that said we both knew this was a level up on the intimacy charts. We lay down, her back a few inches from my front, our heads on the same pillow.

"Can I—"

"Why don't you—"

We both laughed, and I went for it. I reached a hand around her waist and pulled her to me so we were nested close.

"This okay?" My voice sounded particularly low and gruff, even at just above a whisper.

"Yes."

The scent of her shampoo, the warm heat of her body, the soft skin where my hand rested at the curve of her belly —all of it assaulted my senses, and that intoxicated, overwhelmed feeling settled over me. It addled me, so much that I wanted to tell her *desperately*. I wanted to pull her even closer, nuzzle my face into her neck and bare my soul to her. She owned my heart anyway—why shouldn't I?

I had never allowed myself to be enough for other women. We kept it simple, and I avoided the entrapped, caged feeling of barreling toward a relationship not built on love. My heart wanted only one person, and here she was.

But cruelly, I couldn't tell her everything, could I? If I did, wouldn't that confession be too much? Wouldn't I end up thrust back to where we'd been months ago, hardly speaking, and her wishing I'd never changed things between us?

She had feelings for me. She was attracted to me. But love? I'd dreamed of it, but it was too soon. Still far too soon to burden her with my feelings and risk everything we had now. I couldn't tell her and move on when she left. If it was too soon for her, it was too much for me. Because we were coming to the end, even if there was time left, and if I had any chance of salvaging some of my heart to give to someone else, I'd keep that close.

That pulse in my chest, the one trying to gain my attention and push me to push her, to get her to say what she wanted in case it was the same as what I'd only just started admitting, beat steady.

Thankfully, before I spoke those words that would change things, that might be fearfully premature, and that would likely haunt me in ways I'd never live down, she interrupted my internal debate.

"Good night, Nate," she said in a whisper to the dark room.

"Night, Wolfe."

CHAPTER THIRTY-FOUR

Ariel

I'd spent four days in Rome. I'd seen the city from my feet, and that was my favorite way to travel. I'd seen art and eaten gelato and pasta until I thought I'd never need to eat again. I'd genuinely enjoyed getting to know Juliet and Maddie a little, and I hoped I'd see them again. And I could check the box on meeting Annette, which hadn't exactly been a delight, but I was glad I could fit her into the picture of Nate I'd puzzled together.

Though he'd apologized profusely about leaving me solo, I didn't mind it. It gave me time to move from those shamed, frustrated feelings seeing Jim conjured up to a kind of personal acceptance I hadn't anticipated feeling so soon after the encounter.

The truth was, I didn't need to feel bad for running into Jim or his ugliness toward me. What had all the hours of counseling been for if not to face something like this and handle it? Of course, *handling it* could look different for everyone, but in this case, I hadn't crumbled or cracked. I may have stumbled, but I hadn't fallen.

Escaping from Kugelfels, and even being away from my usual routines, had been a beautiful reprieve. It wasn't that I didn't love what I did there—I did. But I could use those routines to keep me moving forward and not stop and address what I felt.

Here in Rome, I had the dual satisfaction of gloriously vivid and beautiful surroundings but also very little to keep me from my own thoughts. That alone time I craved and needed in order to process things felt heightened here in the best way. I couldn't sink into the routines and daily activities. I couldn't go pick up toys at Eric's or help Livie with paperwork or chat with my mom about her Florida friends. I couldn't menu plan or even stress about moving.

So I faced those other, bigger feelings. And not all of them were about Jim. In fact, most of them were those nasty little fears about me.

He'd said I'd be a doormat like I'd been with him. Just thinking of his sneering face, and how true that had been of me while we were together, made me feel ill. And I'd wondered so often in the last few years... could I trust myself? Could I make responsible decisions?

But as I watched pigeons hopping around a weathered stone fountain, the answer planted itself in my chest and rooted into the very core of my being. The water glittered in the sun where it spouted and poured from one level to another. The elegant, lilting strains of Italian conversations left me with company and without disturbance. And my heart answered.

Yes.

Yes, I could trust myself. I didn't need to question every

choice I made from the time I met Jim until I died. I'd made choices that led me to him, and some of them were wrong. But dammit, some of them were right, and he was still poison. I couldn't blame myself for that anymore.

I hadn't stayed there. I was not the same person I'd been when I said yes to moving to Texas, or when I married him, or even when I left him. I'd learned and grown, and I could trust myself.

That answered a deeper question I'd been waiting to ask myself. Could I trust this choice I so desperately wanted to make—could I choose Nate and be right? Could I be with him and not bow to him, not bend and eventually flatten? And the answer to that was also yes. I'd known it all along but had been too afraid of what it'd mean if I heard the answer. Because what it meant was that I would choose Nate and pray he'd choose me and that would, I hoped, be a key in the lock of my future.

It wasn't that Nate held the key. Nate didn't unlock my path forward. It was *me*.

All of that made the trip worth it. Every moment of peace and clarity that came from those heady realizations, and of course, the time with Nate. But especially this morning, as we'd woken and blinked the world awake to find ourselves still nestled together.

His rumbly greeting and quick exit from the bed after kissing my cheek. The butterflies that stayed with me just thinking of our bodies close like that, closer, maybe every night at some point in the not-too-distant future.

Those sweet, fleeting moments gone too soon, we packed and departed quickly. Annette gave me air kisses, then hugged Nate and bid him farewell with a wobble in her voice that made me like her a little more than I had thus far. She did love her son, even if she had the strangest way of showing it.

Maddie had excused herself to meetings after breakfast, so we didn't see her when we left. But Juliet stood at the front of the villa where Paolo loaded our bags into the black sedan like it wasn't odd for her, Nate's ex, to be seeing us off.

"I'm just so happy to have met you. You're lovely. I hope you'll stay in touch." She leaned forward and hugged me.

Surprised, but not ungrateful, I hugged her back. "It was great to meet you, too."

"And maybe I'll see you at the promotion ceremony! I know it's only a few weeks away, so I'm scrambling to work it out with my schedule. I hope I can, and I'll be there to celebrate with you guys." She blew a kiss to Nate who gave her a chin nod from where he stood on the other side of the car, phone to his ear.

She scuttled back inside, and I dropped into the back seat of the car a little more heavily than I meant to.

Promotion ceremony? A few weeks away?

I knew Nate would promote to Lieutenant Colonel, and I knew that would happen soon. Somehow, I hadn't realized it was *this* soon, nor did I realize it was something friends and family came to. I remembered some of Eric's promotions over the years, but I'd missed his to LTC thanks to—well, thanks to the reason I missed everything for approximately three years of my life.

Why would Nate not tell me about this? He hadn't so much as said a word about it, had he? I racked my brain and couldn't remember anything about it. Had Eric said anything? I didn't think so; though lately, I ended up sitting with Livie talking about work or how she was feeling and the funny things the kids said about her now-visible baby belly.

A slick, cold feeling coated my veins. Did he not want me there? Was he embarrassed of me? Was he—

I shook my head and closed my eyes against those thoughts. I'd just come to the conclusion that I wanted to choose him, fully and freely. We'd only just started dating, but I knew what I wanted. This had me seriously doubting that brilliant revelation, but I couldn't just jump to that conclusion.

So much of what he'd done so far was in deference to me. He'd backed off time and again physically to respect my desire to go slowly. I suspected he'd even left me alone more during our time in Italy than he had to simply because he didn't want to pressure me in any way. Could this be something else he didn't want to push me about?

I glanced at him as he ducked into his seat, and Paolo fired up the engine.

"All good?" he asked, threading our hands together.

I nodded, but any verbal response stuck in my throat. I didn't have words yet. I needed time with this before I could just come out and ask him. But I would ask him. I wouldn't jump to conclusions without simply asking why he hadn't told me.

And I prayed with all of me it wasn't going to tear me apart when he gave me the answer.

CHAPTER THIRTY-FIVE

Nate

In the car on the way home from the Munich airport, I could no longer ignore the persistent silence from Ariel.

We'd had a good visit, I thought. My mom had lightened up a little, and the conversation had flowed easily around the table for our last meal all together this morning. I'd been busier than I anticipated, but Ariel knew I'd made plans for the time here since she wasn't originally going with me, and she'd seemed fine.

It was the goodbye that shifted things. Had Maddie said something? Had Juliet? Juliet had hugged her—they'd all seemed downright friendly. My mother hadn't made any parting comments that would hang over us. Had sleeping together—just sleeping, but still—had that changed things for her?

But then, there I went assuming everything had something to do with me. Maybe she was nervous to return here knowing her ex was still lurking and would be for weeks. The rotation would be ramping up tomorrow, thus the reason we were returning today. That I'd snuck away during the first few days of it was miraculous already, but that was only because Eric knew I'd be working incessantly over the summer and forced me to do it.

"Everything okay?" I tried, now for a third time. I was beginning to sound a little desperate, but at this point, I didn't care.

I couldn't look, but I heard her exhale.

"I'm just thinking."

"About..."

The beat before she spoke stretched out like the road ahead. My general measure of patience hung by a thread.

"I'm trying to figure out why you haven't mentioned your promotion ceremony."

"Where did that come from?"

"When Juliet hugged me. She said something about rearranging her schedule and hoping to make the promotion ceremony.'"

Ah. Nerves laced through my chest at the realization that I'd have to ask her. I couldn't put it off anymore. I shouldn't have put it off this long.

"Do you not want me there?" Her question was small.

Oh, good grief. This woman was going to kill me with her tender heart and how little she knew about my feelings for her.

"I one hundred percent, without equivocation or qualification, want you there."

She made a sound like a huff. "Then why didn't you tell me about it? I really like Juliet, but I must admit I felt stupid having her mention it and me fumble around to pretend I knew what she was talking about. I knew you were promoting soon, but I didn't even register you'd have a ceremony. I didn't go to Eric's. I didn't realize..."

I reached over and covered her hand with mine. "I've wanted to talk to you about it, but I... Crap, I'm such a wuss."

I shook my head at myself, annoyed that finding the words, even now when faced with the hurt my reticence to talk to her directly had caused, still didn't come easy. If she only knew what a coward I was—had always been.

"Why are you a wuss?"

I puffed out a breath. "I wanted to ask you for help. With organizing it. I'm doing it with another guy up at the castle, which I arranged, and he's got the programs, but there's some other stuff. And the closer it's gotten, the worse I've felt about asking, and then I didn't want you to feel pressure or like you had to do it or something weird since we're together now."

Her hand gripped mine. Damn, I wished we weren't driving so I could look at her, read her expression, see if I'd just tipped things the wrong way. Five more minutes and we'd be home.

"I would love to help." Her voice was gentle.

"Okay. Good. When we get home, I can talk through what we've got so far."

"Sounds good."

I could tell she was smiling, so I hazarded a quick glance. The lovely curve of her lips rewarded me. If we were a little further along, I could say it—the thought I'd had on the tip of my tongue for how long? The reality that I knew with more clarity every day we spent together. I'd say it—*I love you, Ariel*—and it wouldn't frighten her away.

Not happening, though. She'd been pressured for too

long. Even though my feelings for her were real and genuine and involved protecting her and loving her with every bit of me, they too could act as a form of coercion. She'd want to care for *me*. She was the kind of woman who would help her friends and family, do whatever they needed, even to what might end up being her own detriment. I would not be the source of such a compromise or sacrifice.

So, I'd keep those words shut under lock and key. For good. *For now*, that little voice whispered.

The welcome sight of home greeted us minutes later. We grabbed our bags and shuffled inside. She disappeared with her things up to her room. I washed my hands, gulped down a glass of water, and checked the fridge. We'd left it fairly empty, so I'd run to the commissary before it closed. I didn't want her on post yet—Jim might be trolling around since the rotation hadn't moved to people in the field and he seemed to have plenty of freedom, unlike most of his soldiers, no doubt.

Ariel's hand on my back startled me from my list-making daze.

I turned to her, finishing writing *bananas* on the list when I spoke. "I'll head to the commissary in a few. Did you have anything you—"

She rose on her toes and wrapped her arms around my neck. Her face was inches from mine. My pulse bolted.

"Come sit with me a minute."

Her hold loosened at my neck, and her fingers drifted over my shoulders, then down my arms in a slow caress that left little tingles behind. She clasped my hands and pulled me with her—like I wouldn't go with her. Like there was anything she could ask of me I wouldn't give her.

"What's on your mind, Wolfe?" I asked, making a stab

at not sounding like her initiating touching me made me feel both triumphant and jumpy.

"We need to have a talk. I need your full attention." She stopped next to the couch, and after releasing my hand, gestured to it.

Whoosh—a wave of anticipation and pure nervous energy crashed through me. I plunked down on the couch, not taking my eyes off her. If I'd been confused before, now I was nervous. This sounded serious. But also, the way she looked at me wasn't ... *bad*. It seemed very good. She wouldn't have touched my back or held my hand and led me over here to tell me bad news. Right? *Right?!*

She stood about a foot in front of me with arms crossed and her full bottom lip between her teeth. Her gaze rested heavy on mine, then swept over me, head to toe.

"You've got to stop trying to protect me."

My back straightened. "I'm sorry if I pushed too hard about Rome. I thought you had fun, but I was gone a lot, and maybe you didn't even want to—"

"Not about Rome. Yes, you pushed, but it was good to get away and interesting to see a little slice of your life. I'm glad I met Maddie and Juliet. I'm glad I wasn't sitting here, worrying about running into Jim."

I swallowed. "Okay. Good."

"But with your promotion, you didn't tell me because you didn't want me to feel like I *had* to help, right?"

"I don't ever want you to feel obligated to me. I don't ever want you to feel like you don't have a choice or like you owe me."

Her face softened, and a little smile flashed before she spoke. "The thing is, with you, I don't. I never have, and I can't imagine I ever will. You have always been a safe place for me."

My heart thundered in my chest. She reached out a hand, which I immediately took. She sat on the ottoman next to me. We were close enough that our legs threaded together, one of hers between mine, and vice versa.

I rarely came up short on things to say—I'd made a reputation of being laid back and easygoing, chatty and amiable. But just now, I couldn't find a word. I could hardly hear a thing beyond the blood rushing in my ears. It was like she was telling me something bad, but it was all so good, I shuddered with adrenaline in response.

She squeezed my hand again. "I promise that I will tell you no. Or tell you if something makes me uncomfortable or that I don't like something. I've had time to work on those skills that I lost during my time with Jim, and I want you to know that I pledge to use them with you."

I nodded.

"So that means you should ask me for things. You should... take a little. And I will speak up and tell you if something's not right."

Her blue eyes seemed deeper and more serious with those words. The heavy reality of her words wasn't lost on me. She'd lost the ability to say no—thinking through the implications of that would haunt me. But in this moment, this promise poured water on a part of me I hadn't realized had become parched.

"I'll do the same, then. And you should take a little too." An exhale that sounded like a laugh came out, the tension in my chest, the surging need for her to know this truth blazing in my veins. "Please understand that I've been waiting a very long time for you to take anything at all from me."

Only a quick breath, a beat. And then, Ariel took.

Her body came over me, knees on either side of my hips,

and her hands threaded into my hair. Her lips came to mine and demanded, and oh, good Lord, I'd never been more lost to a moment than this one. She controlled the movement, the breath, but my hands found purchase at her hips, then slipped around to the small of her back, then lower. The heat of her mouth on mine, the feel of her in my hands—I groaned audibly. She hummed in satisfaction and leaned closer, our chests just grazing, the general existence of this event making me wild and unskilled.

"I've wanted this—" I breathed, kissed, touched, "—for so long."

She didn't respond with words but deepened the kiss, pushed against me, and pulled at my hair, pressing her body to mine and causing my entire being to disintegrate into feelings of *finally* and *yes* and *more*.

Nothing in the world could've stopped the progress of the kiss, or my hands, or *her* hands, which now slipped down my chest. I said a silent prayer of thanks to Nick Masters, who'd helped me carve out my abs for the first time in a few years. Ariel's hands on me made every brutal, heaving workout worth it.

"You're... insane," she said, breathless and sounding just as intoxicated with desire as I felt.

"I hope that's good."

She leaned back, her eyes sparkling. "It's very good, Nate."

And then, she made it clear. She took. And it was so, so good.

Ariel

The next day, I woke alone in my room. After making out like hormone-driven teens last night, we did calm down. Nate left to get groceries while I started laundry. It all felt so normal and domestic.

But that feeling of waking up alone, of even going to sleep by myself, had started to seem silly. Granted, the thought of sleeping with Nate sent me into a mild panic. Not that we weren't fairly far down that road, but after that, we'd never recover our friendship. And maybe more to the point, I wouldn't recover my heart. There'd be no way to trick myself into believing that beautiful, safe friendship we had could be a part of my life again.

I'd always loved him. But last night, when he'd admitted to not wanting to pressure me about the promotion cere-mony, it slipped into place like the answer to a question I'd been asking all my life. *I love Nate. I'm in love with Nate.*

He'd prioritized me in ways no one ever had. He'd pushed when he thought I needed it, and he held back for the same reasons. He made mistakes with that—he didn't always know what was right, and he should've just talked to me.

But we'd fallen into this spare, thin way of being around each other since last summer, and so talking through all our thoughts and feelings would take time. We'd done well so far, but I couldn't blame him for not verbalizing every moment of concern he had.

I wanted him to know how I felt, and I desperately wanted him to tell me how he felt. After the time in Italy, I felt both closer to, and farther away from, the idea that we could be together and work out—really work out. I'd kept myself from thinking long term or from running too far ahead, hoping to protect my heart and mind from mistakes I'd made before.

But before I did that, and before we moved forward, I needed to talk to Jim. When I'd told Nate this, he'd gone silent on me. We'd had dinner, had finished cleaning up, and were folding the last pieces of the final load of laundry I'd just pulled from the dryer when I said it.

"I'm going to try to find Jim and talk to him after the X-days." The busier portion of the rotation would mean he and most everyone involved would be out in the training area twenty-four seven for the next two weeks. I hated that I had to wait now that I knew what I wanted to say and that whatever he said to me couldn't hurt me, but after years of waiting to arrive at *this* point, I could do it.

"You—" He swallowed and inhaled slowly. "Okay."

"What were you going to say?"

"It seems like a bad idea to me." His usually smiling face had hardened.

"I can understand that. But I think I need this opportunity. We didn't talk hardly at all during the divorce—our lawyers handled everything, and he only snuck in a few parting shots."

He winced.

"I can handle it. I can."

I could. Part of why I'd been so thrown by him last weekend was thanks to all the times I'd confronted him in my mind in the years before. But I hadn't managed to say any of the things I'd imagined I would—I'd hardly been able to speak at all and then felt so ashamed of myself.

And with a little space and distance this week, thanks to the ridiculous Reynolds villa and gelato and Nate and even Maddie and Juliet, I'd come to a realization. It wasn't the same shame I'd felt so often in that relationship—that of being caught and feeling like I should've known better. Being bruised and lonely and sad and then ashamed for choosing those things. No.

It was frustration with myself for not saying what I'd wanted to say—for not giving myself the closure I'd wanted for years but hadn't seen a way to actually get. I'd never expected him to be here in Kugelfels, but I was so much stronger now than when I left him. I was stronger now than I was when we met, for that matter. And I had things to say.

"I don't want you hurt," Nate said, his voice gruff.

I set down the T-shirt I'd folded and wrapped my arms around him. "Thank you. It won't be comfortable, that's for sure, but I think it's important."

He'd hugged me back, only a nod to acknowledge. He had strong feelings about this, probably wanted to say I shouldn't do it at all, but he just hugged me back for a while, then kissed my forehead, and we finished folding.

A man like that? You don't let go.

Except I did let him go because he had to be up crazy early to dive into the work. I rolled out and resumed my routine, but Livie grabbed me and stared me down when we met for lunch. She'd insisted the day before, said she could sneak out and meet me at one of the little cantinas, so I did as instructed.

Before she even said a word, Bec, Emily, Katie, and Summer walked in.

Livie spoke first. "Eric called. A little birdy told him you're planning to talk to Jim, and he flipped his lid. I'm honestly less concerned about that than I am about your romantic getaway to Italy with Nate."

"Seriously. That man? in Rome? I'd take either one, but both at once? Get the smelling salts." Emily brought her hand to her forehead like she felt faint as we all took places in the line.

"Let's get food first, at least," Summer suggested.

I sent her a grateful smile. I hadn't anticipated talking about all of this with the group. I didn't mind, especially now that I felt steadier and more decided about things. But I'd imagined just me and Livie, so I needed to shift gears mentally.

A few minutes later, we'd all ordered, filled our bowls from the little salad bar cart, and placed our numbers in the center of the table so the staff could find us when the pizza someone had demanded we share was ready.

"So you went on a romantic vacation to Rome with Nate?" Bec asked before taking a bite of lettuce.

"It wasn't like that," I said, chuckling at the eager glint in her eye.

"Explain it, then, please," Emily said, though her please was clearly forced.

"I saw my ex-husband Jim at the fest last weekend. It

threw me for a loop. Nate found out and went into fix-it mode, and next thing I knew, I was walking through the doors of his family's giant Roman villa." The memories of meeting his mother, of seeing Juliet the first time, of the time we'd spent together, flashed through my mind.

"Oh. Damn, I'm sorry." Emily's voice sounded genuinely repentant this time.

"I'm not sure if sorry is right, but I am sorry you had to see your ex if you weren't expecting it." Katie spoke for the first time. She almost always had a soft way of seeing things, but her insights were excellent.

"Thanks."

"So what's this about you trying to talk to Jim?" Livie prompted before devouring a bite of currywurst on a bun.

"It's time. I can't explain it any other way than that. The time in Italy gave me the space to realize that, and the run-in with Jim obviously kicked off that line of thinking."

I poked at my salad but didn't eat. Nerves filled my belly, my appetite nonexistent since I'd seen my friends walk in after Livie. It wasn't so much them as it was knowing I'd have to confront some big things happening. Left to myself, they didn't seem so large, but gauging other peoples' reactions could be extremely intimidating.

"Are you sure?" Livie asked gently.

"I am. Please trust me. I wouldn't do it if I wasn't."

"You know you don't have to, right? You don't ever have to confront him if you don't want to," Summer said and squeezed my hand.

"Yes. I do. Honestly, if I hadn't seen him accidentally, I'm not sure I ever would've wanted to. But the way I reacted last weekend... I just need to do this. For myself."

"Do you want us with you?" Summer asked, and every one of them nodded and chimed in.

"I'll be there."

"Absolutely."

"Name the time."

"Yes."

My heart nearly burst with love and gratitude. "Thank you, but no. I'm going to see how Eric would feel about going with me, but I'm going to speak to him alone."

~

"You say the word, I deck him and we go." Eric's gruff, almost irritable voice cut through the odd haze that'd settled into my mind.

"You're not going to hit him. You'd get in trouble. Plus, I think since we're doing this in a public place, he'll be on good behavior."

I'd planned it that way. Toward the end of the rotation, I'd cornered Eric at his house. He was furious with me for wanting to talk with Jim, but he also knew me well enough to know I wouldn't change my mind. He'd insisted on being there, and I'd told him that was why I had asked him, and why I hadn't bothered telling Nate not to share my plan with him in the first place.

But I knew Jim, or at least I used to, and I knew he'd be angry with me for even thinking I could speak my mind. Or maybe more so, not being terrified of him anymore. I'd planned to meet him outside the PX building. There was a nice little grass area with benches and a fountain. No one would be sitting there this time of day, but there'd still be people milling around. I wouldn't be walled in, and I could walk away any time. And if he got it in his head to touch me or anything else I didn't want, I'd run. And Eric would have my back.

"I'm just saying. One word."

I didn't respond, because all desire to joke around had fled an hour ago when I left the house before Nate got back. He'd asked if he could be here with me, and I'd said no. I knew it'd hurt him, but I also knew it was the right choice.

Jim sauntered up from the left, and my heart shot out of the gates.

"What's this, now?"

"I wanted to say a few things." My voice sounded thin and small, probably a lot like it always used to when I spoke to him. I cleared my throat. "And you're going to listen."

"Oh, am I?" He had that same amused but slightly pitying look on his face. "You here to tell me you're sorry and you want me back?"

My ire boiled over, and that was all I needed.

"I want you to know I forgive you. Not for your sake, but for mine. I also forgive myself. And with all of that, I'm going to forget you, Jim. And I'm going to live a long, happy life without you. I'm with someone who knows how to love, and—"

His face hardened, and his lips pursed into a mean little squiggle. "You'll never forget me, Ariel, because I've got part of you that you can't get back. If some other idiot's signed up for you, you'll do the same as you did with me. You'll forget who you think you are. You'll become a mousy little doormat, willing to obey orders and do as you're told, just like you should."

Molten rage pushed up from my chest and into my throat. "Whatever you think you took, you can have. I'm whole, happy, and I'm not looking back. I hope you'll get yourself some help so you don't hurt anyone else, but I'm pretty sure you won't."

"You little—"

"And you're done. Get out of here before I call the MPs and report you, *again*." Eric's voice brooked no arguments. He'd called the MPs the day he'd showed up to drive me out of the house and he'd seen my arm in a splint. We'd reported the abuse, but I'd let too much slide, and Jim had too many friends in high places for it to get him in much trouble.

"We're not done," Jim spat.

"We're past done. I hope I never see you again, but if I do, you keep walking. Goodbye."

I whipped around and marched back to the car, Eric just behind me. He got in, cranked the ignition, and we were driving off post before I fully caught my breath. I didn't have the same hunted feeling I'd had even weeks ago when I'd fled with Summer.

"Did you say what you needed to?"

I nodded but didn't speak. I could feel the tension in my shoulders, my neck, my jaw, but I couldn't breathe deeply enough to ease it just yet. I focused on the tall pines slipping past my passenger window and dug my fingernails into my wrist whenever I felt the urge to cry welling up. I'd cried way too many tears for myself, for the loss the years with Jim were, for the damage he'd done.

He *had* taken something from me. In truth, he'd taken a lot. But most of that, I'd earned back. I was slowly but surely rebuilding self-confidence, and I'd gotten over my total inability to be around other people before I'd ever gotten to Germany, thankfully. But he'd stolen that hopeful, dreamy girl I used to be from me, and until this moment, I didn't know how or if I'd get her back.

Sitting next to Eric driving like the bank was on fire behind us and the gold bars were stowed in the trunk, I knew. He hadn't kept that either. Because here I was, hopeful for whatever came next. I wanted it with Nate. I wanted a life with him, and I prayed he wanted that with me. But beyond all that, I had hope for a full life, a life of dreams and joy and beauty. A life without isolation or hopelessness.

Some small tenacious part of me had held out and resisted. That was the part that had called Eric instead of staying quiet again. That was the part that had come here. That was the part that had said yes to Nate, and who'd found the courage to love him.

CHAPTER THIRTY-SEVEN

Nate

My mother and Maddie smiled at me with identical bright white grins.

"You do look handsome in that uniform," my mom said with a hint of acquiescence, like my looking good in the uniform compensated for the failure I was overall.

"You really do. Has Ariel seen you yet?" Maddie brushed a mini lint roller down my arm.

A pang shot through me. "No. I actually haven't seen her much in the last few weeks, and then today she was up super early to get ready for stuff, and I've been running around..."

Something major had happened to her yesterday when she spoke to Jim, and we hadn't discussed it. I'd broken down and texted Eric last night because I couldn't handle not knowing, and I couldn't bring myself to pressure her into talking.

Eric's response was vague but disturbing. *"He was his typical trashpile self. She seemed shaken after, but not wrecked. Confirmed she said what she needed to. I think it went as well as it could."*

What could he have said to her in the five minutes they'd spoken? What would make Eric call him that, or was it just his general hatred of the man?

"Seriously? She's barely talked to you? Is she about to ghost you after this ceremony or something?"

I shot her a disapproving frown. "No. She's had a lot going on. I was on rotation and not home for the bulk of that—don't make assumptions. Plus, after you see how good everything looks and realize how much work she put in on a crazy short timeline, you're going to feel bad about that. I thought you guys got along?"

I needed them to get along, and knowing they'd hung out in Italy had made me happier than it probably should have.

"We did. But if she's jerking you around here, I'm not going to stay quiet. It's been long enough."

My stomach flipped. *It's been long enough*—fair. And while I wasn't proud of it, I had a plan for today. Because my feelings for Ariel, those I'd thought couldn't become any more intense or unmanageable, had ballooned out the roof during the rotation and not being with her. I'd worried constantly—about Jim, about her talking to Jim, about how she felt about me. We'd kept in touch via text, but it'd been casual. Sweet notes and wishes for having good days, hoping things were going well, that kind of thing.

Our last real time together had been nothing short of amazing. But then life crept back in, and she'd kept her distance. Or maybe I had. Or maybe the distance had come purely thanks to the rotation and being gone constantly. Whatever the case, doubt yawned ahead and I couldn't shake it.

So today, I'd push. I'd *take*. I'd be honest, like I'd promised her I would. And it would either result in something amazing, or it would be one textbook example of self-sabotaging something good. I hoped to God it was the former.

Returning to the moment at hand, I approached and looked at Maddie, noting that lingering tightness around her eyes and mouth. She looked no more rested than she had when we'd arrived in Italy. Her plan to relax there must not've worked, not that it came as a surprise since she worked full days and then some every day that I saw.

"It's okay, Maddie," I said gently.

She nodded and loosed a sigh. "Okay then."

"All right, it's time to get in there. Let's go."

I held an arm out to her, which she took with a small reluctant smile. My mom had already wandered in to take one of the few seats. The town *burg*, or castle, sat elevated above the rest of the small downtown and the houses of the most densely populated part of town. Great stone walls kept out ancient enemies or, for this afternoon, kept in the guests for the ceremony. Inside the castle itself, the interior was the size of a large swimming pool with two-story ceilings, the walls had been painted a bright creamy white color.

Paired with the bright June sun, the whole room looked lit up. Guests found seats and standing room all over the circular space as I dropped Maddie next to my mom and walked back to the side.

First up, Carl Weldon's promotion. He was a good guy, and it was handy that we could share the festivities because it let us do the ceremony here. I smiled and watched as the commander of the post conducted his oath of office—a unique feature of this promotion since we didn't repeat that at every rank. I laughed and smiled during his speech, but a frantic feeling built in my chest. A little nervous energy, yes, but need, too. I needed to see Ariel. Despite my denial, Maddie's suspicion and concern had joined arms with my own and were running away together.

That, and the reality of what I had planned. *Crap, this could go so, so wrong.*

Just then, a hand gently squeezed my arm. I turned and my heart kicked at the sight of her. She'd worn a light blue dress today, something that matched the infantry cord roping across my right shoulder. Her eyes, her dress, and the blue Bavarian June sky all matched.

"Everything okay?" she whispered, tilting her face up closer to my ear.

"Looks amazing. You okay?"

She smiled, then focused on Carl as he wrapped up his speech. When he finished and everyone clapped, I stood straighter and inhaled slowly. I didn't mind crowds, especially when they were full of friends, but I couldn't deny I was nervous. In fact, I didn't recall the last time I'd been *this* nervous.

Just before I walked into the center of attention, she said, "Nate. Are you sure?"

"Certain."

Her lashes fluttered, and she nodded. I'd told her I wanted her to attach one of my shoulder boards. Traditionally, an officer chose loved ones or friends. If I were married, I'd ask my wife. Eric had asked Delia and Robby, with the help of his mom. Me? I wanted Ariel, and Maddie would do the other side. I had no doubt about it, but the choice held meaning, and she knew it. *Hint number one, Wolfe.*

Once Captain Rob Waverly, the emcee for the event, had introduced Eric, the fun really began.

"Come on out here, Major Reynolds." Eric waved me out to the center of the open space.

He shook my hand, and then I stood to the side. We went through the official motions—introducing my old mentor, now Brigadier General Slocum, calling everyone to attention, and Slocum saying a few nice things about how we met, what a good officer I was, and so on before introducing Maddie and Ariel.

And then, Eric stepped up. Since General Slocum was here, we'd changed the structure a bit, but Eric had insisted he get to say a few words about me. And though I was honored Slocum had made the effort to come, Eric's words made my throat tighten.

"I've known Nate since he was a baby in this Army. He was this cocky little hotshot just out of Ranger school, but just as soon as I thought I had him pegged, he surprised me. The moment I knew I wanted to know him as a friend, he was propping up a fellow lieutenant who'd fallen during a run and bloodied up his knees. It was always like that with him—one minute he's making jokes and winning Mr. Congeniality of a group, and the next he's encouraging some private to think about college credits to help with promotion points. He had that balance of self-confidence and care. And if you're here, you know that well, because the man he is today is just the same."

An amused, accordant murmur rose from the crowd and all eyes pinned on me. I smiled but bowed my head, feeling honored and overwhelmed and so grateful, I might not be able to speak if he didn't wrap it up soon.

But Eric was on a roll, so he continued. "Nate Reynolds is the kind of quality person anyone would be lucky to have in their lives, and the Army is very smart to continue promoting and placing trust in him. And you better believe he's the best if I'm letting him date my sister."

A few guffaws and a handful of stifled chuckles burst out then. I glanced to see Ariel's cheeks bright, but her face smiling and her head shaking. I thanked God she took the joke, and the public announcement of our relationship, that well. Hopefully, this boded well for what I had planned.

"Nate is a man who will make the right choice. He's a soldier who will follow orders with intelligence and integrity. He's a leader in this military who cares for his people and the mission. Honestly, he's like a well-dressed unicorn."

Damn, I was going to have to get him for that one, but he had me laughing along with the crowd.

He turned to me. "I couldn't be happier or more honored to celebrate with you. But first, let's hear the official orders."

Captain Thatcher Wild stepped up to the podium and read the orders announcing my promotion while all the military personnel stood at attention. Then Eric came and administered the oath, in which I swore to protect and defend the nation against all enemies. Then Maddie and Ariel approached, one on each side, and removed the old boards signifying the rank I'd held for the last six years and slipped the new ones into place. They paused next to me for a photo, and then left me to speak.

"Thank you all for coming and celebrating with us. I'm honored to share this day with Lieutenant Colonel Weldon and his family and extremely honored to have Brigadier General Slocum here as well. As for you, Colonel Wolfe?

You'll get yours." I gave him a broad smile, and everyone laughed.

I thanked my family, though simply said "my parents" instead of individual notes of thanks to my mom and dad, because honestly, they'd hardly supported my career, so more than that would've been disingenuous. I spent most of my time acknowledging Maddie and gave Eric some ribbing right back by mentioning that if I was a well-dressed unicorn, he was a grumpy, disorganized werewolf. And finally, I thanked Ariel.

I inhaled slowly, willing the nerves that'd been crawling up my throat back down. This was it. Now or never. Fifteen years in the making, and I was finally going to man up and... be honest.

"Thanks to my girlfriend, Ariel, whom I've known just about as long as I've known her brother, for being amazing."

My eyes flickered to her to find a soft smile and still-flushed cheeks. Good grief, she was gorgeous, and I couldn't believe I got to call her that here in public. She would've merited my thanks as a friend, too, but I loved this new dimension to us. And with that in mind, I pressed on.

"You've been supportive of me in small ways for years, and today especially, you've outdone yourself. Ariel organized the catering and the flowers, which honestly hadn't even occurred to me. So, thank you." And before I lost it, before the bravado of the moment and the plan of the last few weeks slipped away, I continued. "And Eric, I guess I should say thanks again for not murdering me for being in love with your sister for at least a third of my life. Cheers, everybody. Thanks so much. Drink all the beer, eat all the food, and make sure you come say hi before you leave."

I stepped away from the center of the room, a stream of nervous *holy crap, what have I done* obscenities scrolling through my mind like a ticker tape. Loud applause filled the echoing space, but it became muted in my ears. I shook hands, smiled, and thanked the general, the colonels who'd come, all the fellow officers, and NCOs and their families.

All the while, the truth sloshed around in my gut. I'd said it. *Holy shit*, like I'd planned and even rehearsed, I'd said it. I'd just told the room full of people I was in love with Ariel before I'd ever said it to her. And now I had to find her, because she was nowhere in sight.

CHAPTER THIRTY-EIGHT

Ariel

He'd actually just said that. Out loud. In a room full of people.

Could he mean that?

He couldn't mean that. That was insane.

He hadn't been in lo— I swallowed. I could hardly think the word without my stomach tumbling and my mouth drying out. Did that mean he loved me now? Sure seemed like it, but he hadn't told me! He hadn't told *me*.

Maybe it was a joke. Just another little barb at—

"Can I talk to you for a minute?" Maddie ducked to catch my eye.

"Of course."

My voice sounded weird. I felt weird. I felt like I used to when I'd wake up from one of those dreams where you get to school and you're naked. I pressed a hand to my chest and, yes, my dress was still there. *Thank God.*

I followed Maddie out the side exit and onto the cobblestone that paved the castle's grounds closest to the indoor structure. Farther out, it featured grassy lanes zigzagging down terraces until it reached the streets. I'd wandered around earlier, nerves and anticipation at being here, being a part of this, absolutely driving me insane.

Little did I know it would get much more intense. I couldn't have imagined the untenable mix of feeling making my hands shake and my breath come up short.

"So."

Maddie's tone in that one word sent a spike of alarm through me, not that I wasn't already flashing with all kinds of concern all by myself.

"So. Everything okay?" I asked, voice as soothing as I could make it.

"You tell me."

"Sorry?"

"I want you to tell me what you're doing with my brother."

She crossed her arms, and, *wow*, could she pull off intimidating. Her navy suit fit her perfectly, her heels were high and red-bottomed, her hair a sleek spout out of her ponytail, makeup utter perfection.

"I'm—we're dating."

Or, I thought we were. *We are?* I didn't know, because he'd just lobbed a truth grenade into the middle of the room, and I only just now felt the first stabs of anger pressing into my chest as the reality of what'd just happened registered by degrees.

Her eyes narrowed. "Obviously, you know it's more than that for him."

Something had always been a little strained between me and Maddie in Italy, but I'd assumed that was either my self-consciousness and general awkwardness with new people, or the simple fact that my appearance had been a surprise. Or that she wanted Juliet with Nate, and not me. But I hadn't felt she didn't like me, in particular.

At this moment, every second that ticked by seemed to add up to that end more definitively.

When I didn't speak, she did again.

"Listen, you have to realize that what he said was true."

"It can't be," I said, the thought bursting through me like it had from the second the words left his lips.

He can't mean this. He would've told me. We promised we'd be honest.

"It is. He's been talking about you for almost fifteen years, Ariel. He's ended every good relationship he had if he thought you were free. When you got married... I'd never seen him more upset. When you got divorced? He dumped Juliet."

My chest hollowed out. That couldn't be right. He'd always been with someone else. He'd never said a word. Until last summer, he'd never so much as given me a look that made me think he wanted anything from me. "I'm sorry. I didn't know. I didn't—"

"It doesn't matter what happened before. What I'm asking of you is that you don't keep stringing him along. You can't pretend you didn't know anymore. He just told you, so now you know. And I'm guessing that conversation between the two of you is coming very soon, plus *I'm* telling you. If you don't love him back, more than you've ever loved anyone else, you tell him *tonight*. I won't watch him waste any more time on you."

With that, she whipped around and marched off, those red-bottomed heels carrying her away like they were sneakers and not spike-heeled pumps on uneven cobblestone. I stared after her, basically shocked into silence and a numb mind.

She'd been fierce and almost angry, but if what she said was true, it made sense. She must think I'd known and been giving him false hope, or something, all this time. Even if I didn't factor in his breaking up with Juliet coinciding with my divorce, which was insane and scary—and yet also made me feel weirdly... good—Maddie must think I was a monster.

I shut my eyes as a breeze whirled past me, little cherry blossom petals dancing along the stones at my feet.

"Ariel, sorry, do you know where the other racks of beer are?" Thatcher Wild popped his head out with an apologetic smile.

With every bit of control I'd developed over the years of practice, I pushed down the roiling thoughts and smiled back at him. "Of course. Let me come help."

For the rest of the afternoon, I milled around, chatting with people, meeting Eric's friends, Nate's friends, Livie's friends. Bec, Emily, Summer, Katie, and their dates were in attendance, and that gave me a few moments of respite to relax between checking that the large brown bottles of Nate's favorite locally brewed beer hadn't run out or replacing the delicious pretzel bread sandwiches I'd gotten from the caterer. Fortunately, they all seemed to sense I did not want to talk about Nate's pronouncement. I was in hostess mode and loved feeling capable and welcoming, but I knew I'd crash, and crash hard, in a few hours. I hoped I could get everything cleaned up before that happened.

I hoped I'd manage to keep the thoughts pressing in at all corners of my mind at bay for just a while longer.

Nate and I hadn't spoken alone thanks to the crowd of people waiting to congratulate him, catch up, and keep him busy all afternoon. They—he—deserved that. But he'd given me those eyes that made my stomach flip and my pulse race. Whether those reactions were from love or fury, I couldn't tell. The thoughts in my head ran hot and heavy.

My brain: *He loves you!*

Then also my brain: *Yeah, and he told literally everyone else before he told you! Oh and PS, he lied to you for over a decade!*

He'd introduced people to me, and more than one person had congratulated me on Nate's promotion. Like I'd done anything. But it made sense, I guessed—people congratulated Carl's wife. For her, she had put in work—supporting his career, taking care of their kids, generally enabling the success of her husband. She *should* be congratulated.

I'd never done anything like this with Jim. He hadn't had any promotions in the three years we were together, but obviously he'd promoted since the divorce. He'd been a major when we'd started dating. Aside from that, he'd said he didn't like me to be around other soldiers because it'd give me ideas—whatever that meant.

So I did relish being here with Nate, being a part of his celebration in a way that felt meaningful. They thanked me, and though I didn't deserve it, I did feel so proud of him. Not everyone made it this far. Not everyone had this kind of crowd there to celebrate this milestone. People showed up for him because he was that kind of man.

Not that any part of me had doubted him. He'd always

been like this. He could bring people together. He could draw out the best in people.

He could draw out the best in me.

Now I just needed to find out what'd been holding him back for so long, and why he hadn't told me before he shared it with a castle full of acquaintances. Why he'd promised to be honest and then very clearly gone back on that.

I caught his eye as I took a load out to the car. He stood chatting with the general who'd come to support him, and I didn't want to interrupt. Eric hustled behind me, his arms full of empty plastic beer bottle racks and a few long wooden boards the sandwiches had been placed on.

"You head home. Livie and I will get everything else. Mom's going to take the kids back."

"You sure? I signed up for this. I don't mind."

He shook his head. "I'm guessing you have a conversation waiting for you, and you've been here all day. Head home. We'll get the stuff, and we'll get you the caterer's equipment to return tomorrow."

I nodded, a blush heating my cheeks. "Okay. Thanks."

I turned back to the car and shut the full trunk.

"Ariel."

Eric's voice halted my progress in the driver's seat, and I leaned out to hear him. His brow was furrowed, and he looked particularly big-brotherly.

"Any concerns? Want me to tell him to—"

"No. Send him home. I think it's time we finally had this talk."

But before that, I texted Summer, asking her if I could swing by her house. She and Nick had left minutes before, and she responded immediately saying to come any time.

~

I kept my mind blank of feeling, letting the quiet of the car cushion me for the short drive to Summer's. I needed to process this because I knew what lay underneath all of this willful ignoring my feelings.

Fear and hurt. Wild, raving fear that I'd been trusting someone who'd been lying to me for years and hurt because I felt shredded that he'd told me in a room full of people, most of whom I'd never even met.

When I pulled into her driveway, her front door swung open and she shuffled out still wearing her dress and heels.

"That was..."

It crushed in then. My eyes watered and my throat clenched, but I cleared it. "A steaming pile of BS?"

Summer reared back. "You think he lied?"

I crossed my arms, tucking them so tight, it would've been uncomfortable if I hadn't had so much anger crashing through me now. "Oh, he lied. Over and over again. He said he loved me for how long, and yet *this* is the first time he's told me? Really?"

She let out a loud breath. "Oh, wow. I don't think I realized he hadn't told you. That's more of an omission, if anything, but I get feeling blindsided. I figured we just hadn't caught up and..."

I jerked my head to the side in a quick shake. "Nope. That was it."

And if that was the only problem—the delivery—then I'd be fine. It'd all be fine.

But...

"You don't seem happy at all. I guess I figured this was ultimately what you wanted with him, but obviously, that's not quite right."

Her pitying expression made my stomach clutch. "It's—I can't even explain it. I think I need to go and... I don't know."

I couldn't find my words. I wanted to hash this out with her, clarify my thoughts, but I felt like screaming. Me. *Me.* And Summer wasn't the one who needed to hear it.

She reached for me and pulled me into a quick hug. "Do what you need to do. Get it out there, but hear him out too, okay? He's a—"

"He's the best guy, Summer, and honestly, that might be part of the problem."

I slammed my car door, grateful she understood my mood and wouldn't take that personally.

This anger boiling in my belly came from his keeping this from me for so long. Not just since last summer. For far, far longer than that. We'd talked over and over about being open. About going slow, yes, but also about telling the truth. *He* was the one who'd insisted we promise each other to always tell the truth. And who was the one lying all this time? Who'd kept something huge from me for weeks, let alone years?

Add to that that he'd coddled me. *Again.* After promising me not three weeks ago that he'd stop leaving everything up to me. Sure, it was different than Jim's choosing for me, but he was still taking my choices away by never making ones of his own. He'd kept this from me—this huge, unwieldy secret—and he hadn't given me a choice until just now. Until so, so late.

Too late? My aching heart wondered.

Thoughts I so often tried not to entertain flashed through me—*what-ifs.* I'd banished that kind of thinking after a particularly hard but important therapy session. Thinking things like *What if I'd never met Jim?* only served to make me spiral into regret and self-recrimination.

But now?

What if he'd said something sooner?

What if we'd tried earlier?

What if we'd stayed together?

What if we'd been together all this time, living this moment with so many years behind us already?

Those thoughts fueled me despite knowing they weren't helping. I pulled into the house to find the driveway empty —good. I'd have a few more minutes to myself before I faced him. I didn't want to shut down and go cold. And part of me knew I wouldn't.

Not this time. Because the fury that burned in me would have to come out—I couldn't keep it locked up when I faced him now, in private, and could finally confront him about what I'd just discovered was a more-than-decade-long secret he'd kept from me.

CHAPTER THIRTY-NINE

Nate

Eric came tromping back inside, hands empty of the last load he'd taken. But Ariel wasn't behind him.

I'd been stuck talking to Slocum, and as much as I was thankful he'd come and wanted to, I hated that Ariel had taken the brunt of setup and take down. Maddie had disappeared to escort my mom to a car—apparently, she'd overheated or something, but mostly, she needed an excuse to leave. I'd seen Maddie chatting with Emily Wender in the corner a while ago. The crowd had thinned and several people had been helping to clean up, but...

General Slocum offered his hand one last time before he slipped out the door, off to whatever next important thing he had to do. All the other higher-ups had left when the beer had run out a half hour ago.

"Where's Ariel?" I asked Eric as he approached.

"She left."

My stomach clenched and my heart stalled. "What? She left?"

He stared at me a moment, those trademark Wolfe blue eyes stilling me and the rising panic in my chest. "She said to send you home when you could get free. You're overdue for a chat."

That dead beat in my chest started hammering now. "Guess we are."

"Yeah."

I nodded, not sure what else to say. He and I were maybe due for a chat too, but there was one far more important, and it was waiting for me. *She* was waiting for me.

I made the rounds despite my heart tripping over itself, thanking everyone left. So many people had showed—an embarrassment of riches, really. But knowing I might've messed everything up between me and the woman I loved—the woman literally everyone now knew I loved—had me shaking. Eager to get home. Almost irritable to be done with this moment and go find out my fate. *Our fate.*

I'd pushed, and it really could go the other way. She might be scared off, or she might not want to sign up for being with someone who was so gone for her these last few months of her time in Germany. Or she might not be able to stand that my feelings outpaced hers by so much—by so freaking much. If I'd just shot myself in the foot with her, I couldn't go back now. That'd been my plan, after all. Do something I couldn't take back—no amount of ignoring or distancing would erase this like we'd tried doing after last summer. No chance to say I'd misspoken or she'd misinterpreted.

I gathered tablecloths and made sure Ariel's friends took vases of flowers with them. Eric and Livie carried a large arrangement and a few straggler items, and Maddie walked with me to the car. Her own car, complete with driver, sat waiting.

"I hope you make her talk to you," Maddie said, her voice a little gritty and tired-sounding.

"I will. I'm heading there now. And I think she's ready."

She pursed her lips but nodded.

"But listen. At the risk of being an overbearing older brother, you need to get some rest. You need a real vacation. You're exhausted, and I hate it."

Her lips flattened, and I could've sworn tears shined in her eyes before she blinked them away and cleared her throat. "I know. I've booked a trip to a little ski town in Utah this summer. I'm just going to hike and get high off the thin air. Maybe if I like it, I'll work the winter there instead of the city."

Hope for her welled in me. "I hope you do that. Please do it."

She nodded, hugged me, then slumped into the waiting leather, shut herself in, and off she went. I waved, then jogged the half block to my own car and had to mentally talk myself down from speeding after shucking my blues uniform jacket and tossing it into the passenger seat. Last thing I needed was to have a run-in with the *Polizei* on the way to talk to Ariel and have something crazy happen. That'd be my luck, wouldn't it?

My heart hadn't truly calmed since I'd finished my heroic little speech and shared my deepest feelings with a roomful of people. That could prove to be one of the dumbest things I'd ever done, and I knew for a fact nothing but talking with Ariel would tell me which way it'd gone. I couldn't guess, because she hadn't done anything but be gracious and friendly and a consummate hostess, as always, for the rest of the party. No lingering looks or wide smiles or furious glances. Honestly, I would've felt better if she'd done any of that, because it would've clued me in. I was walking in the dark here, completely unable to see what lay ahead for us.

I inhaled slowly and exhaled just the same, pushing out the air and willing the nerves to calm. But I knew damn well the only way they'd truly settle was to see her again, to get a feel for where we stood.

I couldn't have ruined everything, could I?

Yes, you damn well could've, idiot. It's what you do.

She'd looked shocked, then Maddie had pulled her away. And then there was the distance between us—since the rotation, and her talking to Jim, and maybe other things? Maybe her feelings had shifted in the other direction, and there I was, standing up in front of everyone I knew here, spewing my feelings all over everyone.

That was a disgusting image, but thanks, Nate.

My inner monologue was as stressed as the rest of me. Pulling into the drive, seeing her car there, my heart jumped to my throat. All the deep breathing in the world couldn't tamp down the insane beating in my chest and at my temples.

I parked the car and turned it off but gave myself just a second—just a moment to sit in the silence of the car and hope. And pray. For whatever fool reason, this woman had been the unwitting and unrelenting love of my life. Now she *knew* that.

A sick feeling slid over me. I swallowed against it and pushed out of the car. I'd been in battle, and I'd been to war. I'd faced the real potential for death and injury, and I'd seen others meet those realities in ways that changed me. That fear was a primal, bone-deep one. If I'd stood up under those moments, under that pressure and terror, then I could walk into this house and have this conversation with Ariel.

Right?

Seconds later, I'd grabbed my jacket, the bag I'd taken with me, and a small load of things Eric or someone else must've loaded into the back of my car at some point. That was good—having full hands would be useful. Then I wouldn't run directly to her and beg her to talk to me.

The whole day had been surreal, but this minute felt oddly mechanical. Open door, drop keys and wallet, slip off dress shoes and pick them up. No Ariel. *Thump.* My heart beat heavy in my chest.

Ascend the stairs, toss jacket on the bed and bag on the floor. *Thump, thump.*

Stand uselessly for ten seconds, then embrace that I couldn't stay up here and change and pretend like everything was normal. *Thump.* Head back downstairs, shoeless, in my blue pants with a yellow tuxedo stripe, black socks, and white dress class A shirt and black tie.

"Oh, you're back." Ariel had just stepped out of her room. She still wore the blue dress—still looked perfect.

The heavy beats turned to a sprint just standing there.

"Yeah. Didn't mean to startle you." My voice sounded weird. I was *being* weird. Crap.

"Of course you didn't." She shook her head, then glanced toward the stairs with a small lift of her chin. "Do you want to..."

"Yeah. Yes. Let's do it."

Dear God, I sounded like an imbecile. Had I become a plucky teen from a D.A.R.E. commercial? For that matter, did they even have those anymore? Probably not.

Good grief, man. Chill out.

"I thought everything went really well today. How did you feel about it?" she asked as she hit the ground floor.

"It was great—better than great. It looked good, the food was awesome, the beer was perfect—I don't know how you did all that in so little time, but thank you. I know Carl and Cindy were grateful too."

Cindy had been hugely pregnant for what felt like months, and she'd been placed on bed rest recently. Carl and I had insisted she didn't need to do anything. We could keep it simple—the castle setting would be special, and we'd round up some lemonade and a few racks of beer and call it good. Fortunately for us both, Ariel had come to the rescue. Too bad I hadn't manned up and just asked her months ago.

"She already said thank you and handed me a very nice hand-written note today. I'm so glad she could come. Seemed like it was good for her mental health to get out of the house."

"Yeah."

I followed her into the kitchen. She filled two glasses with water from the fridge, handed me one, and moved to the living room. I followed her there too. This was fast becoming a metaphor for my life, and I had to say something or I'd burst.

"So..."*Remember that time I said I'd been in love with you for a minute?*

She sat in her usual spot on the couch, set her drink on the tray sitting on the ottoman, and met my gaze.

"Have a seat, Nate."

My stomach flipped at the sound of my name, but I obeyed. Our time had come, and I'd know if my push had shoved us into something irretrievable. It was what I'd wanted—what I'd resolved to do, even if right now I couldn't quite remember the logic of the decision.

"I'm sorry I said it in front of everyone. But I couldn't stand the thought of a repeat of last summer. I couldn't do that. I said it in a room full of fifty people, or however many, so there were witnesses. So we couldn't pretend and try to go back."

There it was. Exactly that. We'd move forward, or we'd stop.

She got up and paced a few steps away, then turned back and, *holy shit.* The formal veneer was off and she was pissed. I'd never actually seen her angry, but there it was.

"And by *it,* you mean the thing about you being in love with me for the last ten plus years? That *it?*" Her arms were crossed tightly over her chest, her mouth pinched into an unhappy frown.

"Yes. I know it was—"

"It was you choosing for me. Again. *Again.* And we just talked about this. About you not doing that, not smoothing the path or easing the way or pressuring me or whatever excuse you've made for yourself that has justified you lying to me for the last decade, and especially the last few months." Her voice shook, but her words came clear and sharp.

My heart punched against my ribs. "It's not an excuse. I wasn't coddling you or trying to do anything. All those years, it didn't seem right. It... it wasn't right. And since you moved here, I couldn't pressure you with this. It was too much. Ariel, you know how it's been for you, far better than I do. And I—"

"Thank you, Nate. Thank you for reminding me how miserable I've been. So horribly miserable that my best friend, who is apparently so in love with precious little me, that he couldn't just be honest with me and tell me." Her jaw clenched and she shook her head, then looked at me. "I don't get it. I don't understand."

"I couldn't have told you. Look what happened last summer. You flipped out and hid from me. Don't you think I've wanted to?" I shot to my feet and closed the space between us to a little over a foot. "Don't you think I've had the words on the tip of my tongue a hundred times? I have. More than that, probably. Every time, I talked myself out of it, and last summer cleared any misapprehensions about your feelings for me right up. You made it clear."

Her jaw clenched, and her voice was rough. "You were the one who made a promise to be honest. You said we wouldn't lie. I trusted you, and you promised—"

I had to stop her. I hadn't tried to lie. I hadn't wanted to hurt her. My voice came out a little louder to match the intensity of hers.

"I screwed up! I didn't see a better way to do things, but I knew you'd run for the freaking hills if I sat you down and told you I'd been in love with you for years. And you know you would've. It was too much pressure, and it wouldn't have been fair."

"But that's just it. You decided for me, Nate. You used those kid gloves to handle me. Don't you get that's its own kind of pressure?" She thumped her fist against her chest on the first *me*, and it damn near echoed through the room. "I don't want that from you. I don't want that from anyone, but especially not you."

My throat worked before I got the words out.

"How—I don't know. I didn't know." This was the nightmare. All my good intentions, and all my bad ones, they all collapsed into this utter crap heap. I sank down to sit on the ottoman. "I'm sorry. God, Ariel, you have no idea how sorry I am."

A bitter laugh tripped out of her. "You don't get to say you're sorry for loving me. That's not the point."

"I'm not apologizing for loving you—I'll never do that. Sorry, not sorry, not happening. I'm sorry I didn't tell you before I announced it to everyone. That I didn't give us a moment with this, to hash it out before it... became this thing between us."

This huge, air-swallowing thing. Some of the tension bled out, and her hands dropped to her sides.

"I don't know what I would've done before, but Nate, do you know I had a crush on you forever? From, like, day one?"

My eyes shot to hers. "No way. You never gave me a hint. Not anything."

Her head tilted to the right and she slow-blinked. "Unlike you, who just laid it all out there."

I swore, realizing the idiocy.

"If I'd had any idea, I might've made other choices. And I get that I cannot blame all that on you—I don't. But I just... you keeping pressure off me also took choices *away* from me. Maybe I wouldn't have been brave enough to date you back in the day. Or earlier this year. But I would've known it was an option, you know? I would've had the information and been able to make the right choice based on what was real, not based on lies."

I stared at the floor, waiting for her to leave, or yell at me, or anything. A moment passed, then another, and then she sat next to me.

"I'm so mad at you," she whispered, staring at her hands in her lap.

I closed my eyes, crushing them shut against what was obviously the biggest mistake of my life. I saw that now. If I was going to tell her, I should've told her, just us. And a while ago, to say the least.

"I'm mad at me too. And kind of at you, because if I'd had any idea I had a shot with you, I probably would've said something. Maybe. I don't know." I swore under my breath and ran my hand through my hair.

"You know, when I talked to Jim, he said I'd always lose myself in relationships like I had with him. That I was made to obey and do as I was told, and that's how I'd be with you since that's how I was with him."

Her words landed like a roundhouse kick to my sternum as the particular searing rage I associated with thinking about her ex burned into my veins. I let out a disbelieving, pained breath, something that sounded like I'd taken a hit. "He's an a—"

"He's wrong. And I know that. But I didn't always."

Her beautiful eyes flicked over my face. She hadn't touched me yet, but I wished with every bit of me she would. Or I could hug her. Having someone say that to your face... and yet the way she repeated it like it was nothing told me she'd heard that and worse before.

"I used to worry about it, though. I used to wonder how I could be with someone and be normal after being with him. I thought if I got involved with someone, especially someone in the Army, I'd be required to suppress what I wanted in favor of what he did."

I swallowed. My stomach filled with concrete.

"Watching Livie grapple with that and embrace that she could have her adventures with Eric, and seeing Bec and Summer go through similar things has helped me realize that being with someone isn't necessarily a trap or a sentence to *lose* something."

"Good." It burst out, relieved and yet still tense, still walking the tightrope.

"Most importantly, though, has been seeing that I can be myself with you. Not just *someone*, but a person who has been my friend for years and years. A person who I know so much better than I've known anyone I dated. Having your friendship has meant so much to me, Nate. Both before Jim and after. I could be myself with you."

Friend. Friendship.

Oh. Dear. God.

Was I about to be shoved summarily back into the friendzone? Maybe it was better than nothing, in theory, but after kissing her. Touching her. Sleeping next to her...

I tugged at the tie around my neck and ended up pulling it off completely. The knot unraveled in my hand before I tossed it to the side. *I knew it. I knew it.*

Well, this is what you wanted, isn't it? I'd wanted to push her, and after that blow up in which the full extent of my idiocy was on full display for both of us to see clearly, here we were. The verdict.

Ariel waited for my attention to return to her. Once I met her gaze again, she spoke softly. The first soft words since before the ceremony. "I've always been me with you, Nate."

Was this it? The end of us?

Or... the beginning?

I couldn't tell, and my heart was about to beat out of my chest. My throat had dried out minutes ago. Impossible to swallow. I reached for the water she'd poured me and gulped down half the glass. "Please. I—I'm glad. But please tell me what this means. Obviously, I've messed up. I get it. I should've given you the truth and let you decide instead of me being the one to decide it was too much."

I held my breath, hoping it might silence some of that raging pounding that rattled me internally.

Her brow pinched. "It means I love you, Nate. I've realized that I can be your friend and love you and not lose myself. I thought it was one or the other, but it can be both."

It took a beat. Just the drop of a second for her words to filter through all my nonsense. When they hit, I moved. I reached for her hand, and she let me take it. I slid closer on the couch and she did the same. I cupped her face.

"I love you. I love you." Urgent. Sure. Complete.

The idea that I thought I could lay that feeling out and then walk away when she left Germany struck me as the stupidest thing I'd ever even considered. How had I fooled myself into believing a few months would be enough? And how could I ever have imagined that she'd say it back so soon. *Today.* Even after making clear how badly I'd screwed up between keeping my feelings from her and then spewing them out in a crowd, she'd said it back.

Our lips met in a kiss so full—so full of hope—it nearly brought tears to my eyes. And there went my throat locking up again. But it didn't escalate. We pulled back.

Her eyes narrowed. "How long have you wanted to say that to me?"

A pressurized laugh burst out. "I thought I was about to be kicked to the curb. Then I thought I was about to be friend-zoned just now. Can you give a guy a minute to savor the victory?"

She raised a brow. "Really? Victory?"

"Uh, no. The relief. The elation. The backing away from the ledge of impending despair?"

She chuckled.

Adrenaline pumped through me like I'd been in a race. In some ways, I genuinely had—racing against the misunderstandings, the hurt, the years of bad habits piled up between us. I straightened my spine and sucked in my gut and looked her in those beautiful eyes and finally said the words.

"I've loved you, in one way or another, for the better part of a decade. I'm pretty sure it was all downhill with that first conversation when you told me you loved dystopian lit. There's no one moment I just *knew* or anything cheesy like that, but not long after I met you, I found myself comparing everyone I dated to you."

"Why on earth did you wait so long?" The question came out pleading.

"Timing. Cowardice."

She shook her head. "Didn't you ever wonder what would've happened?"

I exhaled through a bittersweet laugh. "You have no idea how much I've thought about telling you—how often and how close I've come more than once. I wasn't lying about that just now. But something stopped me, and now that we're here, I have to believe it was the right call."

"I wish you'd said something."

A grunt emerged before I could help it. "I was right there in front of you for how long? You never gave me a second glance. How could I risk losing you, even if it wasn't the way I really wanted you?"

She sighed, like a weight on her shoulders pressed it out of her. "You were always dating people. Constantly. I never imagined you'd be interested in someone like me, honestly. And you never seemed like you wanted something serious. Or permanent. And that's all I've ever wanted."

I closed my eyes against those words. My efforts to keep myself from her had done their work more than I'd realized. "Well. Shit."

She chuckled and looked down at her hands, which held one of mine between them in her lap. She'd laced our fingers together and squeezed.

"I've always thought of permanence as a trap. You know enough about my parents to know where that comes from."

She nodded, urging me on.

"I kept other people out. I kept you as this... ideal. That hasn't been fair to you, and I get that more today than ever, trust me. But part of that, more than being an excuse not to get close to other people, was because I really did love you. Not like I do now or how I will tomorrow, but I did. And I couldn't ever give someone else my heart when you had it." Speaking of, that muscle in my chest raced, each new confession pulling me wider open.

Her eyes glistened, but then her brow furrowed. "Maddie thinks I've led you on. Have you felt that way?"

I shook my head before she finished the thought. "Maddie is my protective little sister. I haven't given her all the details on you, especially not how things went with Jim. For a while, I couldn't talk about it because I was so angry—not that it's at all about me, obviously. But I don't think she realized that what Juliet and I had was a good friendship, and not much else. You could probably tell from Juliet's reaction to you that she knew about you. She knew why I called things off with her. And she got it."

"I'm not sure she would've wanted to break up."

"Well, I had no choice. I wouldn't want to be with someone who was thinking about someone else while they were with me. So..."

"I've been so angry with you since you blurted it out in your speech hours ago, thinking about how you kept this from me. Thinking about how you were constantly unavailable, and yet, somehow, I was supposed to know you were interested. But I can't blame you. Even last summer, I was so upset with you."

I flushed remembering it. How everything changed. How I'd felt so freaking justified in my choice not to say anything for the years before because of exactly what'd happened. But, somehow, we'd found ourselves here.

"I'm sorry for that. I—I just wanted..."

"What?"

"You."

Her chest rose slowly, but her eyes had me pinned.

"You have me." She pulled me in, but just before our lips touched, she repeated it. "You have me."

CHAPTER FORTY

Ariel

The kiss that came after that—everything that came after that—was pure bliss. The cocktail of love, relief, pleasure, and soul-deep joy that arrived with fighting through hurt and shock, then the confession of feelings, the hashing through our history, and the cathartic tears that slipped out left me exhausted and so happy I could hardly think straight.

"You realize I'm going to ask you to marry me. Like, I know it's super soon, and we haven't even talked about how you feel about getting married again, but I am going to ask."

Nate said this casually, from under me on the couch. We lay side by side, his arms around me and my head on his chest.

"I'm open to it," I said and meant it.

I'd never closed myself off to marrying again. More like, I'd never really imagined I could have someone I'd trust enough to marry, and yet I'd hoped. Maybe like Nate's hope that I'd see him, I'd hoped for someone who'd see me. And he always had. He did.

"Good. How's tomorrow?"

I chuckled, a giddy, gleeful feeling that made me feel about sixteen bounding around my body. "Maybe a touch soon?"

He moved, and we jostled around until we were sitting side by side again. "One thing we do have to deal with, though, is what happens when Eric leaves."

"That's a very unwelcome subject right about now. I'm still basking in the knowledge that you've loved me for a decade. Can that whole issue wait?"

He dropped his head to my shoulder and shook it. "More than a decade. And you're not going to let that one go, huh?"

"Are you kidding?"

He looked at me. "No. But I'm okay with it."

I smiled at his fake self-sacrifice. "Embrace it. It's our love story."

He beamed back at me. "As long as it's *ours*, I'm good with it."

I had to kiss him then. He was too adorable, and I had no reason not to. But before we lost ourselves and another hour of the evening, he pulled back.

"As much as I want that to continue, I want to talk more. About everything. About what you want to do for work. When you want to leave Germany, and if there's any way I can talk you into staying." He pushed a fall of hair behind my ear.

"I don't want to leave if I don't have to. As far as work... I don't know. I feel like I should know, but mostly—" I swallowed the last syllable as nerves crept into my throat and choked out the next words.

His brow furrowed, and he leaned in. "You can tell me anything. Truly, anything, Wolfe. I want to know everything."

I pulled in a slow breath, summoning courage. "I want a family. I always have. I grew up imagining having what my parents had. I know that contributed to rushing into moving with Jim and—everything. But as much as I've tried to find some other path or destiny or whatever, I can't change that part of me. I don't want to. So, I guess you should think about that."

"Me?" He looked truly perplexed.

"Yes. If you want to have kids, and if you mind having a partner who's unambitious and—"

"*Yes*, I want to have your babies."

I laughed loudly, then covered my mouth as that hounding joy and hope squeezed my heart. "Okay then. I guess that clears that up."

The little mischievous pull to his mouth and the happy lines starbursting out around the corners of his eyes might've been my favorite expression on him yet. He looked so happy and playful. Goodness, I loved him.

"We have to talk about the whole *unambitious* thing, though. Okay?"

I swallowed and nodded, not exactly excited to delve into that and possibly muddy the elation, but we should do it sooner than later. I'd finally accepted it, so the time had come. "Sure."

"I think you should do whatever will make you happy and use your skills. If that's exactly nothing, then do that. If it's volunteering, do *that*. If it's something else, do that thing.

But please don't put down my woman, or we'll have to fight."

"Your *woman?*" I bit my lip to hide the pleased smile.

"Oh, yes. Woman, girlfriend, partner, lover, fiancée, wife." He said the last three with feeling, eyes on mine like saying them would will them into existence. "And baby mama as soon as I can work out those last couple." He winked.

"You seem confident, but I can't blame you." If I tried to sound like his joking, silly approach to this didn't still make me all kinds of breathless and restless, I likely failed. "Even if you're insane."

"I think you mean indescribable."

"I mean irritating."

He raised a brow. "No, it's pronounced *inimitable.*"

"More like impervious."

"Love, please, just say what you mean. I'm interesting, and that's that."

I cupped his face and shook my head, a welling of tenderness washing through me. "You're calling me *love* now."

He'd said it two other times, but I hadn't taken it that way. I hadn't been able to see.

He blinked, nodded. "Every time I've ever called you Wolfe, I wanted to say another word. That word. But it's not a word I use lightly, nor have I said it to a woman I'm not related to since high school. So I couldn't toss it around like it didn't mean anything. Plus, you would've asked me about it, and I would've had to tell the truth."

I rested my forehead against his and inhaled slowly. The fleeting sense of loss, of what might have happened if he had spoken up or maybe if I'd not been so determined to be oblivious, snuck in. "You can say whatever you want, whenever you want. I hope you will now."

"I'll ask the same of you."

"I can do that. It'll take some getting used to, but it's always been pretty open between us, except for anything about our relationship."

He made a scoff-snort sound. "True. And now we have to talk about when you leave."

I exhaled. "Okay. Let's do that."

"We're talking like this is going somewhere permanent. I'd fooled myself into thinking we'd date while you were here and call it when you left, but there's no way I can live with that unless that's what you want."

"No. Of course not. Have you been a part of this conversation these last few minutes?" I shook my head at him and his insistence on giving me an out.

He nodded and his Adam's apple bobbed. "We've got time to spend together, and I know we're going to discover things about each other that are messy, but we have good groundwork. I'm going to be here until this time next year, and I don't want to be long-distance that whole time, if we can help it. But I definitely don't want to say that's a deal-breaker, because it wouldn't be. It'd suck, but we can do it if we have to."

"I don't want long-distance either. I want to be with you. That's what I'm trying to say about the work things—I want a family. And I'd already decided I wouldn't go with Eric and Livie since my mom is. I mean, I love them and I'm going to miss them all so much, but I'm ready to stand on my own two feet."

He took my hand and kissed the back. "Then we'll figure it out. You may need to go back for a bit, but we'll make it work. I'll do anything I can to make it work."

"I know you will."

"You do?"

I nodded. "One of the things I've always known about you is that you'd help me. That I could trust you. That's been a constant in our friendship, and I know it even more now. We'll figure it out, like you said, and then you can finally be Mr. Nate Wolfe."

He burst out laughing. "Finally."

He sighed, then kissed me, and our hopes mingled into something bright and glowing and beautiful between us.

EPILOGUE

Nate

"You sure you're ready for this?" Eric asked.

"No doubt." I'd never been more sure of anything in my life.

I would've married her that day—the day of my promotion a little over six months ago. Or that summer, before everyone moved. But I understood—that would've been too soon. For her. And she'd rushed once before.

So, we'd initially set a date for a wedding back in the States when we moved the following summer. We'd managed to figure out command sponsorship for her through her job at the Red Cross, and after six agonizing weeks last summer after she left, she came back to me. Other than rotations and a short TDY, we hadn't been apart. In October, she'd told me she didn't need any more time. She had no doubts, no fears, nothing she was hiding from herself. So, we made the calls.

And now, in the same castle where I promoted, the same place that now stood dusted in twilight and December chill, we'd marry.

"But are you really, really sure? I mean, you've only had, what, like just shy of sixteen full years to think this through, right?" he prodded. Because he'd grabbed hold of the *brother* thing and ran with it.

Oh, good. He's being cute. "Yes, soon-to-be brother-in-law. I am certain I want to marry your sister."

He beamed. "Finally. Long overdue."

He clapped me on the shoulder.

The music began, and that anticipation I'd felt every day for the last few months—the last year, liquefied into pure adrenaline. I clasped my hands behind my back.

"Oh good, we're not doing the *cover my junk* pose like footballers do," Maddie said from next to Eric.

She was a groomswoman. Since we'd opted to marry in Europe, that meant many of my friends couldn't come. It made for a smaller ceremony. I'd worried about that, knowing her first wedding had been at a courthouse and rushed, no family as witnesses. Ariel had assured me that if I was there, and her mom and brother and the kids and new baby were there, she'd be happy.

That Bec and Thatcher flew back had come as a shock to her, but Bec had promised she wouldn't miss it. We'd chosen the week after Christmas, hoping people could swing some leave. Katie couldn't travel due to extreme morning sickness—we could only be happy for them and hope the sickness subsided soon. But Emily was here, Summer and Nick were in attendance, having just recently tied their own knot, and lots of the community who knew Ariel from her volunteering and me from living here for two and a half years.

My parents, both of them, had even showed and had so far kept any commentary beyond congratulations to themselves. I suspected that after Maddie had talked to Ariel—after I'd orchestrated a *let's get past Maddie's grudge-holding baby sister act* meeting, Maddie had adopted Ariel as the sister she'd always wanted. They talked on the phone regularly, and Ariel was my best source of information on how Maddie's mission to actually relax for a few months had gone this fall. I also suspected that Maddie had threatened my parents' lives if they spoke a word against Ariel, which had no doubt helped the overwhelmingly positive conversations we'd had.

"Of course not. We're strong, confident men. The only person here who'd junk-punch me is you, and I'm guessing that's a special gift you'll forgo on my wedding day."

She chuckled. "I haven't done that since I was like twelve."

"A day that lives in infamy."

Eric shook his head. "You two."

Livie, Bec, Emily, and Summer came down the aisle. Then Delia sprinkled white petals arm in arm with a ring-bearing Robby, who bounced along and chatted with everyone he recognized on the way down the aisle. I felt the fleeting sensation that I'd been here before—maybe seeing the kids like this took me back to Eric's wedding eighteen months ago. But the kids were older. Eric and Livie's four-month-old baby boy lay sleeping in his mother's arms in the front row. Livie was a bridesmaid, and Eric, a groomsman.

And I stood here, the groom, waiting for the woman it felt like I'd been ready for my entire life. For this moment to signal a new beginning, the unfolding of years of hope.

Robby slipped into the seat next to Delia and took a big breath. Then the music shifted, and the whole world stopped. My vision tunneled ahead down the petal-dotted aisle.

There she was.

My favorite person.

My friend.

My partner.

My love.

And soon, my wife.

Thank you so much for reading Nate and Ariel's story! I can't believe we've come to the end of the Soldiers Overseas Romance series. If you haven't yet read Waiting on Love at Christmas, don't miss the sweet Christmas novella starring Nina and David.

Get a free novella here: http://www.clairecainwriter. com/newsletter.

ALSO BY CLAIRE CAIN

Veterans of Silver Ridge Series

Small Town Veteran Romance

Love Undercover

Romantic Suspense Light

Back to Silver Ridge Series

Small Town Romance

Exceptional Mission Unit: The Cardinals

Military Romantic Suspense

The Silver Ridge Resort Series

Small Town Romance

Soldiers Overseas Romances

Sweet Military Romance

The Rambler Battalion Series

Sweet Military Romance

Married to the Military Series

Military Marriage of Convenience Romcoms

ACKNOWLEDGMENTS

Wow, this book! I always find ending a series to be the most fun and most challenging. Thank you to the many people who helped make Nate and Ariel's story whole.

First, I have to thank readers for your anticipation of this book! I hope you loved Nate and Ariel's love story. There were times people had suggestions for how things should go for these two, but I've had them in mind since the beginning—since they jumped onto the page while writing a scene in Eric and Livie's book. Then, when Nate hijacked the epilogues of the whole series, I knew he'd have to come last! So thanks for your patience in getting here. I hope you felt it was worth the wait.

To Zee Monodee, who worked tirelessly as my content editor to develop these two and their story into a complete love. You didn't let up until it was done, and I'm so thankful for that. For your vulnerability and honesty in the process, I'm forever grateful.

To Amanda, thank you for helping polish this gem to a high shine.

To my amazing Beta Readers Emma, Amanda, and Ashley. Thank you for your insights, your willingness to spend time with early copies of this book, and for your interest in supporting me as I make these books better! Thanks especially for rooting for Nate and Ariel!

Thanks to Rainbeau Decker for the original cover image —only we know the challenge in getting there, so thank you.

Thanks to Emma Robinson for the beautiful original design and patience with me as I fumble through figuring out titles, tag lines, and blurbs.

Thanks to my husband, who listened to me agonize over making this story the best it could be. Thank you for being a man I'm honored to know and thrilled to turn down the sheets with ;)

Thanks, again, to my readers and Claire's Sweet Reader group members. Your support is inspiring and amazing! You've shaped this book in ways you'll never know!

ABOUT THE AUTHOR

Claire Cain lives to eat and drink her way around the globe with her traveling soldier and three kids, but is perhaps even happier hunkered down at home in a pair of sweatpants and slippers using any free moment she has to read and cook. Or talk—she really likes to talk. She has become an expert at packing too many dishes in too few cabinets and making houses into homes from Utah to Germany and many places in between. She's a proud Army wife and is frankly just really happy to be here.

You can also join Claire's facebook reader group for exclusive content and fun: https://www.facebook.com/groups/clairecain/

Website: http://www.clairecainwriter.com

E-mail: Claire@ClaireCainWriter.com

Newsletter sign-up for new releases, exclusives, and freebies: http://www.clairecainwriter.com/newsletter

www.ingramcontent.com/pod-product-compliance
Lightning Source LLC
Chambersburg PA
CBHW061047190726
48286CB00006B/1651